NEVER EVERS

Also by Tom Ellen and Lucy Ivison

A Totally Awkward Love Story

Freshmen

NEVER EVERS

Tom Ellen and Lucy Ivison

DELACORTE PRESS

Text copyright © 2016 by Lucy Ivison and Tom Ellen
Jacket art copyright © 2018 by Marika Cowan

All rights reserved. Published in the United States by Delacorte Press, an imprint of Random House Children's Books, a division of Penguin Random House LLC, New York. Originally published in trade paperback by Chicken House, London, in 2016.

Delacorte Press is a registered trademark and the colophon is a trademark of Penguin Random House LLC.

Visit us on the Web! GetUnderlined.com

Educators and librarians, for a variety of teaching tools, visit us at RHTeachersLibrarians.com

Library of Congress Cataloging-in-Publication Data
Names: Ellen, Tom, author. | Ivison, Lucy, author.
Title: Never evers / Tom Ellen and Lucy Ivison.
Description: First American edition. | New York : Delacorte Press, [2018] | "Originally published in paperback by Chicken House, London, in 2016." | Summary: "Mayhem and romance ensue when tweens Mouse and Jack meet on the slopes during a school ski trip" — Provided by publisher.
Identifiers: LCCN 2017039050 | ISBN 978-1-5247-0182-6 (hc) | ISBN 978-1-5247-0183-3 (ebook)
Subjects: | CYAC: Impersonation—Fiction. | School field trips—Fiction. | Skis and skiing—Fiction. | Interpersonal relations—Fiction.
Classification: LCC PZ7.1.E44 Nev 2018 | DDC [Fic]—dc23

The text of this book is set in 12.5-point Granjon.
Interior design by Stephanie Moss

Printed in the United States of America
10 9 8 7 6 5 4 3 2 1
First American Edition

For all members of About Time, the Defectors,
Joe's AWOL and Voytek Stanley. But mostly for
Robin, Chris, Harvey and Neil. —T.E.

For Lisa. "I never had any friends later on
like the ones I had when I was twelve.
Jesus, does anyone?" —L.I.

1

MOUSE

"You can't stay in there forever."

I rolled my eyes dramatically even though she couldn't see me and climbed into the tub fully clothed. I lay down and crossed my arms like a snoozing vampire. And then a bottle of Herbal Essences fell on my head.

I *did* realize that living in the bathroom was not a long-term life plan. It was a last-chance act of desperation. At some point I was going to have to either jump out the window or just unlock the door and skulk back out. Not exactly *Braveheart* material. I wonder if anyone has ever locked themselves in a bathroom and come out victorious?

I let my head tilt back against the cold tiles. I'd never been in a bathtub fully dressed before. If I hadn't been having a mental breakdown, it might have been quite relaxing. I turned the tap on with my Converse and a trickle of water came out. I picked up my bright blue Christmas bath bomb and cupped it in my hands under the water. It started to fizz and come alive.

Mum's voice came gently through the door. "If you really don't want to go, you don't have to." She made it sound like *she* was the one whose life was over.

"Do you really mean it?" I thought it would sound defiant but it came out jagged and gulpy.

"You're thirteen, Mouse," she said. "I can't exactly pick you up and drag you there."

An image popped into my head of her hauling me down the road by my ponytail, politely waving to the neighbors. Mums and random pointless comments are like dads and bad jokes. Just *why?*

"But I do think that going on this trip is the best thing to do," she added. "In a week you'll know all the stories and the inside jokes and the gossip, and maybe it won't feel so strange being back there."

Back there. Her saying it made my stomach churn.

"I don't have any friends there anymore. Everyone will be with their groups. I'll be all alone. You don't understand."

I heard Mum sigh and sit down. "I know Connie isn't your best friend anymore, but she'll look after you."

"Everyone thinks Connie is weird. That'll make it worse."

And then I felt horrid. I've known Connie-May forever.

And maybe she's not weird anymore. A lot can change in two years. A lot can change in five minutes, if you think about it.

"Well, I told you to call Lauren," Mum sighed. Hearing Lauren's name out loud made me panic.

I hid the disintegrating bath bomb inside Dad's nearly empty tub of shaving cream; then I got out and started pacing the tiny bathroom. I was going stir-crazy and I'd only been in here ten minutes. Inside the bathroom cupboard there was just an ancient bottle of lice lotion, some eardrops, Mum's toiletry bag and the boot piece from Monopoly.

I unzipped the bag and sat on the toilet seat, opening a heavy gold pot of "bronze sculpting cream." As if *cream* is the right tool for sculpting; Michelangelo didn't go around carving the statue of David with Reddi Wip.

I scooped a big dollop of it onto my fingers and rubbed it into my cheeks.

Next, I took out a medical-looking bottle of "Forever Young youth elixir capsules," squashed one of them open and rubbed the cooking-oil-type liquid onto my nose.

I sprayed myself with the Chanel perfume that Dad got her and put "Monaco Dreams highlighter" over where I'd put the cream.

"I love you," I heard Mum say softly. "I can't bear how hard this is for you. But you are stronger than you think you are, Mouse."

I knew I had to go on the ski trip. It wasn't her fault.

I unbolted the door.

Mum was sitting on the floor, legs outstretched in front of her, drinking tea out of her DANCE MOM mug. She saw me looking at it and cupped her hands to hide the words. I collapsed down next to her and she handed me a cold-looking toast sandwich.

"Weird or not, Connie will be here in five minutes," she said, putting her arm around me.

I opened the sandwich and scooped the jam off with my finger. We both sat in silence. Ahead of us near the top of the stairs was a picture of me in a pale-blue leotard, my grand jeté perfect. When I got in, they put that picture of me in the paper with the headline LOCAL GIRL BEATS 1200 TO PLACE AT BALLET SCHOOL. We both just stared at it.

The doorbell rang.

Mum kissed me on the head. "Mouse, you look like a Smurf. You'd better wash your face."

I walked back into the bathroom and looked in the mirror. "Smurf" was an understatement. A compliment, even. Looking back at me was a huge, blue moon-face with two golden-brown stripes down either side. I looked like a cartoon raccoon that had gone wild with Maybelline. I turned the faucet on full and started to scrub, but it just seemed to wipe the mixture around more.

A little round freckly face and a halo of tight brown curls

poked around the bathroom door. Connie. She flung her arms around my waist and started screaming, jumping up and down with such force that she carried me with her.

"Mouse, your face is so colorful!" she squealed. "I *love* it. Can I do it too or is it your thing?"

"It was an accident." I couldn't fake being excited. But if she noticed, she didn't let on.

"The best things are accidents," she said. "Like me." And then she picked up my hands and put one on each of her cheeks so she had a blue handprint on either side.

She started singing and dancing wildly around the bathroom: "Everybody look left / Everybody look right / Can't you see I'm in the spotlight / Oh I just can't *wait* to be skiing." She climbed onto the edge of the bath and jumped off. "Oh, I just can't *wait* to be skiing."

I scrubbed my cheeks with nail polish remover to try to get some of the blue off. It sort of worked, but I still had faint Smurf-raccoon outlines. I unfurled my hair from its tight bun and pulled it forward to try to hide them.

Connie stopped dancing for a second. "Oh my God, Mouse. Your hair's gotten *so* long. You could basically walk around naked and wear it as a cloak."

I've been growing my hair since I was three. It's the one thing everyone notices about me. There's nothing else to notice, really. I have blue-gray eyes, a ski-jump nose and a little sprinkle of freckles on each cheek. Not as many as Connie, but they are there. I'm tall for ballet school, but average otherwise. Connie looked the same as when I'd last seen her, but different. She had grown really tall. It looked a bit ridiculous. Like she wasn't supposed to *be* that tall, somehow. Like she was on stilts.

She stood next to me and draped some of my hair over her head.

I didn't really talk in the car, just let Connie ramble on to Mum about avalanches and what French people eat for dinner ("Not snails, usually. I Googled it. Phew."). But as we got closer to school, I felt a knot in my stomach.

"Are you nervous, Mouse?" Connie said out of nowhere.

I was so nervous I couldn't speak. And then I saw her. Across the road with Scarlett and Melody. Her hair was in fishtail braids that must have taken ages. We spent a whole week once learning how to do them. She was wearing tiny denim shorts over thick gray tights, and a plaid shirt. She looked the same, just more polished somehow. Like a perfectly colored picture, nothing outside the lines. She wasn't even wearing a coat.

From a distance you could tell that she was still the queen bee. She's not the prettiest—Scarlett is by far—and she's not the sportiest or the smartest; she just *is* that person. The person the other ones follow. The person they want to be. There was a part of me that wanted to be her too. Even though she hated me.

"Ooh, look, there's Lauren Bradley," said Mum brightly, and I felt my insides turn to stone.

JACK

Max tore into his third family-size bag of Cheetos as the bus pulled away from Belmont School for Boys and out onto the highway.

"You know, you can get anything you want in France," he said, stuffing a handful in his mouth and spraying crumbs everywhere. "Like, literally *anything*."

Toddy snorted. "You can get anything you want anywhere. You just have to know the right people."

"Yeah, but that's what I'm *saying*," he sputtered, showering me and Toddy with another dusting of cheesy scraps. "We don't know the right people, do we?"

"We don't even know the wrong people," I said. "We don't know any *people,* full stop."

Max nodded impatiently. "Yeah, exactly. But in France, you don't have to. You can literally buy fireworks and sparklers and ninja stars and *whatever* at the local shop with your chocolate and chips!"

Toddy frowned. "I'm not sure about that."

The three of us were sitting smack in the middle of the bus, where we always sat on school trips. This was our natural position. Where we belonged. We're not geeky enough to sit right up front, near the teachers, but we're also definitely not cool enough to be hanging out in the back with the soccer players and the psychos. We're middle-of-the-bus material, through and through.

Max leaned right over the back of his seat toward us. "I'm *telling* you, boys!" he hissed. "You know Nathan Freeman from the grade above us, yeah? He went on this trip last year. He said, you know how in England we go to the store for some milk or bread or whatever? Well, in France, they go to the store for, like, a baguette and a broadsword and a massive Catherine wheel firework. You come out of their corner stores looking like someone from *Game of Thrones*! That's just how things are over there."

I laughed. "You do realize this is a *snowboarding* trip, Max? We're not going to the Alps to spend five days stockpiling weaponry."

Max clicked his tongue against his teeth and picked out Cheetos. "Dude, the snowboarding is the thing I'm *least* excited about on this trip. In order of excitedness, it goes: snowboarding at number three, buying fireworks at two, and at number one . . ." He lowered his voice to an excited whisper. "Girls!"

Toddy rolled his eyes and turned to stare out the window. "How do you know there's even gonna be any girls there?" he muttered.

"Toddy, have you been living in a cave?" Max hissed. "This

is the *February midterm snowboard trip*! Everyone knows the February midterm snowboard trip is basically wall-to-wall girls! French girls, German girls, random English girls from other schools . . . It'll be a miracle if we get any actual snowboarding done, what with all the girls we'll be meeting."

"Yeah," I said. "I mean . . . considering none of us have managed to kiss *one* girl in thirteen years, I wouldn't bet on that, Max."

Max ran a hand over his shaved red hair exasperatedly. "Listen, Jack. Nathan Freeman was at zero just like us when he went on this trip last year. By the time he came back, d'you know how many girls he'd kissed?"

"I'm sure you're gonna tell us."

"Sixteen," hissed Max. "He says he kissed *sixteen* girls in five days!"

"Yeah, well, Nathan Freeman also says his grandma invented Wite-Out, so he's hardly a reliable source," I said.

"Whatever," Max huffed. "All I'm saying is this week is definitely our best chance yet."

He *was* right about that, to be fair. In my thirteen years and two months on this planet, the closest I'd come to kissing an actual, live human girl was Maria Bennett last October. And that had gone so horribly that I'd barely spoken to another girl since. But I couldn't think about Maria Bennett right now. I'd thought about her way too much over the past few months already.

I pushed all girl-based worries to the back of my mind and jammed my hand into Max's Cheetos bag.

"Hey!" He whacked me hard on the arm. "I never said I was sharing!"

"It's a family-size bag!"

"Yeah, exactly. And last time I checked, you weren't a member of my family. So keep your fingers out."

"You're ridiculous, Max."

Outside, a huge sign with the word SOUTHAMPTON on it flew past. We'd only left Winchester half an hour ago, and we were already only five miles from the ferry. Max licked his cheesy fingers clean and crumpled the bag into a little ball.

"Pass us that French phrase book, Toddy," he said.

Toddy raised his eyebrows. "Oh, right, so you spend all week mocking my phrase book, and now you want to look at it?"

"Well, your mum bought it for you *specially,* didn't she," he said, making his voice go all high-pitched and squeaky on "specially." "So we might as well get some use out of it."

Toddy dug into his backpack and chucked the shiny new French phrase book at Max. He started thumbing through it.

"What are you looking for?" I asked. "I don't think you're gonna find 'I would like to buy some ninja stars, please.'"

"Nah, nah," Max muttered, still flipping through the

pages. "I want to learn how to say 'We're in a band.' Guarantee you the French girls will go crazy for us if they know we're in a band."

"Oh God, you're not still going on about your stupid *band*, are you?"

We all looked up to see the spiky-haired head of Jamie Smith looming over us. That's the problem with sitting in the middle of the bus—you get people eavesdropping on your conversations while they wait in line for the bathroom.

"You guys have never played a gig, and you don't even have a name," Jamie sneered. "You're not exactly a *real* band, are you?"

"Yeah, well, we're working on both those things," Max shot back. "And we're an amazing band, *actually,* Jamie." Sometimes I don't know whether Max is brave or stupid. Jamie's not pure back-of-the-bus material, but he is sort of a psycho. I once saw him punch a junior for taking the last muffin at lunch.

"If you're so *amazing,*" laughed Jamie, "then how come your lead singer bailed at Band Night the other week?" He turned his sneer on me, and I felt myself going red right away. I really didn't need Jamie Smith reminding everyone on the bus what happened that night. I'd spent the last ten days trying to forget it.

"I—I didn't bail . . . ," I stammered, feeling my cheeks get hotter. "I just—"

"You totally did!" Jamie snapped over me. "Everyone saw you! In fact, *there's* a good name for your band: the Bailers."

I heard a burst of laughter from Jamie's best friend, Ed, further down the bus. I suddenly realized everyone was listening.

"Shut up, Jamie," snarled Max. "We're not calling ourselves the Bailers."

"Actually, 'the Bailers' isn't a bad name, to be fair," said Toddy, absent-mindedly.

Max slapped him on the arm. "Shut up, Toddy! We're not the Bailers, because we didn't bail! We just didn't . . . feel like playing Band Night, that's all."

I felt a sudden flash of gratitude. No matter how much of an idiot Max can be sometimes, he always has my back.

"Whatever," Jamie said. "I can't wait to see you guys trying to tell the French girls about your lame band. They'll laugh you off the mountain, man. No wonder you're all still at zero."

There was another howl of laughter from a few seats back. I looked at Max. His face was even redder than mine and you could see the vein on his neck wiggling. He was now gripping his Sprite bottle so tightly that it was shaking.

"You shouldn't shake that," said Jamie. "It'll explode."

"Yeah," said Max, looking him straight in the eye and unscrewing the cap. "That's the idea. . . ."

2

MOUSE

I want to be friends with Lauren Bradley again. I want to pretend the last two years didn't happen. I want to go over to her and say, "Hey, Lauren, I've been kicked out of ballet school now. They don't want me anymore. They probably wish they'd picked you at the auditions instead. You can stop hating me. We can go back to making up dance routines in my bedroom and having sleepovers where we talk until three in the morning."

After I got in and she didn't, she blocked me on Instagram and then I kind of blocked her from my brain. Like our friendship had never existed. I went to ballet school and just erased her from my history. I covered my wall with pictures of Lila, Meg and Kate in our new dorm and shed everything that had come before. Now I couldn't stop myself from looking at her. But she didn't look at me. I hate that girl thing. Where someone just acts like you're not even there. It takes *energy* to do that, to pretend that the space a human form takes up is just thin air. You need control. Lauren must have seen me cross the road, rolling my suitcase with Connie. She must have seen me sign in with Miss Mardle, who was our seventh-grade advisor, and hug Mum goodbye. I used to be her *best friend* . . . but she didn't even glance in my direction.

Walking back through the gates of Bluecoats School for Girls felt surreal, like when you dream about something your waking mind has forgotten. Like trespassing on a memory. It looked exactly the same: that grungy type of old that isn't quaint or majestic but just shabby and clearly a mistake. My mum went to Bluecoats back when it had just been built, and they probably haven't repainted it since. It's concrete and ugly and angry. It's only a few miles from White Lodge Ballet Academy but it could be a thousand. Long before I was accepted, the first time I saw White Lodge, nestled in a park full of deer, I saw a girl and boy through one of its floor-length windows dancing pas de deux. Me and Lauren had exchanged a wide-eyed look, and I'd known then it was all I wanted.

"I am getting really excited and that always makes me need to pee." Connie was jumping up and down on the spot. "You know on one night there is a dancing moose? Minnie Porter said it wears overalls and does the Macarena."

"Hey." A girl flung her backpack on the ground next

to us. At first I didn't recognize her. She had thick, black wavy hair with little braids running through it, and she was wearing ripped-up jeans covered in felt-tip drawings. Her bright green eyes gave her away, though. Keira Avakian. I was kind of stunned by how beautiful she had become. The last time I'd seen her, she'd had a weird short bob that stuck right out because her hair was so thick, and special shoes because she had flat feet.

"Hey, Keira!" Connie launched at her and gave her a hug. They looked a little ridiculous next to each other. Connie with her neat, tight curls and smart ironed shirt that her mum probably picked for her, and Keira with her scruffy, moody coolness.

"It's so early," moaned Keira. "It's like being in *prison*." She shot a death look at Miss Mardle.

"I don't think people get to go on ski trips in prison," Connie said matter-of-factly.

"Hey, Mouse." Keira said it like we were friends, like the last time I had seen her was yesterday.

"Hey." I tried to say it in the same offhand, friendly way, but it came out small and stilted. She just bustled on, unzipping her backpack and rummaging around. It was filled to the brim with food. Cheez-Its and Haribo gummies and two packets of cookies. The opposite of protein balls and packets of almonds—the *fuel for dancing* that my bag was still packed with.

She held out some Cheez-Its, then emptied a few from

15

the bag straight into her mouth. "So how come you left ballet school?"

Girls had started to line up for the bus and the ones around us quieted down suddenly. Obviously Keira wasn't the only curious one.

The brick in my stomach turned to liquid and started jumping around. And then I saw Lauren. She, Scarlett and Melody were all just a few feet away, and none of them was looking at me, but the atmosphere seemed to change. They were waiting for me to speak.

The truth wasn't exactly complicated. It would have been so easy to say, "Yeah, they didn't think I had *realized the potential* I had shown at eleven, so they kicked me out." But I didn't say that. My heart raced and my voice came out squeaky.

"My ballet teacher put me forward for another dance program in Paris. And I start there in September." I said it more to Keira's bag than to her face. I could feel embarrassment creeping into my cheeks. I wanted to take it back straight away, but it was too late.

"Oh, cool," said Keira. "So you're only back here for, like, two quarters?"

I nodded awkwardly and Connie said, "Wow. That is *amazing. Ooh la la, très bon, baguette.*"

A girl in the grade above me at White Lodge had gone to train with the Paris Opera Ballet, so it could have been

16

true. But it wasn't. I waited for someone to call me out on it, but no one did. Maybe Mum *would* let me try out for other schools, and maybe I *would* get into one. If I did, then it wouldn't be a lie, really. I took a deep breath to try to squash it all down.

Keira ate the last cracker, then balled up the packet and hurled it in the direction of the trash can. "I wish I was good at something so I could ditch my parents. And school. Without those two things my life would be really good."

"Well, at least you get to come on the ski trip," Connie said, giving my arm a squeeze. "You can start practicing your French while we're there."

I looked up to smile at Connie but it was Lauren's eye I caught. She met mine for a second, a tiny hint of some sort of smile, and then she looked away and said something to Scarlett and Melody. They burst out laughing like it was the funniest thing they had ever heard. Lauren knew more about ballet than anyone here. She knew about assessments; we had read every book about the Royal Ballet School that existed. I felt sick.

Miss Mardle jolted into action and started herding everyone onto the bus.

"You two sit together," Keira said as we clambered on. "I'm cool listening to my music."

"No, honestly, I would feel really bad," I told them.

"Are you sure?" Connie said. "I don't want Miss Mardle

to think I'm not looking after you. I'm going to take being your Official Buddy very seriously." She put her arm around me proudly.

I sat down behind them. "I'll probably just fall asleep anyway."

"Don't worry," Connie said, beaming, "I'll say everything twice so you hear it too. Like a parrot."

Lauren, Scarlett and Melody walked right past us, but none of them looked at me. I pulled my hoodie over my knees and leaned my head against the window.

We drove out of London and onto the highway. Connie and Keira were listening to music, one set of headphones split between them. So were the pair in front of them and the ones in front of them. All I could see were little sets of wires splitting through the gaps in the seats. Why is everything in life always split in twos?

Every so often I heard Lauren laugh really loudly behind me. I didn't dare look back. It felt like she was doing it for my benefit. To show me how much I was missing out on. Every time I heard her and her friends, I pressed my head against the window and let the sound of the bus vibrating drown them out. I must have actually fallen asleep at some point, because I woke up with Connie's face right next to mine.

"Mouse!" Her eyes were huge. "There's something I haven't told you."

"She's wet herself." Keira stuck her face between the two seats.

"Oh, that's why the floor is sticky," I said, but I didn't have the punch to carry off the joke.

Connie looked at me. "Mouse, can you keep a secret?"

I nodded.

"OK," Connie said earnestly. "I'm not doubting your honor but we need to enact the pact of Cheese Club. Just in case."

She unfurled her fist to reveal two Babybels and pushed one into my hands. "Remember?"

"I thought we could only enact the pact of Cheese Club in the secret meeting place?" I said.

"We amended that in kindergarten at the Science Museum. I still have the constitution." She held her palm of cheese out next to mine and hissed, "Mouse, it's serious. I need Cheese Club. Kiss. The. Cheese."

"OK, OK." I kissed the cheese. "Didn't we disband Cheese Club in first grade, though?"

"Cheese Club never dies."

Connie lifted up her backpack slowly and looked around to check no one could see. I had no idea what she could possibly have in there. She was handling the bag like it was full of explosives. She carefully unzipped the corner.

"Look inside," she whispered.

I bent down and put my face right next to the bag. I

could see some thin metal bars. I pushed the zip a tiny bit more. And then I saw him. Peeking up at me through the cage with little black eyes. A tiny orange ball of fluff.

"Look at his little hamster eyes," Connie cooed. "He remembers you."

I couldn't believe it. "Is it . . . Is that *Mr. Jambon*? Is he still . . . ?" I was a little dazed by the whole situation.

"Yup," Keira said, leaning over. "He's about ninety in hamster years. He's traveling on his Old Age Hamsters bus pass." She laughed like it was no big deal and started to draw a little cartoon hamster with her finger on the window.

"Rub it out!" Connie hissed. "Are you crazy?"

Keira slouched down again. "Yup, that's right. You have brought an elderly hamster skiing, and *I'm* crazy."

JACK

Jamie was still screaming at Max when we arrived at Southampton for the ferry across the English Channel.

"I bought this T-shirt just for the trip!" he yelled as we all trooped off the bus and onto the ferry. "How am I gonna wear it now it's covered in Sprite?"

"I'm sure you can wash it," Toddy offered helpfully.

"It's *hand-wash* only!"

"Well, then hand-wash it, you idiot," muttered Max.

Jamie kicked the metal wall of the ferry, making a loud *bwaaang* sound. We left him moaning to Ed, and headed up to the top deck. There was a restaurant and an arcade and a candy shop, but it all smelled so weird and metallic and sea-sicky that we had to go outside.

"Thanks for that, Max," I said, trying to sound all breezy and offhand, as we stepped out into the crazily windy sea air. "You didn't have to tell Jamie it was all of us who bailed on Band Night."

Max clapped me hard on the back and grinned. "Don't be stupid, man. We're a band. We stick together."

Toddy bumped his fist against my shoulder. "Yeah. I don't blame you in the slightest for chickening out. There's no way I could get up and sing in front of people. I'll be scared enough standing at the back with my bass."

"I still don't see why you can't sing, Max," I said.

"I'm the drummer, Jack," he snapped. "There's no such thing as a singing drummer."

"What about Phil Collins?" said Toddy.

"Never heard of him," Max sniffed. "Which proves my point—he can't be very successful, can he?"

Toddy scrunched his nose up. "I think he is. My dad's got, like, ten of his albums."

"Yeah, well, we're not trying to impress your *dad,* are we, Toddy? We're trying to impress *girls,* get rich and famous, and generally take rock 'n' roll to dizzying new heights."

Toddy nodded. "OK, cool. Just as long as we're not set-ting ourselves unrealistic goals."

Max slapped me on the shoulder again. "Anyway, we've

21

got the perfect front man in Jack. He just doesn't realize it yet. Band Night was a hiccup. Next time, we'll blow the roof off."

Next time. That was the reason Max was being so cool about me bailing on Band Night: he thought it was a one-off. He thought we could just get another gig, and I'd be fine. But deep down, I knew that I wouldn't be.

I love playing guitar and shouting lyrics when it's just the three of us in Max's bedroom, but the idea of standing up in front of a crowd and doing it . . . it just freezes me up inside. That was what happened at Band Night: I froze. I had told Max I wasn't ready, but he signed us up anyway. And when the day finally came, and I peeked out through the curtain at the dining hall full of people, I just knew I couldn't do it. I headed straight for the exit and didn't look back.

We stood at the edge of the deck with our elbows on the railing, watching England disappear slowly into the fog.

"Jamie *is* right about one thing, y'know," said Max. "It's just . . . *depressing* that none of us have gotten a girlfriend yet. You know Ed's kissed ten girls now? *Ten.* He's a month younger than me and he's on double digits."

"Seriously?" I groaned. "That's crazy. I can't see any of us ever getting past single digits."

"We aren't even *on* single digits," laughed Toddy. "We're at zero."

"Yeah, and what's zero if it's not a single digit?"

Toddy opened his mouth to argue with this but nothing came out.

"Exactly," I said smugly, though I didn't feel very smug. The Maria Bennett memory suddenly flooded my head, and this time I couldn't shake it out.

We'd been sitting in the garden at Sarvan's thirteenth birthday party. Maria was the one who'd suggested going outside. I remember thinking that was a good sign. It was October, freezing; the only reason anybody went outside was to hold hands or kiss.

We sat there, looking up at the stars and the black scraps of cloud, and I kept telling myself to lean in and kiss her, but something stopped me. It was weird. It wasn't just getting rejected that scared me (although that was pretty terrifying); it was more the idea of doing it *wrong*. I kept imagining her reeling away in horror because I'd managed to screw it up somehow. So in the end, I just did nothing. I didn't even *try* to kiss her. I froze. Just like I did with Band Night. Just like I seem to do with everything.

"Don't worry," said Max, snapping me back to reality. "We won't be at zero for long." He watched a couple of seagulls hovering a few feet above, and stroked the thin, wispy hairs on his top lip. "I wonder if French girls are into mustaches," he said.

"Oh God," moaned Toddy. "Not this again."

Max had recently become totally obsessed by the fact

that he was pretty much the first in our year to show any sign of facial hair growth. He would *not* shut up about his "mustache." If you could actually call it a mustache. No one else did.

"Oh yeah," I said. "I'm sure French girls are super into real, actual, bushy mustaches. I'm just not sure where they stand on ones that look like three-day-old hot chocolate stains."

"How is this not an actual, real mustache?" Max demanded, pointing furiously at his own mouth.

"You shouldn't be able to count the exact number of hairs in a real mustache," said Toddy. "What's the latest update, twenty-four?"

"Twenty-eight, *actually*," Max fired back. "And that's twenty-eight more than you've got, Toddy. You probably still won't have any pubes by the time you're forty."

Toddy smiled a smile that was half grimace, and I punched Max on the arm. He can be such an idiot sometimes. He knows Toddy is sensitive about how young he looks.

Me and Toddy had both officially been the "short ones" in our class until I had randomly started growing a few months back. Toddy never said anything to me about it, and I never said anything to him, but still . . . I felt bad. What could I do, though? It's not like I could shrink.

Max just doesn't understand what it's like. Even back in sixth grade he was taller than half our teachers. He's big and loud and clumsy, his shaved red hair making him look like a rugby-playing Weasley brother. Toddy is the opposite— small and shy with wonky glasses and an untidy mop of blond hair that he hides behind whenever anyone except me or Max talks to him.

I'm just . . . I don't know what I am, really. I have no idea what other people see when they look at me. That was the whole problem with Maria Bennett, I guess. I just couldn't accept that she might like me.

The wind was picking up on the top deck, so Max opened his battered backpack to pull out a hoodie. I noticed his bag had the words PSYCHO DEATH SQUAD freshly scrawled across the top in black marker.

"You don't honestly want to call our band that, do you?" I said.

"Er, yeah, obviously," he snapped. "A name like that would get people's attention. If you saw 'Psycho Death Squad' on a poster, you'd definitely stop and check it out, wouldn't you? Anyway, it's better than your suggestions."

"I think mine's pretty good, actually," said Toddy.

"Yeah, well, you would," Max shot back.

"The Parallelograms," Toddy said, gazing out poetically at the sea. "I heard it in math. I think it sounds cool."

"Toddy," said Max firmly. "We are *not* naming our band after something you heard in math. We might as well just call ourselves the Massive Geeks and be done with it."

"Yeah, no offense, Toddy, but that's actually worse than Max's," I said. "Mine's the best of the three."

I want us to be called About Time. I think it's got a nice ring to it. I got the idea a while back when I told my dad about Max's "Psycho Death Squad" suggestion, and he said it was "about time Max saw a therapist." I imagine myself telling that story in interviews once we're famous. It always goes down quite well, in my head.

"We do seriously need to decide on a name soon," Max said. "It's getting ridiculous that we still don't have one. All the best bands have names."

"We could vote on it," Toddy suggested.

"How's that gonna work?" snapped Max. "We'd all just vote for our own suggestion." Suddenly his eyes lit up. "I know!" he yelled. "I've got it. This is how we'll decide . . . The trip!"

"What are you on about?" I said.

"Whoever kisses a girl first on this trip gets to name the band!"

Toddy slumped down onto one of the plastic benches, his blond hair flapping about in the wind. "Oh, great. Well, I'm out, then, aren't I?" he muttered.

"Yeah, I'm not sure about that either, Max . . . ," I started, but he wrapped his arm around my shoulder and groaned.

"Jack, you're not *still* beating yourself up about Maria Bennett, are you? That was, like, six months ago, man."

I shrugged.

"Look," he went on, "the point is: I'm not coming back from this trip still at zero, OK? And I'll never get past zero without my wingmen. So, maybe this bet will mean you two at least talk to some girls."

He leaned in closer. "I mean, you *really* don't want our band to be called Psycho Death Squad, do you?"

I shook my head.

"Well," he said, grinning, "then you'd better make sure you find a girl *first*."

3

MOUSE

The bus pulled into the Channel ferry terminal at Dover and stopped at a little hut marked PASSPORT CONTROL.

"Oh my God!" Connie hissed, pulling her bag close. "Do you think they know?"

"No, but what you're doing is probably illegal." As soon as I said it, Connie's eyes went huge and I wished I hadn't. "Well, not *illegal* illegal."

"It's not like she's smuggling drugs," Keira said. "It's only a hamster. Although I did watch a show once where this woman swallowed drugs and took them to another country."

"What if they think I've fed Mr. Jambon drugs?" Connie looked genuinely terrified. She was biting her lip and clutching the bag. "I would never make Mr. Jambon eat drugs. I never even make him eat dry food. I always give him salad."

"Connie, stop acting weird or you'll draw attention to us," Keira hissed. "Why did you even bring it?"

"*Him,* you mean," Connie corrected her. "Mr. Jambon is a man. I mean, obviously he's a hamster, but you know what I mean. He's a man hamster. He's a manster."

"Yeah, OK, great," said Keira impatiently. "Why did you bring *him*?"

"Because my mum always forgets to feed him, and when I went to Brownie camp he got hamster flu and almost died."

"I don't mean to be rude, Con," Keira said, "but he's hardly going to be safer running up and down the French Alps, is he? Look, whatever, they've got no reason to search any of our things, so it will probably be fine."

Connie didn't seem comforted by the word "probably," and she started rocking backward and forward.

I instinctively reached out and put my hand on her shoulder. It felt sort of good to be the one trying to help, instead of the helpless one. "There's no way they could know he's here. It will be fine." It sounded lame and I was pretty sure it wasn't true. If anyone found Mr. Jambon, we would all be in big trouble.

A man handed some papers to Miss Mardle. The bus heaved forward again and drove up the ramp and onto the ferry. Me and Keira exchanged a look of relief. "Don't leave him on the bus," Keira said. "You don't want the driver to hear him hamstering around."

Connie nodded and carefully put her arm through her

bag's strap. "I'll protect you, Mr. Jambon," she whispered into the bag as a teacher I didn't know started telling us the rules about being on the ferry.

We clambered off the bus and up the stairs. I'd never been on a ferry before. It was absolutely massive. We walked past about ten flights of parked cars before we even got to the main deck. Connie was wearing her backpack on her front and was talking into it at random intervals. Keira and I noticed an old couple exchanging a glance.

"Let's go somewhere no one else is," she said.

"I know." An excited grin spread across Connie's face. "Let's write wishes and cast them into the depths of the ocean."

"I don't know if telling the depths of the ocean that I fancy Alfie is going to do anything," Keira said. "It's probably not the depths of the ocean's top priority."

"Do you mean Scarlett's brother Alfie?" I asked. "Do you have a crush on him?" It was still weird that Keira Avakian didn't wear special orthopedic shoes anymore, let alone that she confidently crushed on people. Lauren had always fancied Alfie. She had told me the first time we ever met him at Scarlett's party at the beginning of fifth grade. I wondered if she still did.

Keira and Connie both nodded.

"I think he looks like an ice cream cone," Connie said enthusiastically. "But love is a funny fish like that."

Keira flicked Connie's arm with her finger.

"Do you like anyone, Mouse?" Connie asked as we climbed the stairs to the deck.

I shook my head and felt a little embarrassed. Like I should have some story about a boy at White Lodge. I don't even know if I've ever liked anyone. Like *really* liked them. Like Photoshop-your-face-next-to-his crush. I mean, Lila once *ate* a picture of a boy in ninth grade she wanted.

I guess all I've thought about for so long is ballet. A thud of anger hit me. It wasn't fair that I wasn't good enough. That life could give me something I wanted so much and then just take it away.

"Maybe you'll find someone to like on this trip," Connie said as we pushed a heavy door open and walked out onto the deck. The wind hit us really hard. My hair blew out behind me and the salty spray showered my face.

"I've got quite high standards," Connie shouted over the wind. "I've only fancied one person in my life, and he doesn't even exist." She looked dreamily out to sea. "Oh, Ron Weasley . . . you fictional ginger stud."

"Well, I've only liked one person too!" said Keira, proudly. "Alfie's always been the man for me. And he very much *does* exist. Shame his sister's a bit of a—" She broke off, looking at me. "Sorry, Mouse, I know Scarlett's your friend."

I shrugged to show it didn't matter. The thing was, I had no idea whether Scarlett was my friend or not. And if there were sides, she was on Lauren's.

"Yeah, but you've kissed *three* other boys," Connie

reminded her sternly. "I mean, I totally ship you and Alfie, obviously, but you must have liked those three too?"

Keira wrinkled her nose. "Urgh, *no.* I was just practicing for when it happens with him." She looked at me. "Have you ever kissed anyone, Mouse?"

"No," I said quietly, trying not to draw attention to it. Maybe it was another thing *everyone* had done over the last two years.

"Don't worry," Connie said, smiling. "Neither have I."

"You're not missing out on anything, to be honest," sighed Keira. "It's a little anticlimactic, really. You think it'll be this big, life-changing moment, but it's actually just Elliot Campbell slobbering all over you."

"That's probably not *everyone's* experience of a first kiss," Connie said. "Elliot Campbell doesn't even know that many people."

"Whatever. Maybe we'll meet some French boys in the Alps. I bet French boys are ten times better kissers than English boys."

"Well, obviously," said Connie. "That's why it's called French kissing. You never hear about English kissing, do you?"

Keira leaned over the railings. "English kissing *is* a thing. It's when a boy asks you to dance, drools all over you, and then goes and has a farting competition with his friends and never speaks to you again."

"Hey, guys."

We all turned around at the same time. I had been acutely aware of where Lauren had been every minute for the last three hours, but she had still managed to catch me off guard. Scarlett and Melody stood on either side of her. They smiled at me.

"I haven't seen you to properly say hi." Lauren held her arms out. I stepped forward and we hugged.

"Hey, Mouse." Scarlett hugged me too, then I hugged Melody. The same sort of hollow hug that lasted a split second.

"Your hands match your sweater," Lauren said, smiling and gesturing to where I hadn't quite gotten bath bomb off my hands. "Blue is very in this season. Impressive dedication to accessorizing right there." She was laughing, but in a friendly way. "We're going to get some hot chocolate if you want to come? They might have marshmallows." That had been Lauren's and my post–ballet lesson treat. The knot in my stomach released. If things went back to normal with Lauren, then maybe everything could be all right. I would get my best friend back.

"Yeah, definitely," I said. "That sounds really good." Then I saw Connie grinning at me. I didn't know if the invite was also extended to her and Keira. I couldn't imagine Lauren wanting them to come along. It's not like they're friends. Connie is the type of person Lauren makes fun of

33

behind her back. And pre-hot Keira was too. But it would be really bad to just go back to my old friends straight away, without even thanking Connie and Keira for everything they had done. I looked at Connie and then at Keira; I didn't know what to do.

"Can I meet you there in ten?" I said to Lauren. "We were just going to walk around the deck."

"We've got to talk to the depths of the ocean," Connie said matter-of-factly, and Lauren and Melody exchanged a look. I knew what it meant, but Connie didn't seem to notice.

"OK, well, we'll just be over there." Lauren pointed inside to a neon sign that said SINBAD'S DINER.

Me, Connie and Keira peered over the edge and stared at the ship cutting through the water. Keira got out her notepad and they started writing their wishes. I knew it was mean, but suddenly I wanted to get it over with quickly so I could get to the diner. But however stupid a thing it was to do, it felt like a waste not to write a *real* wish, just in case. Like when you blow out your birthday candles, you always end up wishing for what you actually do want.

"You've got two," Keira said to Connie. "That's cheating."

"I did one for Mr. Jambon," Connie said, patting her bag lovingly.

"Is it about avoiding arrest?" Keira asked.

"Good guess!" beamed Connie. She opened the paper

out to reveal what she'd written: *Please let me avoid hamster prison.*

Keira laughed. "He already lives in a *cage*. How bad could hamster prison be?" She turned to me. "Come on, Mouse, we've both written ours."

I looked at the little blank scrap of paper and decided to write down the only thing I wanted more than anything right now.

"On the count of three!" Keira shouted into the sea.

The wind snatched the papers the second we let them go, and I closed my eyes and repeated the wish in my head again and again.

I looked over at Connie. Her eyes were closed really tight and I could tell she was saying her wish in her head too. I wondered what Connie really wanted.

"Alfie is so hot!" Keira yelled.

"You're not supposed to tell us!" Connie screamed. "Don't hold it against her, depths of the ocean."

I said goodbye to them both and then started to panic. I needed to get the blue off my hands and think about what I was going to say. What if Lauren asked me about Paris? I needed to seem like the kind of person they would want in their group.

I pushed open the door to the bathroom, walked into a stall, locked it and pulled my jeans down. Some blue rubbed off on them.

Suddenly the bathroom door swung open, and I heard Lauren and Scarlett. I opened my mouth to shout hi but froze.

"Connie-May has always been a freak," I heard Lauren say. "It's like *Freaky Friday*. Like actually a seven-year-old is trapped in her body. And Keira looks really, like . . . awkward."

"Ugh, my brother really likes her," Scarlett sneered. "He does swimming with her and he totally hits on her."

There was a beat of silence. I wondered if Lauren had ever told Scarlett how much she had liked Alfie. Maybe she still did.

"Her eyebrows are so crazy," Lauren said. "Why doesn't anyone tell her to do something about them?"

"My brother is pretty weird. So no wonder he likes her."

I could just see them through the crack in the cubicle door as they started putting on makeup and redoing their hair.

My backpack was on the floor in front of me. If they saw it now, they would know I was there. I leaned forward as slowly as I could and lifted it up an inch at a time until it was on my lap. Then, with my jeans still around my ankles, I lifted my legs up and hugged my knees.

I was too scared to even exhale. The thought that they would realize someone was hiding was making me physically shake. And then I remembered that my phone was on loud. I repeated again and again in my head: *Please, God, don't let my phone ring.*

Scarlett walked into the stall right next to mine. She dumped her pink Jansport on the floor and the strap spilled under the gap. I closed my eyes like a baby to try to make it go away. Hearing her pee felt really strange.

"Mouse looks really weird," Lauren said. As soon as she said my name, my cheeks started to burn. "Like a boy. Being that muscular is just really ugly. In fifth grade she was really pretty but now she just looks . . . like a man."

My body felt like it was buzzing with hurt. Like it was numb. I always worried about being so lean and muscular but everyone said I was being stupid.

"I bet she has amazing abs, though." Melody laughed.

"She's probably anorexic," Scarlett said. "Dancers always are." She was literally a foot away from me.

"Guys, don't be mean," Melody said. "I feel sorry for her having to hang around with Eager Beaver and Weirdo Girl."

Scarlett picked up her bag and walked out of the stall.

"I just think it's really messed up that she thought it was OK to just act like nothing had happened." Lauren sounded like she was annoyed. "I'm not *friends* with her. She hasn't really got any friends here, has she? It's kind of weird of her to be like that. Really arrogant, actually. But I guess she *has* always been obsessed with herself."

Ugly. Like a man. Friendless. Obsessed with myself. I had to bite the handle of my bag to stop the tears.

"Why did you *invite* her?" Scarlett said.

"Because knowledge is power." Lauren made it sound like it was obvious.

I heard the door slam and the bathroom went silent again. I could hear myself crying, but I couldn't feel it. I couldn't feel anything.

JACK

"Look!" yelled Max. *"Snow!"*

The whole bus exploded into life as everyone scrambled to press their faces against the nearest window. We'd been off the ferry and driving through France for a good few hours, and everyone was buzzing about when we'd finally see some actual snow.

"Where?" asked Sarvan, who was three seats back from us.

Max jabbed his finger against the window again. "There, you idiots! Look!"

We all followed his finger and squinted. In the distance, emerging out of a cloud, was the ghostly outline of a mountain. You could just about make out its powdery-white peak.

"Oh yeah," said Toddy. "Bit disappointing."

Everyone sat back down, grumbling.

"Unbelievable," Max grunted. "You try to do something nice . . . Some people . . ." He turned to me. "D'you know what I mean?"

I nodded, but I was barely paying attention. I was just thinking about the bet.

Max was definitely going to win it. That was probably why he'd suggested it. But still, maybe he was right. Maybe a bet like this *was* exactly what I needed to finally stop worrying and get some courage. I promised myself right then and there that no matter what, I wouldn't be gutless again. If there was another Maria Bennett situation this week, I wouldn't chicken out. I would take a deep breath, close my eyes, lean in and go for it.

Outside the window, the snowy mountains on the horizon were getting gradually bigger. I felt a little jolt of nervous excitement in my chest. Next to me, Toddy still had his head buried in the phrase book. Since getting back on the bus, we'd decided we would try to memorize the most pointless French phrases we could find, then see if we could slip them into conversation during the trip.

"All right," Toddy said, pushing his glasses up with his middle finger, "what about this one: *'Avez-vous ma trousse?'*"

"What's that mean?" I asked.

"'Do you have my pencil case?'"

Max nodded. "Pretty good. Five points if you can get

that into an actual conversation with an actual French person. But you get much better results by mixing and matching from the vocab sections. Like, check this . . ."

He grabbed the book and flicked to one page at random, then another.

"OK . . . *'Ma perruche . . . est dans la zone piétonne.'*"

"Which means . . . ?"

"'My parakeet is in the pedestrian zone.'"

I laughed. "Yeah, that is good. Fifteen points if you can use that one."

"I still prefer *'Monsieur, votre grand-mère était un blaireau,'*" Toddy said.

"What was that again?"

"'Sir, your grandmother was a badger.'"

We all exploded into laughter.

"It's the 'Sir' that makes it work," said Max, wiping his eyes. "They think you're being all respectful with the *'Monsieur,'* and then—*bam!*—you hit them with the *'blaireau.'*"

"It's a classic sucker punch," I said.

"Thing is, we can't use any of these phrases till we get to the resort, can we?" Max said. "So, what about coming up with some challenges we can do now, on the bus?"

"Like what?"

"I dunno. Like mooning out the window."

"Max, we're not gonna give you points for showing your butt," said Toddy.

"Why not?"

"Because you obviously won't."

"I obviously *will*!" Max huffed. "If you'll give me twenty points, I'll pull a moonie."

Toddy shrugged. "All right. Twenty points for a moon."

"You do realize these 'points' have no actual value in the real world, Max?" I said.

"Yeah, but—" He stopped mid-reply and suddenly yelled, "Ugh! Oh my God, that's *rank*!"

I was about to ask what he was talking about, when a sharp, nasty tang hit the inside of my nose.

"Oh my God," I croaked. Bus farts are the worst farts known to man.

Max slapped both his hands over his mouth and pressed his face against the window.

"Vass meffalee munna damie thiff!" he said.

"You what?" said Toddy. "Oh man, what's that *smell*?"

Max moved his hands up so they were just covering his nose. "I *said*—that's definitely one of Jamie Smith's."

"Yeah," said Toddy, pinching his own nose, hard. "Cat food. Why do his always smell like cat food?"

With one hand still clamped to his face, Max shouted back down the bus at Jamie. "Hey, Jamie! Why do your farts always smell like cat food?"

"Because that's what your mum serves for dinner," Jamie yelled back.

He was rewarded for this with a loud cheer and a flurry of high fives. Max slumped back down into his seat grumpily. "That doesn't even make sense," he grunted. "Why would my mum serve cat food for dinner?"

Toddy rolled his eyes at me, but before he could reply, Mr. Flynn was bounding down the aisle toward us.

"All right, boys! Settle down. We're nearly there now."

You can usually hear Flynn coming a mile off because of his booming voice. He's quite short, with slicked-back hair and a black goatee. He talks like he's about sixty, even though my mum says he can't be more than thirty. We were all excited he was on the trip, because he's a real pushover.

"How are we all doing back here, then?" Flynn asked us, waving his hands about dramatically. He inhaled heavily and let out a loud, satisfied sigh. "Will you just smell that mountain air, eh, lads?"

"We're on a bus, sir," I said. "All we can smell is Febreze and Jamie Smith's farts."

Flynn wrinkled his nose. "Hmmm. Yes. It is a little . . . cat-foody back here."

"Sir," Max said, rubbing his top lip, "can I ask you a question about facial hair maintenance?"

"Yes, Mr. Kendal, you may," said Flynn, stroking his goatee proudly.

"Well, sir," said Max, "as you can see, I've got a mustache these days—"

"You may need a magnifying glass to confirm that, sir," I interrupted.

"Shut up, Jack," snapped Max. "Anyway, sir, do you think I should be shampooing it? Do you shampoo your beard?"

I groaned and stood up. "I can't listen to any more of this. Excuse me, sir."

I squeezed past Flynn and jammed myself into the tiny bathroom.

As I slammed the door behind me and straightened up, I whacked my head on the ceiling, painfully. It was only stuff like this that made me realize how much I had grown recently.

"Haven't you changed, Jack!" That was what my parents' friends always said when they saw me nowadays. But it was weird—I didn't *feel* different. I looked at myself in the little mirror. I didn't even *look* that different really, apart from the height thing. Same small, sharp brown eyes that curve upward at the edges. Same thin, pointy nose that I definitely got from my mum. Same deep, O-shaped dimples on either side of my mouth that double in size when I smile really widely. Same bushy brown hair that always sticks up at the front, no matter how many times I splash it down with water.

I pushed my face right up against the glass to check out my top lip. Nothing. Some of the hairs around the side of my mouth were getting sort of darker, but I was still a long way off even Max's crappy attempt at a 'stache. Maybe I could just color the hairs in with a black marker? Would anyone notice that? Maybe that was what Max was doing.

Suddenly a loud burst of shouting and laughter erupted above me. I flung the door open and sprang back up into the aisle.

I saw what everyone was going nuts about and burst out laughing too. Another bus full of school kids was driving alongside us, all going equally mad, because Max was standing up on his seat with his pants around his ankles, his bare behind pressed firmly against the window.

4

MOUSE

I crept back onto the bus before anyone else. I stared out the window the whole time people were clambering on, trying to be invisible, waiting for Lauren to walk past and confront me. When Lauren, Scarlett and Melody finally got on, they seemed louder and more giggly than ever. As they got closer my hands started to shake. They passed me, and the giggles stopped for a beat, but then they all just carried on walking down the aisle, louder than ever.

"How was the diner?" Connie asked brightly as she and Keira plonked down in the seats in front of me and the bus rolled out of the ferry's belly into France. "We got slurpies. Half blue raspberry and half bubblegum. See?" Connie stuck her tongue out and it was bright blue. "Now I match," she said, pointing at her blue-handprinted cheeks. I tried to smile. She looked at me more intently and then glanced toward the back of the bus. Her eyes clouded a little.

"You OK, Mouse?" she said softly, and I nodded.

I leaned my head against the window and pretended to sleep. Then Keira and Connie fell asleep for real, heads resting on each other, hair intertwined like their headphone wires, their legs flopping over each other. I didn't have to make conversation and pretend to be OK. I pulled my head inside my hoodie like a tortoise as I watched the French highway flicker past.

I listened to the music from *Swan Lake,* closed my eyes and tried to remember the steps, but I couldn't drown out Lauren and the things she had said. I felt hot, damp tears building at the corner of my eyes but wiped them away quickly. We hadn't arrived at the resort yet and already I wanted this whole trip to be over. I didn't even want to go home; I just wanted to go back in time and be a better dancer.

Finally, I actually did sleep. I dreamed weird dreams where me and Lila were jumping from bed to bed in the White Lodge dorm, and then I was playing in the kiddie pool with Connie when we were little, but she still had blue handprints on her face. Then Mum was hugging me and I heard Lauren's echoing laugh, mingling with Melody's and Scarlett's. As I opened my eyes the dream got muddled and I realized they really were laughing. Everyone was.

The whole bus was going absolutely crazy. Everyone was pointing and screaming. Even Connie was jabbing me with her finger. "Butt!" she screamed through hysterical laughter. I looked outside to see another bus driving next to us, and this pale, wide dough of backside pressed up against the window.

Everyone was taking pictures and yelling, and the boys on the other bus were going mad too. Connie put her hands over her eyes but kept shouting "Bum!" like she was calling for help, and I could hear Lauren screaming "Oh my God!" Miss Mardle came marching down the aisle doing her best stern face. The other bus overtook us, and the butt disappeared.

"All right, ladies! That'll do! It's just a bottom! I've got one, you've got one, everyone's got one!" Her Welsh accent got more exaggerated when she was flustered.

"Miss Mardle's got a butt!" Connie announced, and everyone burst out laughing again.

"Yes, yes . . . ," said Miss Mardle patiently. "I do hope you're not all going to go into wild hysterics every time you see a few boys. There *will* be boys at our hotel, you know."

"What?" said one girl near the front. "Are you serious, miss? There'll be boys there?"

Miss Mardle looked like she instantly regretted saying anything. "Erm, well . . . yes, Nadia. What I mean is, there will be a few other school groups staying there too, and chances are that some of them will include members of the male gender. . . ."

The rest of her sentence was drowned out by everybody screaming and yelling in excitement again. Miss Mardle clapped her hand to her face and retreated back to her seat.

Suddenly another ripple of commotion shot down the bus. I looked out the window again, and saw what everyone was shouting about—a huge billboard with a boy's grinning face on it.

The boy was incredibly, *amazingly* good-looking. He had big blue eyes that were looking slightly down, like he was shy, and a kind of half-smile that showed little dimples on each cheek. His light brown hair was messy and swept sideways, and he was topless and had that kind of perfectly tanned skin that only celebrities have. He was wearing a tattered black leather jacket, and his jeans were so low that you could see his whole torso, and underneath was the word ROLAND.

Keira whistled. "If that's what all the boys look like in this country, then I'm *definitely* up for some French kissing."

"It's not very practical to go out without a shirt in the snow," Connie said.

Keira whacked her on the head. "Don't even pretend you'd pick Ron over him."

"Ron is my one true love," Connie said without taking her eyes off the poster. "But I might let Roland English-kiss me. To warm me up for Ron."

I heard Scarlett behind us saying, "He must be, like, a French singer or something."

Lauren said, "I don't care what he is—he's definitely the hottest boy on the planet. He's amazing. We need to Google him the second we get signal."

Finally, as the sun was starting to set and the stars were beginning to show, we passed a sign for Mercier, the town we were staying in. The bus pulled into the hotel parking lot, and as I stepped off a blast of freezing air hit me. The fact that we were in the middle of a mountain range felt real for the first time. I hugged my jacket close to me and looked around. It wasn't actually snowing, but a thick white blanket covered pretty much everything—the ground, the cars, the roofs of the buildings. It all felt so strange and distant. Even the air smelled different.

I waited as far away as possible while they were sorting out our bags so I didn't have to be near Lauren. I knew I'd have to speak to her at some point, but I just couldn't face it right now.

Miss Mardle came over and said, "Matilda, love, I've put you in with Connie, as she's supposed to be looking after you. I remembered you and Lauren were friends, but I'm afraid there wasn't space in her room."

I breathed an inward sigh of relief, and said, "That's fine, miss."

Connie beamed so widely she almost shone. Then she

turned to Keira. "Did you know that I thought Mouse's real name was Mouse until third grade?"

"Yeah, you also thought your dishwasher was haunted," said Keira.

"It was!" yelled Connie.

Miss Mardle interrupted, "Yes, look, girls, this is all fascinating, obviously. But let's head inside to the rooms now, as it's completely freezing. I'll need you all back in the lobby in about half an hour. The hotel's putting on a movie night for us. Connie, *please* make sure you wash your face before you come down."

Connie sighed and nodded, and we walked into the hotel with everyone else, making sure to keep a few feet behind Lauren, Scarlett and Melody. There were more posters of Roland stuck up all over the lobby.

"He's following us," I heard Melody say.

"I wish he *was* following us," Lauren said.

The woman at the reception desk pushed her glasses up her nose and peered at the poster with us. "You like Roland, eh? All the girls love Roland. Do you want to know a secret? Some people are saying he's right here in this town at the moment, making his new music video." She raised her eyebrows at us and smiled. "Maybe you will see him. . . ."

I saw Lauren mouth "Oh my God!" at Scarlett and Melody, and the three of them hurried off into the corridor, giggling.

Even though I hated myself for it, a bit of me wished I was with them.

JACK

Flynn unlocked the door and we charged past him into the room.

"Well, here it is, boys," he said. "Your home for the next five days."

The room was small, dark and very, very neat. Everything in it was a kind of weird browny color—the walls, the beds, the tables, the lamps. Even the sink in the bathroom.

"Nice!" said Max, dumping his bag on the floor. I looked out the window at the dark, starry sky. You could still see the outline of the mountains underneath it.

"Unpack your stuff quickly, and then come straight to the main hall," Flynn said. "Since it's too late to do anything else, the hotel is putting on a film night for us this evening."

He shut the door, and we turned our bags upside down and emptied them onto our beds.

"Right," said Max. "That's the unpacking done. Let's go and look around."

The entire hotel seemed to be covered in posters of some French singer called Roland. He looked like your typical boy-band clone—big, cheesy grin plastered across his face and a sideswept mop of brown hair covering his forehead.

He was wearing skinny jeans and a tattered black leather jacket. His confidence seemed to burn right off the poster.

"What. An. *Idiot,*" said Max, jabbing his finger against Roland's super-smug face. "See, this is exactly the kind of moron we're up against. Our band—whatever it ends up being called—needs to be the exact opposite of this guy and all the other commercial *X Factor* stuff."

Toddy squinted up at the poster. "He looks a little like you actually, Jack," he said.

"Shut up, Toddy," I laughed.

"No, seriously. He's got your nose, at least."

I looked at the poster again. He was sort of right. The little sharp, pointy nose and cheek dimples were a bit like mine. But the big blue eyes, smug grin and bulletproof confidence were about as far from me as it was possible to get.

Max checked the hall behind and in front of us, then pulled a pen out of his jacket and scribbled a big black mustache on Roland's upper lip. He checked the coast was clear again and added a speech bubble coming from under the mustache with the words *Je suis un loser* inside it.

He stepped back to admire his work. "What d'you think?"

"You know 'loser' isn't actually a French word?" I said.

Max sighed. "Course it is. 'Loser' is universal. It's one of those words that's the same in every language, like 'internet' or 'weekend.'"

"I'm fairly sure that's not true."

"Well, I'm fairly sure it is."

"I think the more interesting thing here," Toddy interjected, "is that you've drawn a mustache on him and *then* called him a loser. Are you trying to say that people who have mustaches are automatically losers?"

Max rubbed his few whiskers on his top lip defensively.

"No, obviously not, *Toddy*," he snapped. "It's not the mustache that makes him a loser. What makes him a loser is the fact that he's a loser."

"Ah, yeah, that makes sense," Toddy said, nodding. "Thanks for clearing that up."

We turned the corner into the main sitting room of the hotel, which was the same chocolatey-brown color as our bedroom, except it was about fifty times as big. There was a huge log fire blazing in the fireplace at the far end, and above it a massive TV screen. Tons of chairs were laid out in neat little rows, nearly all of them filled with kids of various ages. And about half of them girls.

"Oh my God!" hissed Max, grabbing my arm. "I told you!"

My stomach did a mini backflip as I glanced around the room. There were so many girls I didn't even know which ones to look at. Max was clearly having the same problem. His face was twitching wildly in all directions, like he had ten flies buzzing in front of him.

"They're all so . . . so . . ." His voice tailed off. "What's the word?"

"Hot?" I suggested.

"Yeah," Max said dreamily. "Exactly. Hot. They're all so hot."

We settled down into three free seats near the back as Mr. Flynn came bounding up the aisle toward us.

"What we watching, sir?" I asked as he sat down in the row in front of us.

"*Romeo and Juliet,* Jack," said Flynn.

All three of us groaned loudly. "Oh, what?" Max whined. "Firstly, I've already seen that, and secondly, it's awful. You literally can't understand a word anyone's saying. It should have subtitles or something."

Flynn smoothed the side of his goatee down with his thumb. "*Romeo and Juliet,* Mr. Kendal, is not 'awful.' It is Shakespeare's finest work—a boundary-trampling fusion of love, jealousy and family loyalty. A tragedy of utterly Dionysian proportions."

"You should have subtitles as well," muttered Toddy.

"What was that, Lewis Todd?" Flynn snapped.

"Nothing, sir."

"I can't believe we've spent all day on a bus just to sit inside and watch the guy from *Inception* in a Hawaiian shirt," said Max. "Can't we go out and explore, sir? Have a look around the town or something?"

"No, you most certainly cannot, Mr. Kendal. You will sit here quietly and soak up the words of England's greatest writer."

Max snorted. "If he was England's greatest writer, how come he didn't write in *English*?"

"It *is* English, you dummy," said Toddy. "It's how English people talked in the olden days."

"Yeah, well, no wonder the olden days were so awful, then. That's probably why they never got around to inventing TVs and iPhones and stuff—because no one could understand what anyone else was saying."

Suddenly the lights went down and the big screen flickered into life. Flynn whispered, "Quiet now, lads."

I tried to concentrate on the movie, but it was way more interesting to look around at all the girls in the hall. On the other side of the aisle, about ten seats away, my eyes fell on one chair that was totally hidden by hair: a long, straight, brown wave of hair that draped all the way down the metal seat-back and halfway to the floor. I followed the hair upward until I saw the girl it was attached to.

Even in the darkness, I could tell she was cute. Really cute. She looked sort of sad and serious at the same time. She was wearing an oversized gray hoodie and sitting in this weirdly rigid way—straight back, hands crossed in her lap, and feet pressed together on the floor.

I couldn't stop looking at her. It was weird. Every time

I tried to focus on the film, my eyes just drifted right back across to her.

I was starting to quite enjoy this secret little game when, suddenly, during the part where Leonardo Whatshisface and Juliet are flirting through the fish tank, she turned her head sideways and looked straight back at me.

5

MOUSE

The second I noticed him, he looked away. He might not have even been looking at me in the first place. There were about a hundred people in the hall. He could have been looking at anyone.

But then, suddenly, he turned again, and we locked eyes. It was only for a second, but a second that definitely happened.

I looked back at the screen straight away. I sat up and stared dead ahead. I tried to move my eyes without moving my body, but since I'm not a gecko, that didn't work.

He had dark hair that stuck up a little at the front. The boys next to him were whispering to each other and every so often he absent-mindedly whispered something back, but he was actually watching the movie. Or at least, trying to. It made me like him. He was wearing a woolly blue sweater with a hole in the sleeve that he was sticking his thumb through. His friend said something and he smiled and shook his head. He was good-looking, but when he smiled he was gorgeous.

I'd only noticed him in the first place because I'd been glancing around, trying to figure out where Lauren was. She was sitting behind me, somewhere, but I still didn't know exactly where. I felt like once I knew, I would be calmer somehow. It's weird how knowledge makes you feel more in control. Like an animal, trying to figure out where the next attack might come from. But then I saw Scruffy Sweater and forgot to look for Lauren.

I snuck another glance at him, but he was still staring straight at the screen. Watching Leonardo DiCaprio look at Juliet made me want to look at him even more. It was like Leo's stares were catching.

It was kind of nice not to be expected to talk. A break from pretending to be OK. I could just exist in the dark with Connie and Keira next to me, passing me candy every so often. But it was like once I knew the boy was there, I couldn't un-know it.

"The sex part is coming up now," Connie whispered to no one in particular.

Watching sex scenes with your parents is horrendous, but it turns out watching them with a bunch of people your own age is also really bad. Some boys started to laugh as Leonardo's shirt came off, and I felt my neck get hot.

I obviously couldn't bear to look at Scruffy Sweater during the sex scene. Once it was over, though, I couldn't help but dart my eyes over to him. He was holding his hand out to his friend next to him, who filled it with gummies.

Keira tapped me on the knee. "Who are you looking at?" she hissed.

"No one," I whispered, turning back to the screen.

"You *are*!" she hissed again. "You so *are* looking at someone!"

She sat up and stretched so she could see over me.

"Please don't," I whispered, grabbing her arm. "Please, Keira!"

"Who?" Connie went to stand up, and I pulled her back down into her seat. Keira burst out laughing. Miss Mardle shushed us from the back of the hall.

"Come on, which one are you looking at?" Keira whispered after a few minutes.

"Keira, I *beg* you," I pleaded.

"What? It's not against the law to look around a room."

Both Connie and Keira were now scanning the hall. Connie even had her hand over her eyes, like she was a sailor looking for land.

My stomach flipped in panic and I could feel my face flooding with heat.

"Which one is it? It's the one in the blue sweater, isn't it?" Keira whispered triumphantly, slumping back down into her chair and getting out some Starburst.

I shook my head furiously.

"Liar," Keira laughed. "You are the worst liar ever."

Keira pulled her knee up to her chest and started drawing stick people on her jeans. Then she drew a heart and put "Mouse" on one side of it and a big question mark on the other. I shook my head again but I could feel my face was redder than ever.

At the end of the film, when Romeo and Juliet died, I wanted to cry, even though we've watched it twice already in English. We even learned a scene from the ballet in sixth grade. I had been one of the guests at the ball. Afterward, in the dorm, we had all talked about what it would be like to dance it for real, at the Royal Opera House. The memory stung hard in my chest.

The lights came on and we got up, filtering out of the hall. I tried to look for the boy, but he'd been swallowed in the crowd behind us.

"This place smells like the PE changing rooms," Keira said as we walked back down the hall.

"Look, Mouse, there's the bathroom," said Connie loudly. "If Loverboy wants to kiss you, there's the perfect place!"

"It's not exactly the *perfect* place, is it, Connie?" Keira was kicking a Coke can down the hall.

"Guys!" I whispered as forcefully as I could. "He could be right behind us!"

"I know what we can do," Keira said, grinning, and another wave of panic washed over me. "A love spell."

The panic melted. A love spell probably didn't involve anything embarrassing. Not publicly embarrassing, anyway. It might be *insane,* but no one would ever know it had happened.

Keira groaned. "Oh, wait, no. We don't have the main thing we need for a love spell."

"Amortentia?" Connie said.

"No, we don't know his name." Keira stamped on the Coke can in frustration. "We have to know his name for the spell to work."

Connie stopped dead in the middle of the corridor. "Don't worry," she said. "I'm on it." Then she turned and ran back toward the hall.

JACK

How do you know if someone's looking at you because they like you, or just looking at you because you're looking at them? It's basically impossible to tell.

The girl with the long hair was out the door pretty much as soon as the lights came on. I definitely heard her and her friends giggling at some point. I really hoped they weren't giggling about me. Or maybe it's a good thing if girls are giggling about you? Who knows? They should cover giggling in biology.

Just as I was about to ask Max for his views on the female giggle, the tall, curly-haired girl who had been sitting with

Long Hair Girl came slinking back into the hall. Out of the corner of my eye, I watched her walk to within about five or six seats of us and start looking at her phone. She literally just stood there, by herself, checking her phone. What was she doing?

Flynn came over and clapped me on the shoulder.

"There you go, boys," he boomed. "That wasn't *so* bad, was it?"

"Yeah, sir, it was all right, I suppose."

"'It was all right, I suppose,'" Flynn repeated loudly. "I'm sure the Bard would be delighted with that eloquent appraisal, Jack. Now let's get back to the rooms, please. Big first day of snowboarding tomorrow."

Everyone in our group started shuffling toward the exit, and I noticed the curly-haired girl scurrying back out ahead of us. As she disappeared into the corridor, I felt Max grab my shoulder tightly.

"Oh my God," he hissed. "Look how hot *they* are!"

He was staring at three random girls who were standing near the entrance, checking their phones and glancing around the room. One was blond, and the other two had darkish brown hair, but apart from that, they all sort of looked the same. Like, with these huge, round eyes and red, pouty mouths and kind of scarily perfect prettiness about them. They almost didn't look real.

"Three of them, three of us," whispered Max.

"So?" I said, with a slight sinking feeling.

"Well, the numbers add up, don't they?"

"I don't think it really works like that, Max," I said, frowning.

"Course it does."

"What, so if Demi Lovato, Rihanna and Taylor Swift walked in, we'd have a shot with them too, would we?"

Max wasn't paying attention. He was properly transfixed by these girls. "We've got to go and talk to them," he mumbled.

Toddy kicked at a bit of loose carpet on the floor. "You can't be serious, man."

Max rolled his eyes and groaned. "Oh, come on, Toddy. What are you afraid of?"

I knew exactly what Toddy was afraid of, because it was the same thing I'd been afraid of that night with Maria Bennett. He was afraid that no fit girl in their right mind would be interested in someone half their height who looked about half their age.

"He's right, Max," I said. "I know we said we'd try harder with girls on this trip, but there's no way we can just go over and talk to girls *like that*. I mean, *look at them*."

Max leaned in toward me. "You do realize that if we *don't* go and chat to those girls, then Ed or Jamie or somebody else will? Do you really want to stay stuck at zero while those guys get even further into double digits?"

"Well, no, but—"

"You *do* want to win the bet, don't you? Because I *definitely* do."

"Yeah, but, Max—"

It was too late. Max was marching toward them. I don't think I'll ever stop being impressed by Max's confidence. Or maybe it's not confidence—just craziness. Either way, I felt myself being dragged along behind him, like I was attached to his jeans by an invisible rope. I turned to look at Toddy, and he shrugged, sighed and followed us.

The girls looked even better close up. I felt like I was on autopilot, like I wasn't really even in my body. My tongue felt twice as heavy as normal and my knees twice as weak. I had literally no idea what to say to these girls. Luckily, Max piled straight in, like he always does.

"All right!" he said as they turned to look at us. "How's it going? I'm Max."

The girls flashed their pouty smiles at him. They were about our age, maybe a little older, though it was hard to tell. The blond one giggled and said, "Hi, I'm Lauren," and the other two sounded off with their names, which were Scarlett and Melody.

"I'm Jack," I said, feeling my face temperature shoot up about ten degrees. Toddy said nothing at all. He just kept staring down at his shoes like it was the first time he'd ever seen them.

"So," Max said with a huge grin. "Crap movie, right?"

The girls looked at each other. "I actually really liked it," said Melody.

Max didn't miss a beat. "Yeah, it was great, wasn't it?" he said, nodding. Then, as the girls looked understandably confused, he added, "We call all great things 'crap.' It's a slang thing, y'know. So, what was your favorite part?"

I couldn't tell whether they thought Max was a hilarious maverick or a total idiot. Probably the second.

"I really love the language they speak in," said the ultra-, ultra-hot one named Scarlett. "I wish people still talked like that."

"Totally," Max said. "The language *is* the best part. One kid next to us said he needed subtitles. What a *moron.*"

The girls all laughed. Toddy and I exchanged a sideways glance.

"Where are you guys from?" asked Max, and Lauren said, "London."

"Cool," said Max. "We're from Winchester."

"Ladies!" shouted a woman at the entrance in a fluffy pink sweater. "Come on now, time to get back to your room."

"Ah, that's our teacher," said Lauren. "We'd better go." She grinned quickly at Scarlett and Melody and then said to Max, "Hey, if you want, though, you guys should come and knock for us later. We're in room twenty-two."

Before any of us could answer, they all walked off, giggling. Seriously, what is it with girls and giggling?

Max turned to me and Toddy, his eyes nearly boggling

out of his head. "Oh my *God*!" he hissed. "Amazing! And you two wanted to go back to the room without talking to them!"

"Okay, smart move," I conceded. "You did well there."

"*Quite well,*" snorted Max. "Three ridiculously hot girls just invited us to their room! And they don't even know we're in a band yet! *Imagine* how insane they're gonna go when they find out we're in a band! They'll probably be begging us to go out with them."

"Seems unlikely," I said.

"We can't actually go and knock for them, y'know," said Toddy quietly. "I mean, we'll get in so much trouble if we get caught sneaking down the halls at night."

Max clicked his tongue against his teeth. "God, Toddy, would you think outside the box for just one second, man? Room twenty-two's on the ground floor—it's like ten doors down from our room. So we don't need to sneak down the hall—we'll just climb out our window and then go and knock on theirs!"

"You'll probably get in more trouble wandering outside the hotel in the middle of the night," said Toddy.

Max snorted. "Fine, Toddy, don't come. Whatever. I don't think they'll particularly care whether you're there or not. You weren't exactly the life and soul of the conversation, were you?"

"Chill out, Max," I said.

"What, are you wimping out too?"

I glared at him, but as nervous as I felt, I knew this was a seriously big deal. Invitations to knock for girls in the middle of the night don't come along every day. In fact, this was the first one that had come along in thirteen years.

6

MOUSE

"She's actually crazy," Keira laughed as we opened the door to our room.

"It's *awful*," I said, but I couldn't help laughing along with her. "I'm going to have to go around in disguise for the rest of the trip so he doesn't see me."

"Are you group-crying?" Connie burst in behind us. "Let me join in."

"*What* did you do?" I was laughing and horrified at the same time. "Did you speak to him?"

"I employed masterful spy tactics, *actually*." Connie beamed.

"Does that mean you marched right up and said, 'We're going to do a spell on you, what's your name?'" Keira climbed on her bunk.

"I won't bother next time, then," Connie said, crossing her arms over her chest, making a *humph*ing sound.

Keira chucked her bag of Starbursts at Connie but she didn't notice. It hit her head and exploded wrappers and candies everywhere.

"Sorry, Connie." Keira leaned over the bunk. "That was supposed to be a thank-you."

"Did you actually do something?" I asked. My heart started to race a little at the thought of her talking to him. "Seriously, what did you say?"

Connie climbed up the ladder. "Well, I didn't *say* anything, actually."

Most of me was relieved but a tiny sliver was disappointed. Maybe he would have said, "Your friend is enchanting, would she like to gaze through a fish tank with me sometime?"

"Thank God," I said, slumping down onto my bed. "So what did you *actually* do?"

"I did exactly what you told me to," Connie said proudly. "I found out his name."

Me and Keira both yelled at the same time, "What is it?!"

"Do you really want to know?" Connie said, climbing onto the bunk with Keira. "It might ruin the mystery."

"What is the point of having a crush if you don't know their name?" Keira picked up a pillow and put it on Connie's tummy before sitting on it.

"Romeo and Juliet didn't know each other's names." Connie squirmed. "I can't breathe."

"It's *called Romeo and Juliet,*" Keira said. " 'Romeo, Romeo . . .' Remember?"

"Yeah, but they don't know in the beginning—it gets the romance going. Keira, I'm gonna vom!"

"I don't have a crush on him," I said. But even I could hear how weak it sounded. "I only . . . looked at him."

"That's how it all started with Juliet," Keira said. "A couple of looks through the fish tank and then—*boom!* True love."

"Maybe we should all ask for fish tanks for Christmas," Connie said.

Keira wailed, "Connie, can you please just shut up and tell us his name?"

"It's not actually physically possible to shut up *and*—"

"Tell us his name!" me and Keira both screamed at the same time.

"OK, OK . . . Look, if you guess his name, I'll tell you. That makes it more fate-ish."

I groaned. Keira said, "Is it Leonardo?"

"No." Connie wriggled herself free from Keira and reached across to the top of the wardrobe and got Mr. Jambon out. He purred in her hand as she fed him a piece of carrot.

"Leroy?" said Keira. "No, actually not Leroy. Link?"

Connie shook her head. "It's not a fancy name. It's just a normal boy name."

"George?" Keira said, and started doing a tiny braid in her hair.

"It's exactly like George but not George. It's the most like George you can be without being George."

"Porge?" I said.

All three of us simultaneously burst into hysterical laughter. It was the first time I'd really laughed in ages. I could hardly breathe. Each of us kept trying to speak but couldn't because we were laughing so hard. It was like crying; once I started I couldn't stop.

"OK, OK," Keira said at last, wiping her eyes. "Not Porge, then. What about John?"

"John is super close." Connie started waving her arms about. "It's actually closer than George. It's the most John name without being John."

"Jack?" I said.

Connie squealed and leapt into the air. "Yes! It's Jack. Oh my gosh, it's actually Jack!"

"Oh my God, it's definitely true love," said Keira. "*You* guessed his name!"

"So how did you find out if you didn't speak to him?" I asked.

"I just stood near him and pretended to check my messages," said Connie. "And then their teacher came over and called him Jack."

"No way," Keira said, shaking her head.

"I think Jack suits him," Connie said.

"We don't even *know* him," I laughed.

Keira jumped down to the floor and walked over to the window and opened it. "Jack, Jack, wherefore art thou Jack?"

Connie was rocking and unable to speak she was so hysterical. I covered my eyes in mock horror. Keira shut the window and pulled the curtains closed dramatically. She went over to her bag and rifled through it before taking out a book. In purple sparkly letters on the front it read *The Teen Witches' Book of Spells*.

"Right," said Keira, opening the book. "Love-spell time. Let's do this."

I had absolutely no idea what was happening, but I went with it.

"First," said Keira, "we need to form a coven. But we have to do it right. Magic is a powerful and chaotic art form. It's about the energy you bring to the spell. This is not some childish game—it's deadly serious."

"Can Mr. Jambon be our mascot?" Connie said, giving him a kiss.

Keira sighed. "He can be our *familiar*. You don't have mascots in magic."

Connie whispered, "Did you hear that, Mr. Jambon? You're a *familiar* now."

Keira tapped the book with her finger. "Now, the next thing is to cast a circle. Let's make one with our clothes."

We all rolled our clothes into sausages and made a weird little oblong circle between the bunks. Keira looked at the book. "The only problem is we are all supposed to have a wand."

"We need to go to a wand shop." Connie said. *"Monsieur, où est le shop de wand?"*

"No, maybe we just need to go outside and find some." She studied the book. "It says here, 'You will find the right wand for you when you go looking for it.'"

"Can't we use a temporary wand?" I said. "I mean, surely we can improvise and then find proper wands tomorrow?"

"Well, it doesn't say you can't improvise," Keira said.

"Exactly. Maybe *the right wand for us* is right in this room?" I suggested. "Maybe the right wand for us isn't a wand. Well, maybe it's not even wand-*shaped*." I reached into the bottom of my bag. "Maybe the right wand for us is a headlamp."

"I think you're right," Connie said. "And I think we should dress up."

Keira rolled her eyes. "I swear you're *obsessed* with dressing up. As what?"

"Ourselves," said Connie. "Our witch selves. Group hug!"

She screamed, and she and Keira jumped at me. I squealed as they squeezed me, and jumped along with them.

Connie put on her lion onesie and drew war paint on her cheeks in purple marker. Keira drew tiny stars next to her eyes, and changed into an all-black outfit, except for brown socks with owls on them.

I rifled through my bag again. "I don't really know what my witch self is."

"I know," said Connie. "Your witch self should be Juliet. Because Jack is your Romeo."

Connie started wrapping the bedsheet around me, and then made me a crown out of a belt and a T-shirt.

"I look like a Roman," I said.

"Or a mummy?" Keira offered.

"I think it's perfect," Connie said. Keira drew a heart on my cheek in red felt-tip to complete the effect.

"OK, now we have cast the circle and embodied our true witch selves," said Keira. "Next, we need to find the spell." She flicked over to another page. I suddenly wondered if the book had a spell to make you a better dancer. Or maybe even turn back time.

"Got it," Keira said, and smiled. "Irresista-spell."

Connie squealed. "Jack and Mouse, sitting in a tree, K-I-S-S-I-N-G!"

"Er, it's a bit more complicated than that," Keira said. "We need paper and a pen. A true belief in magic. A full moon—I can't see it, so let's presume it's full. A hair from your head and a mason jar."

The only thing we didn't have was a mason jar, so Connie scooped her suntan cream out of its pot and rinsed it out.

As Keira was the most experienced witch, she took control. "OK, so, Mouse, you need to stand in the center of the circle."

"Oh, I'm getting a little scared," Connie whispered.

"Don't be silly. It's not a hex, it's a totally white magic spell," Keira said. "The first rule of teen witchcraft is not to wish harm on others."

"Yeah, but we could be opening a vortex into another world," I said, smiling.

"OK," said Keira, "you have to put the hair from your head into the jam jar."

Keira pulled one out and handed it to me and I dropped it into the sticky pot.

"Now you have to write his name and put it in the jar."

"This feels really weird and psycho," I laughed, scribbling his name down.

"OK, now we're going to hold hands, and we all have to sing, 'Name is written / Hidden singing / Compel the object to my bidding / So mote it be.'"

"'So mote it be'?" Connie burst out laughing.

"And then we all have to sing his name three times and Mouse has to sing it into the jar."

"I don't know if I can remember all that. Can we practice?" I said.

We stood in a circle and the others held hands and I held the pot and we all started chanting the song.

"Now!" Keira shouted, and we all shouted, "Jack! Jack! Jack!" and then Connie yelled, "Wherefore art thou, Jack!"

There was a pause, then Connie screamed, Keira hit the floor and I froze in terror.

Someone was knocking at the window.

JACK

Me and Max locked eyes in panic.

"Why are they screaming?" he whispered. "They told us to come!" He jumped to the left of the window and pinned himself against the wall, out of sight.

"Maybe they were expecting us to knock on the door, like normal people," I muttered.

Suddenly the curtains were flung open and I was face to face through the glass with the tall, curly-haired girl who'd been hanging around at the end of the movie night. She widened her eyes at me, then squealed and flapped the curtains shut again.

Max was still standing flat against the wall, his eyes darting about like a nutcase.

"What's going on?" he whispered. "Is it the girls or not?"

"It's *a* girl," I said. "Just not any of the girls we were looking for. I think we got the wrong room."

Max unpinned himself from the wall and peered up at the window.

"What are you on about? The curtains are still closed."

Before he could pin himself back against the wall, Curly-Haired Girl flapped the curtains open again and yanked up the window.

"Hi!" she said, grinning. "Come inside, you must be freezing!"

Me and Max looked at each other and shrugged. We had been wandering around the outside of the hotel for a good ten minutes, trying to figure out which window belonged to room 22. Despite wearing two hoodies and a jacket each, we were both absolutely frozen.

"Er, yeah, OK. Thanks," I said, trying not to sound too pathetically grateful for the chance to get out of the cold.

I pulled myself up onto the window ledge and looked around the room. I saw that there were two other girls inside, and one of them—sitting in the middle of the floor—was Long Hair Girl. I felt my heart jump right up into my throat.

She wasn't wearing the gray hoodie anymore, but what she was wearing was absolutely insane. She had a bedsheet draped over her, a belt tied around her head and a massive red heart drawn across the side of her face. The two other girls were rocking the same strange hippie look.

I became suddenly aware that my nose was actually dripping from the cold. I ran my glove over it, hoping none of them had noticed. In proper lighting, and closer up, Long

Hair Girl looked *seriously* hot. Even the fact she was dressed like a crazy person couldn't disguise it. The combination of the shock and the cold and her serious hotness was too much, so I just hung there on the ledge for a few seconds with my mouth open. The girls just stared back at me.

Finally, Max broke my trance by yelling, "Can you get inside, Jack? I'm freezing my face off out here!"

I hauled myself through the window and tumbled into the room.

"Well, this is a surprise," said Curly-Haired Girl.

I stood up and brushed myself off. My heart was beating so hard I could feel it bumping against my T-shirt.

"Er, yeah, sorry," I stuttered. "We were actually . . ."

I caught eyes with Long Hair Girl, and something inside me said not to tell them that we'd been looking for another group of girls.

"We . . . were actually just bored, so we thought we'd go for a midnight walk," I said.

"Nice idea!" said Curly-Haired Girl. "Midnight walks are my favorite kind of walks."

"I, erm . . ." I tried to think of something to say. "I like your outfits" was the best I could come up with, and I felt the sudden urge to curl up in the corner and die.

"Thanks!" said Curly-Haired Girl. "We made them ourselves. Well, except I didn't make this lion onesie. I got it for Christmas from my Auntie Alison."

She beamed at me. The other two girls looked mortified and slightly in shock. Behind me, Max hauled himself onto the window ledge and propped himself up on his elbows.

"What's up, ladies?" he said with a grin. "What's with the dressing up?"

Suddenly, there was a knock at the door. We all froze. Outside in the hall, we heard a woman's voice.

"Girls? I thought I heard some commotion. Everything all right in there?"

Curly-Haired Girl mouthed, "Oh no!" and Long Hair Girl suddenly sprang up and whispered, "It's Miss Mardle!"

"Jack, let's go, man!" hissed Max, dropping off the windowsill and back onto the snowy ground outside. I made to follow him, but there was another knock at the door and this Miss Mardle woman's muffled voice said, "Girls? Are you OK? I'm coming in now."

The door clicked and started to creak open. Long Hair Girl mouthed the word "Sorry." Before I could ask what she was sorry for, she shoved me into the closet and quietly shut the door.

In the darkness, over the sound of my heart thudding in my ears, I could hear the girls getting grilled by Miss Mardle.

"I thought I heard someone screaming in here," she said. "What are you all up to?"

"It must have been another room, miss," said the third girl. "We were asleep."

"Asleep? Then why are you all dressed so strangely?"

There was silence. Then one of them coughed and said, "This is just . . . what we wear when we go to sleep, miss."

"Right . . . ," said Miss Mardle. "I don't mind you having fun, girls, but just try to keep it down. And get some sleep. We've got a big day ahead tomorrow."

"OK, miss. We—"

I didn't hear what came next, because I was suddenly flooded with shock, pain and cold, horrible terror.

Something was in the closet with me.

7

MOUSE

Connie was staring openmouthed at the closet. She might as well have been holding a sign that said BOY HIDING IN THERE! I didn't know where to look. Panic was immobilizing me. Luckily, Keira was much cooler under pressure than either of us.

"OK, miss. We'll try and keep it down," she said. "We were just a little, you know, excited or whatever for tomorrow." Keira somehow perfectly pulled off her trademark underwhelmed-by-everything tone.

"OK then, girls," said Miss Mardle, backing out the door. "I'm excited too. Night, then."

"Sleep tight, miss!" Connie chirped, slightly manically.

I could feel the panic starting to melt. She was inches from leaving the room.

And then, from inside the closet, there was a loud thud.

Miss Mardle stepped back in. "What was that noise?"

Connie had gone white and was still staring at the closet like she thought it led to Narnia. *Why* wasn't he just keeping still in there? We could get *expelled* for having a boy in our room. Kicked out of two schools in one month. Surely that would be some sort of record?

I looked over at Keira, but she was busy eyeballing Connie, willing her to look away.

I curled my hands into balls to try to stop them trembling, and somehow managed to get out, "Oh, sorry, miss . . . I put three jackets on the same hanger in there. One of them must have fallen off."

Miss Mardle nodded. She seemed satisfied. And then there was another thud.

"There goes the second one," I said, mock-breezily, and Keira laughed a little too loud. *What* was Jack doing in there? Was he *trying* to get us into trouble?

Miss Mardle frowned and took a step forward, toward the wardrobe. Suddenly Connie snapped into action.

"Miss Mardle," she said, her whole body shaking. "I am a really good person. I raised three hundred dollars in the trash-fashion show last year and I also do guerrilla gardening with Miss Ford and I'm on the school council. . . ." Her voice started to quiver like tears were coming.

I looked wildly at Keira. It was all over. There was no way Miss Mardle wouldn't check the closet now. Another faint knock came from inside. Jack had clearly gone mad. We had to get her out of the room. Quickly.

"Can I talk to you privately, miss?" I blurted desperately. She didn't move, so I walked past her and out into the hall.

"Of course," she said, her eyes still on the closet. Then she followed me out, shutting the door behind her. I had done it. My heart was still racing, but as long as she didn't go back in there, then we might have got away with it.

But now I was standing opposite Miss Mardle, alone in the hall. And she was waiting for me to say something. Something that was apparently so important I couldn't say it in front of anyone else.

"It's all just really . . . hard," I said lamely. She put her hand on my shoulder and gave it a little squeeze. The weird thing was that even though I was making up a lie on the spot, it was actually true. I opened my mouth to say something else but nothing came out. Lauren and the ferry and all the trauma of the last month—it was all there, but it was too big and too true to tell her.

"I know, dear," she said. "I know."

We stood in silence for a bit. Was that enough? Did that merit a private discussion out in the hall? I thought about lying and telling her my parents were getting divorced. For a split second I even contemplated hugging her.

"I just wanted to tell you, that's all." It hung there, sounding ridiculous.

Then she said, "Thank you, Matilda." She put her arm around my shoulders. "I think you're very brave. Night, dear. Get some good sleep." And she walked back down the hall.

I nearly fainted in relief.

When I stepped back into the room, Keira pounced on me. "I literally love you, Mouse! You are a legend!" she whisper-shouted, squeezing me. It was like we had won some kind of fool-the-teacher competition.

And then the closet door burst open and Jack came flying out across the room.

"There's a rat!" He was jumping up and down on the spot. "In there! A massive, huge *rat*!"

Keira laughed. "What?"

Jack was fidgeting on the spot and ruffling his hair. His face was bright red, and it looked like he was sweating. "It bit me! Right on the ankle! I'm telling you, there's a rat in there!"

Connie still looked a little shell-shocked, but without saying a word she got on her hands and knees and crawled right into the wardrobe, her lion's tail swishing as she rustled about. Then she reappeared and held out her palm to reveal Mr. Jambon. "My hamster is *not* a rat," she said.

She and Keira burst out laughing, and Jack went even redder. He was rubbing his ankle and staring down at the floor.

"Yeah, well, you should check again," he muttered. "'Cause there's definitely a rat in there as well."

"I would have thought exactly the same thing," I said, and he looked up at me. "France is known for its killer closet rats, after all."

He smiled a kind of thank-you smile and then looked down and shoved his hands in his pockets. Him being so near me felt like too much, like I might implode. So I just focused on a spot over his shoulder where Keira's bra was hanging on the end of the bunk. His hair was dark and thick, sticking up all over the place. He was even cuter than his outline at the film night had suggested.

He looked at Mr. Jambon. "You brought a *hamster* on a school trip?" He sounded impressed. "That is quite an . . . insane thing to do."

I saw him look me up and down, from the T-shirt crown to the bottom of the bedsheet dress. I didn't know what to do, so I just put my hand over my cheek to cover the red felt-tip heart. And just left it there, trying to seem casual, like I always stood like that, my hand glued to my cheek. I was trying desperately to think of an explanation for why we were dressed like this, when there was another knock on the window.

Connie screamed, "The spell's still working!"

"Shut up!" Keira whispered. "Mardle will come back."

"What spell?" asked Jack, but we all ignored him.

Keira walked over to the window and opened it. The same freezing-looking boy with shaved red hair was peering over the ledge.

"What's going on?" he hissed. "Did you get caught?"

Keira shook her head. "Your friend did get savagely bitten by a killer hamster, though," she said. "He could have died."

Max snorted with laughter.

"It was a rat, *actually*," Jack snapped. "There was definitely a rat in there as well."

"I don't think they even *have* rats in France," Connie said.

"Yes, they do," I said, and something made me smile at Jack, to make him feel better, maybe. "What about the rat in *Ratatouille*?"

Jack smiled straight back at me and a little dimple appeared in each of his cheeks. My stomach jolted. "Exactly," he said. "Thank you."

"That rat's American," Connie said. "He has an American accent."

"He lives in Paris!" Jack said.

"And he's called Remy." We both said it at exactly the same time.

"You said the same thing at the same time." Connie clapped her hands. *"Spooky."* She looked over-meaningfully at me and Keira.

"Thanks for pushing me into the jaws of death," Jack said, nodding at the closet. "I'm Jack."

"Oh, we know," Connie said, nodding. Keira visibly winced and gave Connie a Death Eater stare.

"We know *now*," Keira amended. "I mean, you've just told us, so obviously we know. Anyway, I'm Keira. Hamster trafficker over there is Connie." Connie was letting Mr. Jambon crawl on her head. "And that's Mouse."

All the things that usually come naturally started to feel hard. Thinking, speaking, standing in a relaxed way. So I settled for shifting from foot to foot, my hand still clamped to my cheek.

Jack laughed. "Mouse? Why do people call you that?"

I opened my mouth to speak, but Connie answered for me. "'Cause in kindergarten, she used to have her hair in two big buns, like Minnie Mouse. Plus, y'know, she looks like a mouse." Connie broke off and started miming a mouse cleaning its whiskers. "Squeak, squeak, squeak," she said. Mr. Jambon started squeaking on cue.

I was cringing inside. I was trying to look normal while giving myself orders in my head. *Don't smile too widely; try to stand in an effortlessly cool way. What is an effortlessly cool way of standing? Stop standing weirdly.* But Jack just stood there, smiling at me. So I just kept smiling back.

From outside, the other boy said, "And if anyone cares, I'm Max, and I'm about to get frostbite. Jack, can we go now, please?"

Keira popped her head outside the window. "My God, it's freezing out here. What room are you lot in?"

"Room ten, back down the end of the corridor," said Max, who was shivering but still managing to gawp at Keira in a not-very-subtle way.

Jack turned to me and said, "Sorry, we better go, but see you tomorrow maybe?"

I nodded and couldn't think of anything to say, so I nodded again. And then again. I almost looked like I was bowing or something.

Jack climbed out the window awkwardly, flashing his boxers, which were covered in little goldfish. Then he was gone.

"That. Was. Wild," Keira said, when she'd closed the window.

"I'm really, really scared now," Connie whispered. "If we can make boys just randomly appear, what else can we do? What about global warming? Should we do something about that?" Me and Keira sat back in a circle. "But it *really* happened," Connie went on. "Like, we made *that* happen. We summoned him."

Keira patted her hand. "Calm down, Connie. Maybe we did conjure him to our window, or *maybe,* just maybe, he loves Mouse and he came to find her."

I shook my head. "No. I definitely don't think so. No."

Keira groaned. "Oh, come on, Mouse. He only found out your room number and snuck out to come and see you. Face it, you are a boy-magnet. Or a Jack-magnet at least." She picked up a pen and wrote JACK on the other side of the heart on her jeans in huge purple letters.

"Keira, stop!" I wailed.

"Or maybe we accidentally summoned the powers of darkness and they just made them come here like zombies. . . ." Connie still sounded scared.

"Maybe," said Keira. "Either way it's good. We're either true witches or Jack wants a piece of the Mousester."

I smiled and let myself think about it all for a second. The movie, and how there had been that moment that definitely happened. I couldn't stop smiling.

"Aaaaaah," said Connie. "You *love* him."

"I might not even see him again," I said, staring at Keira's knee with his name now scribbled on it, and praying she didn't wear those jeans again this week.

"Well, he came to your balcony," Connie said, and then she dramatically put her hand to her forehead. "What light through Mouse's window breaks?"

Keira laughed. "What you need to do now is show him that you like him back."

I blushed. "No way. No. Definitely not. Whatever it is you're thinking—no."

JACK

"All right," whispered Max, "now let's find room 22."

I stared at him in disbelief, watching his words dissolve into thick, puffy clouds of smoke. We had started crunching back through the snow toward our own window. My fingers were so cold they were stinging, the freezing wind was making my eyes stream and my ankle was still throbbing from whatever it was that had savaged me in the closet. Plus, my phone said it was now coming up to midnight.

"You're not serious?" I hissed at him. "After what I've just been through?"

I was still trying to figure out what had actually happened in that room. There was no way I was up for breaking into a whole other room full of girls now.

Max was grinning and blowing on his hands. "Jack, obviously it was quite fun hearing you make a fool of yourself and get attacked by a hamster in a closet, but I would still quite like to do what we actually came out here to do, and meet some pretty girls."

"Firstly, it was a rat, not a hamster, and secondly, I thought Mouse and those girls were pretty too." Despite all the madness that had happened in that room, the one thing I couldn't stop thinking about was the way Mouse had smiled at me. She was *so* cute—but there was something more about her that separated her from the other girls I'd met. . . . A weird kind of calm, maybe; a stillness that put you at ease straight away, even when you were rambling on about *Ratatouille* or whatever.

"Yeah, yeah, they were hot," Max conceded. "The one that was all in black is, like, *really* attractive, and so's the one with ridiculously long hair. The curly-haired one's a little strange, though. And yes, Jack, it was definitely a tiny baby hamster. I saw it. Anyway, let's stop whispering like idiots out here in the freezing cold and go find the girls we were actually *supposed* to meet. Who actually *invited* us to their room."

"What if their teacher's still prowling about? Do you realize how close I came to being caught back there?"

"S'all right, we'll just make less noise this time, won't we? Anyway, once we get inside, the only sound I'm gonna be making is this . . ." He started kissing his own hand dramatically, making horrible, soft smooching noises.

"So, what, we're all gonna sit and watch while you kiss your own hand?"

"Shut up, Jack, you know what I mean. Anyway, if we don't knock for them, then we've totally blown any chance we might have had with them for the rest of the trip. They'll think we're complete idiots."

I thought about it. He did have a point. Although, at that moment, all I really wanted to do was get back to my warm bed. And maybe think about Mouse's smile some more.

"OK, fine," I said. "But how are we even gonna find them? We thought that last room was room twenty-two, so we clearly have no idea where we are."

Max raised his eyebrows and grinned. "Well, Jacky boy, that's where you're wrong. I saw their room key by the bed. It said 26, which means . . ." He broke off, counted four windows down from Mouse's room, and then jabbed his finger triumphantly. "*That* one must be room twenty-two!"

He started trudging back the way we had come, and I slouched after him. When we got to the window, Max stopped and looked up.

"It has to be this one, right?" he whispered. "I mean, I'm pretty sure it's this one."

" '*Pretty sure*,' " I muttered. "You're not positive, though, are you? What if this is a *teacher's* room, Max? It could even be Flynn's room."

Max shrugged. "So? If he sees us, we'll just say we were sleepwalking."

"*Sleepwalking?* What, outside? Together?"

"Yeah."

"Bit of a coincidence, don't you think, that we both happened to be sleepwalking at the exact same time, in the exact same place?"

Max shrugged again. "Stranger things have happened. Probably."

"Great," I said. "That's what you can tell Flynn, then. 'Stranger things have happened, sir. Probably.' "

"God, Jack, are you gonna be a total wimp all your life, like Toddy?"

I sighed. "All right, this is what we'll do. You knock on the window, and then we'll both jump out of the way, just in case it's not their room."

"Yeah, OK."

Max gulped and raised his fist up toward the window. He banged loudly, three times, and we both leapt flat against the wall.

For a second, nothing happened.

"No one screamed, at least," Max whispered.

"They're probably just calling the police instead," I said.

Suddenly the window was yanked up, and a head poked out. It was the blond girl called Lauren. Max stepped away from the wall, out of the shadow.

"Oh my God!" Lauren squealed. "It's you guys! We thought you would . . . y'know, knock at the door."

Max grinned. "Erm . . . well, we thought it'd be more, like, *Romeo and Juliet*–y if we came through the window."

Lauren laughed and yanked the window right up. "Well, come in, then."

Max raised his eyebrows at me and piled straight through the window. There was nothing I could do but follow him.

8

MOUSE

"I'll only do it if we say the note is from all of us."

Keira rolled her eyes at me and groaned. "Mouse, don't be ridiculous. It needs to be from you. We can't send a *group* love letter. He'll think we're crazy."

"That ship might have already sailed, to be honest," said Connie, nodding at my bedsheet dress while stroking her own lion onesie.

"I just . . . Please . . . ," I stammered. "I really don't want to make it awkward. I'll die of awkwardness."

Keira groaned even louder. "We're only putting a note under his door, Mouse. It's not like you're proposing to him. I mean, he literally walked through the freezing cold to serenade you at your window. How much more proof do you need that he likes you? Do you want him to get your name tattooed on—"

"His butt!" Connie interrupted. "Imagine if he got 'Mouse' tattooed on his butt!"

"I was going to say his chest, but whatever," said Keira. "Mouse, I would totally be the same if there was any doubt about whether he liked you or not, but there isn't."

It wasn't true. It couldn't be true. But Keira seemed so sure. Like there was no other explanation. Her certainty was growing this tiny, shiny new me that knew boys and had *things* with them.

Connie rummaged in her bag and pulled out a pen. "Special occasion gel pen." She held it under my nose. "Cotton candy. The smell of *luuurve.*"

Keira tore a page out of her notebook, and we all sat in the coven circle and stared at it.

"You have to write it, though," Connie said to me. "Otherwise the aura might get confused."

She handed me the pen. I stared down at the page. "I don't know what to write. What do you write to someone you don't know?"

"Don't overthink it," said Connie. "Speak from your heart. What about, 'Dear Jack, it was lovely to meet you this evening. Thank you so much—'"

"Connie, it's not a letter to her freakin' granny." Keira grabbed the piece of paper and stared at it. "What about, 'Hey, Jack, I like you too. Mouse.' Or 'Mattie,' if you wanna be hot. Do you wanna be cute or hot?"

"I can't be the person who decides that, can I? Can't someone be both? Can I change my mind?" Everything was getting complex.

Keira shook her head. "You're either one or the other. It's a fact."

"What are *you*?" I asked.

"I haven't decided yet either. It's a big decision." Keira smelled the gel pen and wrinkled her nose. "This smells like school ravioli."

"Can't we write the note from all of us, instead of just me?" I asked again.

"But what would we *all* want to say to him?" Keira sighed dramatically.

"We could ask him a question," suggested Connie. "Like . . . who's his favorite Muppet? Or what does he think happens to you when you die? Or . . ." She scrunched her face up, thinking hard.

I took the paper from Keira and stared at it and then put it on the floor and wrote, *Hey, Jack. See you at breakfast tomorrow. Thanks for coming to see us.* I held it up to them.

"It's not exactly *I wanna smooch your face off, hot stuff,* but it'll do," said Keira. "Are you going to sign it?"

"No."

"Why don't you draw a little mouse and a kiss?" Connie blew a kiss toward the note. "Do you need to address it? Room ten, the Brownest Hotel in the World. The Mountains. France."

I ignored her and folded the piece of paper up.

We opened the door as quietly as we could, but as soon as we stepped into the hall the lights switched on automatically.

"Just try and be as quiet as possible," Keira said.

We half walked, half crawled to the end of the hall, past some vending machines and a fire exit, then turned the corner. Everything was completely silent, except for an old-fashioned ticking clock on the wall.

"It's one minute to midnight," Connie said. "The witching hour. I'm scared."

"Shhhhh. We're witches, aren't we?" I reached down and held her hand. We both grinned at each other. It felt like we were ten again, sneaking about in the night at a sleepover.

"There it is. Room ten."

As she whispered it, my stomach jolted. When we were in the room writing the note, I hadn't really thought we would actually end up here. Now it felt too real.

"I think we should go back," I mumbled. "I don't want to do it anymore."

"Come on, Mouse, you've got to *make* stuff happen. Otherwise you'll just stay exactly the same forever." Keira said it in an offhand way but it made me think. She was right: I didn't want to stay like this.

I looked at the note folded up in my hand and opened it.

"Connie, I hate you." I hit her on the arm. "You drew a mouse."

Connie giggled and Keira smirked. "Well, it looks like a deformed lion, if that makes you feel better," Keira said.

"Are you are a lion or a mouse?" Connie said, pointing at the room.

"Be a lion-mouse," Keira whispered.

"A louse," giggled Connie. "Or, actually, no . . . not a louse. A mion."

We all looked at the door and I took a step forward. I looked back at them and Keira mouthed, "Go on."

I took another step forward. Room 10 was only a few doors away. I closed my eyes and took a deep breath.

Then I looked back at them. "I can't," I hissed.

Connie tiptoe-ran at me and hurled herself into me like a football player. She grabbed the note from my hand. I tried to catch her tail but she was at the door and shoving the paper under the crack with a little yelp before I could get her.

We turned and ran and only stopped in a burst of quiet laughter when Connie tripped over her onesie feet. My heart was beating like when the curtain goes up on opening night; this weird rush of adrenaline was going through me.

As we were helping her up, we heard a laugh from the room we standing outside. It's weird how people laugh in really peculiar ways. I would know someone's laugh any-where. And I knew the one we could hear coming through the door was Lauren's. Knowing she was there made me heavy suddenly. I didn't want her to see us. Dressed up like stupid kids. She would laugh at us with Scarlett and Melody. Talk about how lame we were. How weird. All of the fun of it just disappeared because she was close by.

Keira rolled her eyes. "I'm sorry, but she's so annoying. Even her laugh is annoying. It reminds me of our burglar alarm."

And then, unmistakably, we heard a boy's laugh. We all froze and looked at each other. Keira took a step forward and put her ear against the door. She didn't need to.

"Jack, you're such a loser!" a boy's voice guffawed. I felt my stomach turn to ice. Then Jack's voice came through, muffled, but clear enough.

"Yeah, whatever, Max, it was your idea in the first place."

There was a burst of laughter, and then we heard Lauren say, "You guys are *so* funny!"

I took a step back. Connie and Keira glanced at each other and then both turned to look at me. It was like a balloon had popped.

We tiptoed back to our room, and I went into the bathroom and shut the door behind me.

I was an idiot. Lauren had probably *sent* Jack to our room as a trick. They were probably all laughing at us now, about how I had believed that he would like me.

This feeling of empty disappointment just seemed to follow me everywhere. It was there at White Lodge when they told me I hadn't realized my potential and I would never be a ballerina. It was there in the ferry bathroom as I listened to Lauren say I wasn't good enough to be friends with them. And it was here now, stronger than ever, as I digested the fact that Jack had never really liked me at all.

There was a faint knock on the bathroom door and Keira poked her head around it. "Mouse, I'm really sorry. I feel like it's my fault. Like I stirred everything up."

She came and put her arms around me and then Connie did too.

"Group hug," Connie said sadly.

"I don't understand what they're doing. I mean, are they just, like, randomly knocking on girls' windows?" Keira sounded almost impressed.

"What horrid, awful people," Connie said. "We should write them another letter saying 'We take back our first letter.'"

I looked up. All three of us were entangled in a cuddle. I met Keira's eyes in the mirror and panic jolted us both.

"We need to get the note back," I said, and she nodded.

Going into the hall for the second time, I didn't even think about Miss Mardle. It would be worth getting sent home to get the note back.

Connie was holding the coat hanger we had brought in front of her like a sword, swinging it from side to side, to deter attackers.

We crept past Lauren's room and stopped to listen.

"They're still in there," Keira whispered.

We crept further down the corridor and stopped by room 10.

"Right, Connie, you need to be quick 'cause they could come out at any time."

Connie crouched down on the floor. Her lion hood fell forward, covering her face. She slowly pushed the coat hanger under the door and moved it along the carpet.

"I think I can feel the note." She ran the coat hanger along the floor again and stopped it. "It's definitely there."

She closed her eyes in concentration and pressed her cheek firmly against the door. Which then opened, sending her tumbling onto the carpet face first.

A boy with floppy blond hair and glasses stood there, looking down at us, holding the note.

JACK

I was woken up by a sliver of hot white sunlight that fell through the curtain and came to rest slowly on the tip of my nose. I blinked my eyes open, feeling woozy from lack of sleep and already like I was catching a cold. It'd be so typical if I managed to get sick before we'd even got up a mountain.

All the madness of last night came rushing back to me. The crazy moment in Mouse's room with the closet rat-hamster. And then the depressing part in Lauren's room afterward.

Lauren and those girls were the exact opposite of Mouse's group. Chatting to Mouse felt easy and natural and fun, and I wasn't constantly worrying about sounding like an idiot. But with Lauren, Scarlett and Melody, I got the feeling that one misplaced word or one uncool reference, and they would have sent us straight back out the window.

They'd just mainly gone on about themselves, their school in London, bubble tea and *Pretty Little Liars*. At one point, I'd been sitting so close to Lauren on her bed that our knees were almost touching, but I never felt like anything could happen. It almost seemed like they were just . . . humoring us. Keeping us in their back pocket until they met some legitimately cool boys.

After about forty-five minutes of giggling and boring conversation, Max and I finally crawled back out the window, both still very much at zero. As we trudged back to our room through the snow, Max had muttered about how we needed to keep trying with them because they were so gorgeous, but I was much more interested in seeing Mouse again. Even as I'd fallen asleep, her long hair and big gray eyes were the last things flickering through my head.

I sat up and stretched out in the sunlight. I opened the curtains and really saw the Alps for the first time. Under the blazing sun, the white mountains were actually sparkling.

They looked like huge scoops of melting ice cream. The idea that we would be trying to snowboard down them in about an hour suddenly felt real and completely terrifying. I shook my head and told myself to get a grip. This trip was supposed to be about finally getting some guts, after all.

I heard the splash of the sink from the bathroom, and Toddy emerged through the door.

"Ah, finally! You're up."

"Morning," I croaked.

"OK, so a weird thing happened when you two were gone last night. Here, wake Max up—I don't want to go through this twice."

I chucked my pillow at Max, who was just a misshapen lump under his comforter. He groaned and popped his head out.

"What?" he whispered. "Why?"

Toddy started speaking, slowly, as if he was still trying to piece the story together in his head. "OK, so listen. At about midnight last night, I was just about to go to bed, when I heard this sort of scratching outside the door. I looked over and saw this little scrap of paper had been pushed underneath it. So I walked over and picked it up, right, but as soon as I did, I could hear whispering right outside. I opened the door, and there were three girls just lying on the floor in the hall, poking a coat hanger under our door."

"What?" Max was now fully awake. More awake than I

had ever seen him in my life. He sat bolt upright in bed, his eyes burning a hole in Toddy. "What girls? What did they look like? Did they mention me? What happened?"

"They were like . . . quite pretty, I guess," said Toddy. "One had, like, really long brownish hair, one had sort of wavy black hair, and one had curly hair."

Me and Max swapped openmouthed grins. "Oh my God!"

"So what happened next, Toddy?" I asked.

"Well, I said, 'Is this yours?' because I was holding the note. And the black-haired one said, 'Yeah.' And then the curly-haired one said, 'Can we have it back, please?'"

There was silence.

"And then what?" urged Max, slapping his own face in frustration.

Toddy looked at us blankly. "Well, I gave them the note back and then they left."

More silence. Max's left eye was twitching. He looked like a malfunctioning robot.

"You . . ." His knuckles were white from gripping the bedsheet. "You . . . gave them the note back?"

Toddy nodded.

"Did you *read* the note first?"

Toddy shook his head.

"So you have no idea what the note actually said?"

Toddy shook his head again. "They asked for it back," he said simply. "What else was I gonna do?"

Max jabbed his finger at the window, furious. "So if I *ask* you to throw yourself off that mountain, will you do that too? Because that is literally what I am now asking you to do, you absolute, *absolute dummy*!"

Before Toddy could defend himself, Flynn banged on the door.

"Breakfast time, boys! Make sure you eat—we've got a big day ahead. Snowboarding all morning and afternoon, and then we're going ice-skating in the evening. Chop-chop!"

Max was still fuming as we got dressed and headed out. He was even too busy moaning at Toddy to enjoy everyone laughing at the Roland poster he'd defaced.

To be honest, I didn't care that Toddy hadn't read the note. Just the fact that Mouse and her mates had *put* a note under our door was something. Notes under doors are generally a good thing, I figured. Surely you wouldn't put a note under someone's door unless you liked them? Notes under doors should be added to the curriculum, along with giggling.

Breakfast was a bustling, shouting, every-man-for-himself type of thing. You grabbed a tray and loaded it up with strange French cereal and slightly stale croissants and weird, horrible tea that tasted wrong no matter how much sugar you put in.

As we ate we told Toddy what had happened last night.

"Basically," said Max, "we had *two* different dates with *six* different girls in the space of *one* night! That's probably never been done before in the history of dating. We could probably get into the Guinness Book of Dating Records."

"No such thing," said Toddy, through a mouthful of cereal.

"Yeah, well, you wouldn't know about it even if there was," sniped Max. "The only way you'd get into the Guinness Book of Dating Records is through being the least dateable guy in history."

Toddy swallowed his cereal and nodded thoughtfully. "OK, cool. Well, as soon as someone invents the Guinness Book of Dating Records, I'll start to worry about that."

Max thumped Toddy's arm. "Hey! So, those are the note-girls, right? Those three?"

I turned, and my stomach fluttered a little at the sight of Mouse's long hair swishing as she walked into the dining hall with her friends.

Toddy nodded. "Yup, that's them."

Max was squinting at Keira. "Actually, that Keira girl is pretty cute." He turned to me. "We should go and talk to them, Jack. Try to find out what was in that note."

Before I could answer, Ed Deacon, who was sitting farther down the table, jumped in. "As if you guys met all these random girls last night," he laughed.

"We did, *actually,* Ed," sniffed Max. "Like I said—six girls, two rooms, one night." He added, "You do the math," even though there wasn't really any math to do.

Jamie, who sat next to him, cracked up. "How many numbers did you get, then?"

"Well, it wasn't . . . 'Getting' is a broad term, isn't it?" Max spluttered. "We were basically just laying the groundwork for some *serious* stuff tonight."

"So in other words, you got zero girls?" sneered Jamie.

"Same as every other night of their lives, then," said Ed, and the two of them burst out laughing.

"Shut up, Ed," growled Max.

"I don't believe you even *talked* to those girls, let alone sneaked into their room," Jamie shot back.

Max stood up, scraping his chair loudly across the floor. "Right. Fine. Jack, let's go."

I had no idea what he meant. "Go where? What you on about?"

He nodded over at Mouse, Connie and Keira, who were now sitting on the other side of the busy hall. "Let's go and talk to those *hot* girls, who we know *really well,* and who we spent last night with, and then maybe these *absolute idiots*"—he indicated Ed and Jamie—"will shut up."

"I don't know, man . . . ," I said. I wasn't sure I was ready to speak to Mouse again yet. Especially in front of half my class. I felt like I needed more time to prepare.

"Of *course* the lead singer of the Bailers doesn't want to go over there," Jamie cackled, and I felt my cheeks flush slightly.

Max gave me a stern, let's-prove-them-wrong type of look. I sighed and stood up. "Fine."

As we walked over, I could feel Jamie and Ed's eyes on our backs. I thought I saw Mouse smile at me, but as we got right up to their table they didn't seem to have even seen us.

"Hey!" I said brightly. But Mouse didn't look up from her cereal.

Max added, "How's it going?"

None of them answered. Something was definitely wrong. Then Keira stood up with her tray and said, "Yeah, we were just going, actually." She didn't even look at us.

Connie and Mouse both stood up too, and the three of them walked over to the counter, dumped their trays and left the hall.

I could hear the laughter from the other side of the room. I felt that same hot, sticky humiliation I'd felt at Sarvan's party and on Band Night. What had happened? What did we do wrong?

"What. The. *Heck?*" hissed Max. He shook his head and ran a hand across his stubbly hair. "Girls are *crazy.*"

I was about to agree when a tap on my shoulder spun me round.

"Hey, guys," said Lauren, smiling. She was dressed all in white—white furry pompom hat, thick white scarf, white ski suit. She looked seriously amazing. I noticed the laughter on the other side of the room had stopped.

"Um, hi, you all right?" I offered. Melody and Scarlett

were on either side of her, and Max was not-very-subtly boggling his eyes at Scarlett, who also looked pretty unbelievable with her hair pulled up into a high bun through a bright red scrunchie.

"So, listen, Jack," Scarlett said to me, with a weird, twinkly grin on her lips. "We were just saying last night, after you guys left . . . you look a little like that Roland guy. The one on all the posters."

Max suddenly found his voice and burst out laughing. "Yeah! We were saying that too!" He whacked me on the shoulder. "Poor guy. Must be tough, being a dead ringer for the biggest loser in the whole of France."

Scarlett answered him, still looking at me. "I don't know . . . Lauren really likes Roland, actually, don't you?"

She nudged Lauren, who smiled at me and shrugged innocently. I got the sudden sense that they'd rehearsed this whole thing.

Scarlett carried on, "And if she likes him, and you look like him, that must mean . . ." She wrinkled her nose in mock confusion.

Lauren grinned and pinched Scarlett on the arm. "Yeah, don't make it *too* obvious, Scar. . . ."

All three of them giggled, while me and Max stood there trying desperately to follow what was going on.

"Anyway, maybe see you tonight if you're going to the ice rink too?"

"Yeah!" said Max. "We'll be there."

"Cool, see you then."

They glided off to get breakfast, and I tried to process what had just happened. I turned to Max, but he was busy flicking highly insulting hand gestures in Jamie and Ed's general direction.

9

MOUSE

"We should have brought our food with us," Keira said as we marched purposefully out of the dining hall.

"Shall we run back in and get it?" Connie glanced back. "I was going to get a coconut yogurt."

"You can't let the team down now for a yogurt." Keira linked arms with us, dragging us down the hall and out into the brilliant sunshine. Seeing an awe-inspiring mountain range *right there* made me feel like I was on a movie set. Home and White Lodge felt like an alternate universe.

Connie lay down in the snow and started making an angel, and after watching her for a couple of seconds, Keira did the same.

I stretched out next to them and stared up at the massive expanse of blue. I felt tiny next to the mountains and under the endless sky.

"I sort of wish we had stayed to see what Jack was going to say," I said. The snow was deeper than I thought, and with all my padded clothes I felt cocooned in it and even a bit sleepy. "Now we'll never know."

"Yeah," Keira said from inside her snow-angel outline. "Now that we've done it, I do kind of wish we had let him say loads of stuff and *then* walked out."

"No way." Connie was indignant. "We don't need to hear what he has to say. He's a two-timing love rat. And a hamster hater."

"Connie, he didn't two-time me," I laughed. "To do that you have to be going out with someone. Or at least have kissed them. I think you're being a little harsh. I mean, we spoke to him for about five minutes and that's it. Does that mean Alfie is—"

"I love you, Alfie!" Keira shouted randomly at the sky, like he had appeared there. Like for someone to say his name without her affirming her love for him was unlucky.

"Yeah, but he's not two-timing you, is he?" I felt like I had proved my point.

"I wish," Keira said. "Then he would have to have one-timed me."

I had gone over it all a million times in my head since last night: Whether Jack had really been looking at me during the movie. Why he had come to our room, why he had gone to their room. What he was thinking. What he was doing.

Whether he liked me at all. Whether he *had* liked me and then just liked Lauren better.

Keira and Connie had talked about it a bunch before we fell asleep. I didn't mind them going over it, but I didn't know what to say. The whole thing was so confusing. Jack must fancy Lauren. And who could blame him, really? I would choose Lauren over me. It felt like I had landed a role in a film without even auditioning. It was weird being one of those girls. One who is always in the drama. One who flounces out of places, all Scarlett O'Hara. It was so far away from who I was.

Last night I dreamed I was dancing. It was the first time I've dreamt about ballet since leaving White Lodge. In my dream I danced and danced. When I woke up I felt tingly and alive and wanted to dance again.

I had wriggled out of my sleeping bag carefully, passed Connie and Keira and gone into the bathroom. I'd closed the door and looked at myself in the mirror, wound my hair into a bun and rolled my pajama bottoms up. I had warmed up properly, the same way I've done for years. As I'd stretched I felt my body elongating and waking up. I still had bruises from falling, but they were fading. And the calluses on my feet and weird bumps on the ridges of my toes were less cracked. But it felt good. To be totally consumed again, to be blank apart from that. In the mirror there was a little fleck of toothpaste. I'd focused on it and started to turn in the tiny space, catching my eye as I came back round. Spinning. Dancing.

Now we lay encased in our snow angels, staring at the sky, until the others came out from breakfast. We got our stuff and snaked down behind Miss Mardle to the ski rental place.

"It feels crazy to be doing this," I said, staring up at the mountains. "I wonder who invented skiing? They just look so . . . huge. Surely it's dangerous. It's weird they even let us do it. They won't allow sodas but they'll let us throw ourselves down a mountain." Everyone just presumed I would be good at it because of ballet. But it seemed like the opposite of ballet. So imprecise and wild and dangerous.

"Forty-five people a year die skiing," Connie said matter-of-factly, and then told the girl behind the counter her shoe size.

"So, what, if only forty-four have died one year, do they, like, push a random person off a mountain?" Keira said as she was handed her boots.

"It's an average," Connie shot back haughtily.

I chewed on my coat cord and took deep breaths as I was handed a ginormous pair of boots. Everything felt so heavy and restricting. The thought of wearing them and being locked into skis made me feel a little sick. I like being in control of my body. I didn't want to give it to a mountain and weigh it down with all these things.

"Well, if anyone's dying, it's not you," Keira said to me. "You're gonna be *amazing*. You can balance on your toes. You're strong and über-coordinated. If anyone's gonna be dying, it's ol' Crazy Bones." She pulled Connie's ponytail of curls and it sprang back. "She can't even make it through Uno uninjured."

Keira seemed so sure that I would be good at it. But what if I wasn't? And she didn't even know that I wasn't the dancer I made myself out to be. What if it was going to be another thing that I just didn't quite realize my potential in? My life was just a series of "not quite good enoughs," really.

"Maybe we should have done a don't-die-skiing spell," I said as we filtered into a room to get the boots on.

"Do you think skiing's popular in the witchcraft community?" asked Connie, wandering over and picking up a random souvenir pen and flourishing it to see if it had wand potential.

"Connie, you really don't seem to be taking the coven seriously. But, I dunno," Keira said, "I can't really see Professor McGonagall and Glinda bombing down a mountain in one-piece jumpsuits. Plus, they could just fly to the bottom."

Walking around felt unnatural. Like I was in a spacesuit getting ready for a moon landing.

"*She's* more likely to be one of the forty-five," Connie whispered quite loudly.

Lauren was wearing all white. Even her bobble hat was

white, trimmed with fake white fur. Only her sunglasses were black, framed by her blond hair. She looked like a celebrity. "If she's caught in an avalanche, they'll never find her," Connie hissed.

"Here's hoping," Keira said. "Is that why you're dressed as a huge highlighter?"

Connie was impressively orange. Keira was all in black, as usual. I looked down at myself: a hodgepodge of things my mum had borrowed or bought in the clearance section at T.J. Maxx. It hadn't crossed my mind that looking cool while skiing was a thing.

"OK, OK, let's do this!" a girl shouted, and clapped her hands above her head. "I'm Tania, your instructor," she said. "Let's head on over to the bunny slope." Her accent was harsher than French. German, maybe.

She wasn't that much older than us but she didn't look like anyone I'd ever seen in real life before. She had cropped hair dyed bright blond with silver glitter running through it. She looked like she'd just walked out of a club.

The bunny slope didn't exactly sound top-of-a-mountain scary, but I felt sick. I looked back at the ski shop and wondered if I should ask to go to the bathroom and then just not come back. Would they even notice I wasn't there?

Maybe it would be OK after all.

We all got into a line and were kind of conveyor-belted to the top of the slope. When we got there, we huddled around Tania, who said, "Right, I'm gonna put you in pairs."

My stomach tightened because we were a three. I didn't have a natural pair. Girls shuffled closer together, showing Tania who they wanted to be put with. Making the decision easy for her. Connie and Keira stayed close to me, but I looked down to try to melt into the background.

"You and you," Tania said, but I didn't realize she had pointed at me, let alone seen who she had paired me with. I saw Keira's face and knew straight away. Scarlett and Melody were exchanging looks with Lauren. She didn't move at all, just stayed next to them in a three.

"Who didn't pair up yet?" Tania said.

I didn't know whether to move or not. It was like a showdown—one of us would have to move first. Lauren kept looking at Scarlett and smiling a kind of this-is-awkward smile.

I unsteadily took a step forward. Lauren looked at me and then back at Melody and Scarlett. Then she hugged them both like she was leaving them forever, and started to walk toward me.

We didn't speak as Tania taught us how to practice sliding on our skis, pointing them toward each other, guiding each other in turns. We stood side by side, facing outward, not even letting our sleeves brush. Tania told us to get started and we watched everyone find a spot and start, giggling as they did it. I tried not to think about the ferry. Or the note. What if the boy with glasses had read it? And then told Lauren what was in it?

Lauren went first. She was naturally good. She is tall and strong and has always been athletic. But she has a long torso to match her long legs. Too long for ballet school. Not the Royal Ballet physique. It's stupid and ridiculous, really, that there can be an "ideal torso length." At first we did the moves without talking. I didn't know what she was thinking. The last time we had actually spoken to each other was when I had agreed to meet them in the diner. Neither of us mentioned it, but we were probably both thinking about it.

The first time I tried to move, I fell over. And not in a graceful way, but hard, right onto my shoulder. Lauren reluctantly gave me her hand to help me up and I took it. She pulled, and as I moved she fell backwards and suddenly we were both lying together in the snow. I started laughing a little bit, and then when I heard she was laughing too I let myself really laugh.

"Do they even know you're here?" Lauren said, sitting up.

"Who?"

"The Opera Ballet."

For a second my mind just froze.

"Yeah, I mean, I guess if I got injured, that would . . . be bad." I wondered if it sounded as lame as I thought it did. And before I thought it through, I said, "Do you still dance?"

The tempo between us changed. It felt horribly electric.

118

I'd said the word. The word that had bound us together and then torn us apart. *Dance.*

She looked down and something about her face became weirdly real. She shook her head. "I stopped after I didn't get in. I kind of wish I had kept it up. It was weird, it was like it was gonna be that or nothing. It's hard to explain."

If there are bits of your heart that change when you are rejected, mine and Lauren's had changed in the same way. Just at different times. And when it had happened to her, I hadn't really *got* it. It *was* hard to explain. I had tried. My mum hadn't been able to understand even though she loves me and wanted the dream almost as much as me. No one could really get it. Except for maybe Lauren. I opened my mouth to say something but the lie just sat there inside me, stopping me. I couldn't tell her now. I wanted to hug her and say sorry that I had just forgotten about her. That I got why she had stopped speaking to me. I would have hated her too, if she had got in and I hadn't. "I love dancing at parties, though," she said.

"I *hate* dancing at parties. I never do. I get so embarrassed." I picked up a stick and started swirling patterns in the snow.

"You're not *still* shy?" Lauren rolled her eyes. "You're like those girls on the edge of the dance in *Grease.*"

"A wallflower," I said. "Yeah, I know. I am. But I can't help it."

She laughed. "Scarlett and Alfie had a party at Christmas and I made them play the same song again and again so I could dance to it for hours."

"Do you still like Alfie?" I giggled.

"Ugh, no, I forgot about that phase." She crinkled up her nose and shivered like it was painful to remember it.

"Keira really likes him," I said. "They swim together."

"Cute," she said. "He probably likes her too. She's really pretty."

"Who do you like, then?" I asked. Inside, my stomach tightened, but only a fraction.

She looked around and leaned closer. "I met this boy last night."

And then Lauren described Jack. And how he spoke and how he dressed and how he had a friend who was a lunatic and how he looked a little like Roland. I listened like it was all new information, until Tania called us back.

As we pigeoned over to the group, I could feel Lauren harden and separate, like some kind of spell had been broken.

I shuffled back over to Keira and Connie. "Are you OK?" Keira asked. "Was she all right with you?"

I nodded. They hadn't said anything after the ferry, but I think they knew something had happened and could probably guess along what lines.

"Yeah. She was actually nice."

Keira raised her eyebrows, but before she could say anything, a trickle of girls started scurrying across the bottom of the patch of mountain we were on. Some of them were carrying posters or banners they had obviously made with the entire contents of an art supply store. They all consisted of a jumble of illegible French words, but one word was clear: ROLAND. The trickle turned into a steady flow and then a kind of gushing, squealing river.

"What's going on?" Lauren demanded.

Tania shrugged. "Only one way to find out."

JACK

Max spent the whole morning discussing the two breakfast "incidents." By the time we'd all got our lift passes figured out and were in the shop renting boards and boots, Toddy had started listening to his iPod to block him out.

"Keira and them are hot, but clearly insane," Max reasoned as he pulled on a snowboard boot the size of a loaf of bread. "Lauren, Scarlett and Melody, on the other hand, are hot but *not* insane. The choice is clear."

I nodded. "Well, yeah. But there isn't a choice at all, really, since Mouse and Keira won't even speak to us. What did we do? You don't think they saw us go into Lauren's room."

"Course not," Max sniffed. "We were like ninjas.

Anyway, who *cares* if they saw? We need to concentrate on Lauren's group now. She clearly likes you, so that means it's very likely that Scarlett likes me."

"Solid logic there, Max."

As I took my boots and board up to the counter, I wondered whether Lauren really *did* like me. It seemed way too good to be true. Surely there were other, much cooler, guys on this trip she'd rather hang out with?

Me and Toddy both ended up with boards that had decent graphics on them—a snake for Toddy, and a silhouetted guy with a gun for me—but Max got stuck with a really embarrassing one that was bright purple with a huge glittery unicorn. His only consolation was that he managed to sneak *"Ma perruche est dans la zone piétonne"* into his conversation with the French guy who was setting him up, for which Toddy awarded him fifteen points.

Max was keen to find a fireworks-and-ninja-stars shop, but he didn't have time; Flynn marched us all straight out of the board store to the bottom of the mountain. One by one, we stepped onto this enormous conveyor-belt thing that whirred us up a short distance to one of the beginners' slopes.

It was like being on the moon or something. Apart from the odd clump of snow-covered pine trees, there was just endless whiteness stretching out everywhere you looked, with the zigzagging wires of the ski lifts buzzing away overhead. It was amazing.

Our instructor was a tall skinny dude named Sebastian, who told us to call him Basti. He didn't look that much older than some of the seniors at school. He had a huge stiff blond hairdo that was about half the size of his face, and a ridiculously fancy accent. His first words to us were "If you guys can keep it down today, that'd be awesome. I was out all night at a party." Flynn did not look impressed.

Basti showed us all how to click our boots onto the boards and tighten them up. Then we stood up, wobbling, in a circle around him.

"OK, so how many of you have snowboarded before?" he asked.

Only a couple of hands went up. Jamie's was one of them.

"Whoa, right, OK," he said. "So you're all basically never evers."

"We're what?" asked Max.

"Never evers," sniffed Basti, as if we should all know what the hell that meant. "It's an American phrase. I picked it up when I did a season in California in my year off. It means you've never ever snowboarded before."

Max nodded, and I heard Jamie whisper to Ed, "That's not the only thing those guys have 'never ever' done." We shot them death stares while they cracked up.

Basti gave us a short and intensely boring speech about safety on the slopes, and then made us all skate around slowly in little circles, one foot strapped onto the board, the other pushing against the snow. After that, he made us strap both feet in and slide around on our bottoms. The sun beat down and sparkled off the slope, hurting my eyes, and the snow made funny squeaking sounds under the weight of the boards.

Finally, after we'd all fallen over about twenty times, Basti said we were ready to try it for real. "First off, watch me," he said. We were on a pretty tame slope, with a load of little kids messing around at the bottom while their moms chatted to each other. Despite that, it still looked scary from up at the top; there was no way we were getting down without falling at least once. Basti shifted his weight so he was pointing downhill. He glided slowly down to the bottom, making big S shapes in the snow, and then carved right around, to stop himself.

Max scratched his head under his helmet and shrugged. "Don't see what all the fuss is about. Looks easy."

"Looks ridiculously hard, more like," I said. "You really think you can get down to the bottom without falling over?"

"Definitely."

Toddy dusted some flecks of snow off his glasses and said, "Max, the statistical probability of you falling over is very, very high."

"Yeah, well, so is the statistical probability of you . . ." He thought for a second. "Being an idiot."

"Nice," Toddy said, putting his glasses back on. "Classic comeback."

"Off you go, then!" Basti shouted up at us. "And remember what I told you: You shouldn't ever be aiming straight down the slope—you want to glide gently across it, turning right and left. Tilt forward then backward with your toes and heels. Try to feel your way into it."

I looked at Max and Toddy, who shrugged as if to say "You first." Jamie smirked and set off, making it all the way down without falling. We saw Basti clap him on the back proudly.

Max pushed off, and so did Toddy, but within about three seconds, they'd both fallen flat on their backs.

I shifted my body sideways so my left foot was pointing toward the bottom of the slope, and felt myself start to move forward slowly. I leaned back very gently on my heels and turned the board left. I wobbled, flapped my arms about, but somehow managed to stay standing. I was picking up speed. I leaned forward slightly on my toes, still gaining momentum. Again, I wobbled. Again, I didn't fall. Maybe this was it; maybe snowboarding was my "thing." I'd waited thirteen years to find something I was actually, really good at, and this was it!

I was gaining speed, but all my focus was going into trying not to fall over. I tried to turn again, to slow myself down, but my body wouldn't do it. It just kept pointing me straight ahead, down the slope.

I heard Basti yell, "Not so quick there, buddy!" but

I didn't really have any idea how to stop. Arms flapping madly, I whizzed straight past him and Jamie and carried on down the hill, still picking up speed. I could hear Basti's shouting and Jamie's faint shrieking laughter ringing round the slope behind me.

Just as I was considering how difficult it would be to unclip my boots and jump off smoothly, the edge of my board caught a bump in the snow. I slammed down, flat on my back, with a painful crunch. Even then, I didn't stop. I carried on sliding.

Though big clumps of powdery snow were streaming into my eyes and mouth, I could see I was aiming straight for a huge blond lady in a neon-pink ski suit. I tried to call out, but my mouth was so full of snow I couldn't make a sound. There was nothing to do but close my eyes and hope.

I heard a loud scream, then felt the full weight of the woman as she thudded down on top of me. All the air whooshed out of my lungs. I opened my eyes to see her huge, bewildered face pressed right up against mine. She was lying sprawled out on top of me, and for some reason, the first thought that popped into my head was that this was now probably the closest I'd ever been to kissing a girl.

She looked like Thor's sister. I was having quite a lot of trouble breathing.

She suddenly found her voice and started screeching at me in some weird language or other—Russian, I think. I turned my head and saw Max, Toddy and the rest of the class sliding down toward me on their butts, literally crying with laughter.

"That was *epic*!" Max yelled. I tried to say "Help me," but there wasn't enough breath in my lungs. All I could do was watch as he aimed his iPhone. "Say *'fromage'*!"

By lunchtime, I was in total agony. Not only due to the massive Russian woman breakdancing all over me, but also because the backs of my legs had completely cramped up. Basti said it was because I was "using muscles I had never used before," but I think it was just because I was falling over every two minutes.

"I don't think I'll ever get the hang of this," I said as we sat down on the benches outside a big restaurant that overlooked the beginners' slope. Max and Toddy groaned in agreement.

"Trust me, it's all about day three." Basti winked. "It all starts to make sense on day three."

"Well, if I've still got a body left by day three, that'll be great," muttered Toddy.

We had lunch—an amazing tinfoil-wrapped baguette that had a burger *and* fries stuffed inside it—then, as we were about to head back, Basti said we could quickly go and have a look at the "thing that was happening" further up the mountain.

"What thing?" Flynn asked.

"You guys haven't heard? That French singer, Roland. He's filming some music video up at the next slope."

"Oh my God!" said Max, jabbing me in the chest. "Your loser twin brother!"

"Shut up, man. He doesn't look that much like me."

"Yeah, well, we'll be able to judge for ourselves when we see him live in the flesh. Plus, if it's a music video thing, there might even be some, y'know, industry types we can talk to. About the band."

"What, our band with no name?" said Toddy.

"It's not gonna have no name for much longer, my friend." Max smirked. "Once I work my magic on Scarlett at the ice rink, we will officially be Psycho Death Squad."

Flynn agreed we could go and have a look, so our whole group, led by Basti, took the magic carpet a little higher up the mountain. There was already a huge crowd at the top. We shoved our way through, with Flynn shouting "Don't get lost!" and "Stay together!" but when we finally got to the front, there were just loads of lights and cameras, two massive white trailers with their doors closed, and tons of bored-looking people milling around holding clipboards.

"What a rip-off," said Max.

"Do you think he's already come and gone?" Toddy asked.

I said nothing at all. Mainly because standing right beside me, her shoulder almost brushing mine, was Mouse.

10

MOUSE

I panicked and pretended not to see Jack. Which was ridiculous, as he was right next to me. And the more people turned up to look at what was going on, the more compact the surroundings seemed to get.

Connie and Keira were taking pictures of the superfans: girls wearing jackets with Roland's face printed on them and headbands with boingy capital *R*s. One girl had stickers of him stuck all over her face.

The longer we all waited, the more intense the atmosphere got and the more awkward it was that me and Jack hadn't spoken.

A girl in the crowd made herself a human battering ram and launched herself right into the gap between me and Jack in a desperate effort to get closer to the front. She fell hard, right in front of us.

"Are you OK?" I said, and held out my hand to get her up. She nodded but looked a little teary and said something in French. Jack bent down and picked up her Roland sunglasses from the snow and handed them to her. She smiled and squinted at Jack, her eyes flickering for a second with excitement. Then she shook her head to herself before saying thank you to both of us in English and pushing back into the crowd.

To *both* of us. Like we were there together.

And then we were looking right at each other.

"This is a little crazy, isn't it?" Jack smiled at me.

A little crazy that you came to our room last night after we magicked you there from a purple sparkly book? Or a little crazy that we curved you this morning and have been standing here for the last ten minutes ignoring each other? Either way, it was indeed all pretty crazy.

In my head I repeated "Don't say anything stupid" in a stern voice. I tried to look casual by tucking my hair behind my ears. And then untucking it again. He pointed over at a group of hard-core fans who were each holding a huge cutout letter from Roland's name.

"It says LANDOR," I said. "They're not that dedicated if they can't stand in the right order."

"True. Or maybe 'Landor' is a secret word only the biggest fans know."

"It must be weird for him, all this insanity. He looks about our age. Are you in seventh grade too?"

Jack nodded. "Weird for him? It must be *amazing* for him. Look at how many girls have turned up to stare at a patch of snow that he may or may not walk on."

"Is that your dream, then?" I said. "To have girls waiting around in the snow for you?" I laughed, but suddenly felt self-conscious. Like I was some straight-edge nun-in-training telling him off for having immoral thoughts.

But he laughed too, and I thought I saw him blush slightly. "It would be nice, I guess. . . ."

"Well, you need to get famous first," I said, catching Connie's eye a few feet away from me. She crossed her arms like a teacher who is really disappointed in your behavior. I looked away from her quickly and back to Jack. I saw Max and the little blond boy who'd given us the note back standing on the edge of the crowd, near Miss Mardle. They didn't seem to have noticed Jack talking to me; they were watching the cameramen like everyone else.

"So, what could you get famous for doing?" I asked. "Are you any good at singing? Maybe you could ask Roland to form a duo. You do look a little like him." It was me who blushed this time. Roland was *hot*. Even in his cringeworthy, topless-in-the-snow posters, it was undeniable. I had pretty much just told Jack I thought he was hot too.

If he had noticed me basically saying out loud to his face that I liked him, he didn't show it.

"I can't really sing at all," he said. He shuffled around in the snow like he was weighing things in his head. "Though I am . . . in . . . I'm sort of in a . . . band."

"Well, there you go, then." I smiled. "It's definitely gonna happen. Just a matter of time." Jack being in a band did add to his hotness. Boys in bands are just attractive. Way more attractive than boys who do sports, definitely cuter than ballet boys. Boys in bands are edgier and artsier. And they might write a song for you. Which is kind of hot. "What do you play?" I asked him.

"Guess." He mimed twiddling a guitar in a really exaggerated fashion.

"Oh, right," I said. "The trumpet. Cool."

We both laughed, and for a second, it felt so easy and comfortable between us. Like I'd known him forever. "No, I'm supposed to be guitar and vocals," he said, taking off his beanie to ruffle his thick, dark hair. "But I'm not really . . . front-man material."

"What material are you, then?"

He blinked and looked down at his beanie, then back up at me. "I don't really know, to be honest."

I nodded. "Yeah, me neither. Or maybe I thought I was one kind of material but I'm not."

He shrugged and smiled. "Well, at least we're in the same boat. The Unidentified Material Boat." My stomach full-on flipped over, like being at the top of a roller coaster.

"What's your band called, then?" I asked.

He sighed and pulled his beanie back on. "Well . . ."

"Are you actually *in* a band?" I folded my arms. "Or are you just trying to look cool?"

"No, I *am* in a band, I swear," he laughed. "We just don't have a name at the moment."

"Well, you need to think of one, because you can't really move on to superfans unless you have a name."

"I know, I know." He nodded apologetically. "We're working on it. If you've got any suggestions, just let me know."

"Let's see. . . . If I think of one, I think you should make me an honorary member."

"Done." He held out his gloved hand. I shook it with my mitten and felt a little jolt because we had touched, even if it was only through two layers of wool.

I tried to think of a band name but my mind went blank. "All I can think of is the Beatles."

He frowned, mock-serious. "I'm pretty sure there's already a band called the Beatles."

"Yeah, you're right. The Beatles are called the Beatles. I think the more random, the better," I said. "It's probably best to just close your eyes and then name the band after the first thing you see when you open them."

He closed his eyes and I took the opportunity to look at him. His dimpled smile really was amazing. Then he opened them and I looked away.

"The Ski Lifts?" he said, looking up at the wires above us.

"Hmmm . . . Not that catchy. Try again."

He closed his eyes but kept smiling.

"You need to look in another direction," I laughed.

He twisted his body on the spot, then opened his eyes again at the LANDOR letter-carrying girls, who were shuffling into the right order now, and getting increasingly hysterical.

"The Girls Who Can't Spell?"

"That's good," I said. "I like that. But it suggests there are girls in the band. Are there?"

"Well, you." He grinned. "If you can think of a name that doesn't totally suck."

I closed my eyes and said, "What about . . . Killer Wardrobe Rats?"

It was the first time anything about last night had been mentioned. He looked down sheepishly. "Well . . . as if *anyone* brings a hamster on a school trip."

"Shhhhh." I put my finger to my lips, glancing over at Miss Mardle.

Suddenly there was a huge surge in the crowd. All the girls started screaming "Roland!" again and again and again. It was getting insane. I looked around for Keira and Connie and suddenly saw Lauren, looking straight at me like she wanted to kill me. I felt a sharp pang of guilt and tried to move a step away from Jack, but there wasn't any room. There was another surge forward and he knocked into me hard.

"I'm so sorry!" he shouted.

I jolted forward into a gap in the crowd and realized that I didn't know how to steady myself or even stop myself from moving. I lost my balance, and the last thing I saw was the sky being swallowed up by loads of people above me.

I could hear people shouting in a foreign language and someone yelling my name. And then lots and lots more screaming. And then I was pulled to my feet and away from the crowd.

The embarrassment was overwhelming. I could feel how many people were looking at me, and my cheek was stinging.

I was the last person to see that the guy who had pulled me to my feet was Roland.

JACK

It took me a few seconds to see what everyone was gasping and shouting and screaming about. At first, I thought they were all pointing their cameras at Mouse lying on the ground, which seemed a little harsh really. But then the crowd shifted, and I got a clearer view.

It was like something out of a movie. A really, *really* awful movie.

Roland was wearing the same ridiculous stuff he had on in the posters at the hotel: the skinny jeans, the black leather jacket and a pair of huge sunglasses. He was about my height, and our hair was the same sort of color and length, but his was all floppy and swept sideways. He grinned this bright-white superstar grin and knelt down to take Mouse's hand. Then he pulled her to her feet, and for a second they both just stood there, looking at each other. All you could hear was the whir of iPhone cameras.

Roland pushed his sunglasses up into his hair, revealing his big blue eyes, and said something to Mouse in French, but she just blinked and shook her head, saying, "Erm . . . sorry, I don't . . ."

"Ah, you are English?" he said in his gloopy French accent. Mouse nodded. "I was asking, are you all right?"

Mouse nodded again. She looked like she couldn't quite believe what was happening, which was fair enough, really, as it was pretty unbelievable.

He gently put his hand on the side of her face, where she had fallen. There was a collective intake of breath from the girls around me, like they were all about to faint at the same time.

Then he whipped a black beanie out of his back pocket and handed it to her. "Well, this is my very favorite hat. And I give it to you—my very favorite English fan."

The crowd suddenly found their voice again. I had to shove my fingers in my ears as girls broke out into screams all around me. It was so loud it drowned out what happened next, which was Roland whispering something to Mouse, and then beckoning over a frantic-looking woman with a clipboard and a headset. The woman listened as Roland said something I couldn't hear, and then, suddenly, all three of them turned and started walking back to one of the massive white trailers.

Mouse span round to boggle her eyes at Connie and Keira, who were standing a few feet away from me in the crowd; then she disappeared into the trailer behind Roland. I couldn't figure out what the hell was going on. Was she being very politely kidnapped?

I could hear Connie gabbing away loudly with her own theories. "Oh my God, he's clearly just fallen in love with her at first sight! Maybe he's asked her to marry him!" She gripped Keira's shoulder. "Keira, they might literally be getting married in that trailer now!"

"I suppose that's a possibility," I heard Keira say. "I wonder what *is* going on."

A group of hysterical little Rolandettes started screaming at Connie. "Who is that girl? *Who is that girl!*"

"She's our friend, actually." Connie beamed proudly. "So we'll probably be bridesmaids at the wedding. Do you want an autograph?"

I felt Max and Toddy squeeze through the crowd and stand right next to me.

"Well," said Max, nodding at the trailer. "There goes any chance you had with Mouse, eh?"

"Shut up, man." It did feel pretty unfair that she'd suddenly been spirited away by the most famous guy in France after we'd had such an amazing conversation. I couldn't get over how easy and fun it was to talk to her.

"Were you speaking to her before?" Max asked.

"Yeah."

"And?"

"And what?"

"*And* did you find out what was in the note?"

"Will you shut up about the note? It doesn't matter what was in it."

Max looked horrified. *"Of course it matters!"* he hissed. "It could have been about me!"

Connie was still rambling on about what might be happening inside the white trailer. "This is literally the craziest thing ever!" she said. "Maybe we'll get to actually meet Roland!"

I felt Max bristle next to me. "These girls are just too much, honestly." He shouted over at Connie, "Even if you did meet Roland, you'd probably just ignore him the next day for no reason, wouldn't you?"

Connie and Keira both turned to face him slowly, their eyes narrowed to tiny slits. "Excuse me?" Keira snapped at Max. "Did *you* say something?"

"Yeah, I did, actually," Max huffed. "Just that, like, it was a bit ridiculous to not even acknowledge me and Jack when we came over to say hi this morning, that's all. You might even say it was downright *rude*."

I tried to kick Max's shin to shut him up, but there were so many legs next to mine that I couldn't get a real swing going.

"Um, are you crazy?" Keira shot back at him, jostling three little French girls out of the way, so that she and Connie were now standing right beside us. "Do you really think we were just going to be all nice and sweet to you after what happened?"

I felt a flash of confused panic burst through me. Max was clearly equally stumped. "What do you mean 'after what happened'?" he demanded. "What did we do?"

Keira coughed up a short, hollow laugh. "Oh, come on. We weren't born yesterday, you know."

"Yeah," said Connie, fiercely. "We were born thirteen years ago. That's a *lot* longer ago than yesterday. It's like . . ." She broke off, dreamily. "How many more days is that than yesterday? What's 13 multiplied by 365?"

Keira swatted her away impatiently. "It doesn't matter, Connie. The point is—they know *exactly* what they did."

Max squinted in confusion. "What the hell are you on about? We behaved like perfect gentlemen. Except when Jack got bitten by that hamster. Is *that* what you're angry about?"

"Rat," I corrected him, wishing he wasn't talking quite so loudly. "It was definitely a rat."

"For the last time, Mr. Jambon is a Dwarf Campbell's Russian *hamster,*" said Connie firmly. "And he doesn't *usually* eat humans. He only eats salad." She frowned at me. "Your ankles must taste like salad, that's all."

"They eat nuts as well, actually," said Toddy quietly. We all turned to look at him, and I saw his neck start to redden slightly. "I mean . . . I used to have a hamster too, and I fed it nuts all the time."

"Nuts," Connie said, smiling. "Good idea. I'll give Mr. Jambon some nuts tonight."

"Honestly, the only nuts around here are you girls," Max snapped at Keira.

"Well, I'd rather be nuts than morally bankrupt," she fired back.

"You what?" he laughed. "I've got *loads* of money! I've got fifty euros on me right now just to spend on fireworks and ninja throwing stars!"

Keira let out a loud sigh. "*Morally* bankrupt, you idiot. It means you've got no morals."

Max stood up straight. "Okay, that's it. I didn't come here to be insulted."

"That's a shame, because you're very good at it," said Keira, and Connie doubled up laughing.

Max jabbed his finger at Keira sternly. "Right. From now on, don't speak to us on this trip. Keep away from us, yeah? You do your thing, we'll do ours. And never the train shall meet."

"Twain," Toddy corrected him.

"Or the twain." Max nodded.

"Fine by us," said Keira. Max spun around angrily and barged through the crowd, with me and Toddy following him. I heard him huffing, "That Keira is ridiculous. How can someone so cute also be such a tool?" He stopped and turned to me. "Thank God we've got Lauren and Scarlett as backup. You need to focus all your efforts on Lauren now, Jack. Trust me—" He broke off and nodded at the white trailer. "Just forget about Mouse."

11

MOUSE

"OK, so the Roland ground rules: No speaking to Roland. No looking Roland directly in the eye. No touching Roland. No pictures with Roland. And absolutely *no* social media. OK? Great. Go ahead and sit down, honey."

The bonkers-looking woman with the clipboard pointed at a sofa where two girls covered from head to toe in Roland merchandise were sitting. As soon as we'd entered the trailer, Roland had been ushered straight back outside by more flustered women with clipboards, and I'd just stood there, trying to figure out exactly what I had got myself into. All I knew was that Roland had definitely whispered to me, "You want to be in my video?" and nodding had seemed like the only appropriate response.

"Um . . . this isn't homeroom, honey. Daydream on your own time, okay?" The woman jabbed her finger again at the sofa. She was wearing short leather shorts that kind of flared out like a tutu, with these really thick knitted Nordic socks that came right up her thighs, leaving a tiny strip of bare leg at the top. Her sweater had PEANUT BUTTER AND JELLY YOU IDIOT across it in gold letters. Her hair was in two Heidi-type braids across the top of her head, a hairdo that seemed to accentuate her eyebrows, which already looked like they had been stenciled on from a Build Your Own Vampire kit. I had been expecting her to speak French but she was actually American.

I followed her finger to the sofa and sat down between a girl wearing a Roland visor and a girl who had those sneakers that light up every so often. They looked at me suspiciously and started muttering to each other in French. They were both really, *really* pretty. And then I heard some muffled sobs coming from a closed door.

The crazy Nordic socks woman rolled her eyes. "OK, so it looks like . . ." She clicked her fingers and shook her head.

"Valentine," the girl with sneakers said.

The woman nodded. "Right, so it looks like Valentine is too . . ." Another loud sob came from the bathroom. "Basically, Valentine's not in a good place right now."

The girl with sneakers looked genuinely shocked and then her lip started to wobble. "Valentine is not going to be in the video with us?"

Nordic Socks looked like she was losing patience.

"Honey, she is clearly too overwhelmed right now. If she broke down in tears because Roland was in the *next trailer,* she's hardly going to cope with *physically* being in his presence, is she?" More sobs. "But we are gonna hook her up with a signed calendar and five tubes of Roland-brand I Love Your Smile minty-fresh toothpaste. It's gonna be perfect, honey." She shouted the last part at the bathroom door. "So, anyway . . ." She smiled at me. "It's actually worked out great because . . . what's your name, baby girl?"

"Uh . . . Mouse." As soon as I said it I wished I'd said Matilda. Or Mabel or Marmaduke, or *any* name that isn't Mouse.

"Mouse," she repeated. "God, I *love* the British. You kooksters."

"Mousse?" said the girl with the visor, raising an eyebrow.

I shook my head and then did the same mouse impression Connie had done for Jack. "Mouse."

Visor and Sneakers exchanged a disgusted look.

"Anyway, Mouse is going to take Valentine's part in the scene," said Nordic Socks.

Sneakers eyed me suspiciously. "I haven't seen you on Instagram. . . ."

"Did Mousse enter the competition?" Visor Girl sounded almost angry.

"Nope, but little Mr. Perfect says he wants her in the

video, so she's in the video." The woman winked at me. "You obviously had quite an effect on him, honey." I blushed, and Sneakers and Visor shot me the darkest of dark looks.

"Anyway, hair and makeup in ten, ladies," said Nordic Socks. And then she disappeared out the door again, and it was just me, Visor, Sneakers and the muffled sobs coming from the bathroom.

I didn't really know what to say, sandwiched there between them. "Is Valentine OK?" I offered.

Neither of them answered. They just sat there talking in French across me. I took a deep breath to kind of steady myself. I looked at the door. I wondered if I could just leave. Run back outside to Connie and Keira. And Jack. I thought about the band-name conversation, and started randomly daydreaming about going to one of his gigs and him dedicating a song to me. Then Sneakers tapped me on the knee.

"So, how big a Roland fan actually are you, Mousse? Do you know his middle name? Do you know his favorite food?"

"Etienne. Prawn vindaloo," said Visor proudly, and Sneakers shook her head. "I know *you* know, Chloé. I was asking *Mousse*." She turned back to me. "Do you know how he got the scar on his thumb? Or what his Cambodian tattoo means? Or—"

She was interrupted by another clipboard-holding woman opening the trailer door. "You," she said, pointing at me. "Come." I smiled goodbye to Sneakers and Visor—who looked like they genuinely wanted to murder me—and followed her out.

As soon as I stepped out, I remembered we were halfway up a mountain, and that there were hundreds of screaming girls waiting. We walked three steps to another trailer and went in, the noise disappearing as the door shut behind us. Every single surface was covered with makeup and coffee cups and cans of Diet Coke.

At the back of the trailer there were rails and rails of clothes and a table laid with fruit cut into hearts and stars and a tower of vegetables with a beet perched on the top. Who eats a *whole* beet? The trailer was so full of things that I hadn't noticed a human being nestled among it all: Roland.

He was standing in the middle of a square plastic bath mat laid out on the floor. For a second I didn't realize what he was doing. He took his monogrammed sneakers off and then his black leather jacket and T-shirt, revealing his tanned, super-toned body. He was stripping, right in front of me. I closed my eyes, in case he didn't realize I was there. In case he was going to get fully, completely naked. I half opened one eye. He was peeling off his jeans. A woman was standing next to him holding a kind of plastic gun hooked up to a machine. And another woman was holding a paintbrush. Now he was wearing only his boxers.

"I'm here," I squeaked.

The women laughed. "Just because you have your eyes closed doesn't mean we can't see you. Take a seat. We need to get this done and dried before we get on to you. Eat something, if you like."

I picked out a single carrot stick and sat down on a pink plastic chair. Roland held his arms out and the first woman started spraying him with a thin brown mist. Every so often the other would use her paintbrush to kind of shade his stomach or his shoulder and then take a step back and admire her work. They chatted over him, like he wasn't human, like he was a giant Ken doll. He just kept his arms out like he was playing freeze tag. He stared straight ahead at the wall with a blank expression on his face. He didn't seem to have even noticed I was there.

The women muttered something in French to Roland and then left the trailer. I looked down and realized I was squeezing the carrot stick in extreme panic. I was alone with mostly-naked Roland.

Still not looking at me, he reached over to the table and picked out a handful of almonds. He had clearly been told about the "fuel for dancing" too.

"So, what is your name?" he asked, examining the almonds carefully before popping one in his mouth. His French accent made it sound like every word was coated in honey.

I carried on looking at the carrot and prayed for an

avalanche. All I could think about was Nordic Socks telling me *No speaking to Roland.* I looked up. He was still standing in just his white boxers, which were now a kind of muddy-brown color. Our eyes met. *No looking Roland directly in the eye.* I looked down again and shut my eyes. Like I had accidentally eyeballed Medusa.

I heard him laugh. "Let me guess: Cooper has been telling you those ridiculous 'ground rules.'" He pronounced "ridiculous" like Lumière from *Beauty and the Beast.* "Cooper is OK, but she used to work for Mariah Carey, so I guess she thinks I am just as much of a diva. But I am not Mariah Carey, am I?"

I looked up at him and met his big blue eyes properly. It was only then I realized I'd snapped the carrot stick in half. "No, you're not Mariah Carey," I said.

He smiled at me, his dimples deepening in his cheeks. He was *gorgeous.* Looking at him was how I imagine it must be to see a lion on safari. You've seen it tons of times in pictures, but up close it's totally different. Even though you know it's real, it feels like it can't be. Every single thing about him was perfect. Every corner, every feature. He looked airbrushed and filtered and framed in midair, even in brown-stained boxers.

"So," he said again. "What is your name?"

"Mouse," I said. "Like the animal." And I was so used to doing it that I did the mouse impression without really thinking.

Roland laughed. "I love it." And then he did a mouse impression and laughed some more. "Will you give me your honest opinion, Mouse?" He pronounced it "Merssssss," like it had about six Ss in it.

"Uh . . . yeah?" I said.

He reached into the clothes rack and pulled out a black T-shirt with ROLAND across it in silver glitter. "I am being told to wear this in the video. What do you think?"

"Um . . . It's very . . ." My mind went blank. "It's very *you?*"

He blinked and then burst out laughing—deep, roaring, bellowing laughs that rang all around the trailer. "Yes . . . ," he said, looking at the T-shirt and then at me. "It *is* very me. But is it . . . *too* me?"

"Well, it is a *little* weird to have your own name on your T-shirt," I said. "I mean, my mum sews my name into my clothes, but that's just on little tags at the back, not a giant glittery splash across the front."

Why was I telling the hottest boy I'd ever met about my *mum's* sewing skills? I felt myself blushing, and I looked away. When I looked back at him, though, he was watching me closely with a weird smile on his face. His dimples and nose made me suddenly think how much he and Jack looked alike—apart from the eyes and the different hairstyles. They could have been brothers. Or cousins, at least.

"What will I have to do . . . in the video? I mean, it's

really . . . nice of you to have asked me." Before I could stop myself, I added, "Why *did* you ask me?"

He didn't break eye contact with me, just kept smiling his wide, gorgeous smile. "Because there was . . . I don't know." He shrugged. "Because everyone wants to be in my videos, and because, y'know . . ." He winked at me mischievously. "You're cute, Mouse."

Just as I was letting that sentence sink in, Nordic Socks flung the door open, flanked by the French makeup women. "Roland honey, they need to borrow you a minute in the other trailer. Mouse—you're ready for makeup now."

Roland flashed me another grin and grabbed an overly fluffy robe off the door. He stepped into it and left. The two makeup women sat me down and started pulling out tubes of foundation that were about eight shades darker than my skin and painting it in lines on my cheeks and nose. "I love your hair," one of them said, picking up bits of it and holding it up to the other one. "I think we can do something interesting with it."

Ten minutes later, I was ready. My hair was parted into long, Nordic Socks–style Heidi braids, and I had never worn so much makeup in my life, even for ballet performances. I had bronzed cheekbones and shiny pink-glossed lips, and my eyelids had been covered in a million different pots of identical-looking gray shadow.

Visor and Sneakers had also been made up. Visor was

dressed in a pink all-in-one ski suit, and Sneakers was in navy pants and a woolly sweater with snowflakes. I was handed a white all-in-one ski suit. It looked exactly like Lauren's. I imagined her face when I came back out of the trailer wearing an outfit identical to hers.

I held it in my hands without moving. "Is there another color?" I said quietly, trying to sound offhand.

"OK, people, we need to start getting *real*," Cooper shouted from the other end of the trailer. "We are doing this in *five minutes*."

I went into the tiny bathroom and pulled the ski suit on. I was hot with nerves and the thick layers of foundation were starting to melt. I got some tissue and patted my forehead. Some of the makeup came off, leaving a white patch.

I realized I was shaking violently. I heard Cooper say, "Girls, you look amazing. You beat twenty-five thousand other fans to be in this video, so you enjoy every doggone minute, OK?"

She ushered us out and the cold air and the screams hit us all at once. "Whatever the guy over there with the red hat tells you to do, you do it, OK?"

Sneakers and Visor had linked arms and were huddling together.

Cooper led us out in front of the crowd and the cameras. I tried to get closer to Visor and Sneakers for safety. I saw Connie at the side near the front, jumping up and down with excitement. Keira was next to her, smiling. She gave me a thumbs-up. Miss Mardle looked like she was watching a horror film. I felt like I was in one.

I couldn't see Jack anywhere but I did see Lauren, her face blank and unreadable among all the screaming open mouths around her.

The man in the red hat approached us. "OK, all you have to do is dance, girls. Roland will sing one verse, and you just sway and jump around behind him. We'll do it a few times over. Just dance like you're at a Roland concert."

I have never been to a concert, let alone a Roland concert. I hate dancing when there aren't steps. I don't dance at parties or weddings.

The crowd suddenly got ten times louder as Roland emerged from the trailer and stood waving at them in front of us. He was wearing a plain black short-sleeved T-shirt— without his own name on it. He turned around and shot us a wink, and Visor and Sneakers both made a soft, whimpery sound, like they'd just sunk into a too-hot bath.

The red-hatted man went back behind one of the cameras and held three fingers up at us. Then two. Then one.

Then music started blaring out from somewhere, and Roland was jumping around in front of us, mouthing French words I couldn't understand while the crowd went crazier than ever.

Automatically, I started swaying on the spot, feeling totally ridiculous. I looked at Sneakers and Visor; their faces were frozen into Instagram pouts and they were waving their arms around in time to the beat.

I couldn't help scanning the crowd, wondering if Jack was watching.

JACK

Mouse was amazing. Really amazing. Max had bustled us all the way to the back of the crowd, so we couldn't see as clearly as I would've liked, but she definitely looked cooler and more at ease than the other two girls. They were posing and pouting and generally looking super try-hard, but Mouse just kind of swayed elegantly, like she was in her own world. Like she didn't even realize the crowd or the cameras were there.

Max stood next to me bad-mouthing Roland and the song he was prancing around to—which was a kind of cheesy, jittery Euro disco, so sugary it almost set your teeth on edge—but I couldn't take my eyes off Mouse. Even with her long hair in those weird bunches, she still looked so, so hot.

Once they'd finished filming and she'd been taken back into one of the big white trailers, we all headed back down to the beginners' slope, and the rest of the afternoon passed in a blur of constant falling over. By the time we got back to the hotel at five, we were all in so much pain we could barely walk.

"How are we supposed to ice-skate when we can't even stand up?" Toddy moaned as he flopped down onto his bed.

"We're not *gonna* be ice-skating, are we?" said Max, rubbing his battered legs while simultaneously checking himself out in the mirror. "We'll be too busy meeting girls to do any ice-skating. Speaking of which, we need a game plan for tonight."

Me and Toddy both groaned, but Max just carried on as if he hadn't heard. "Jack, you go for Lauren. I'll go for Scarlett, and, Toddy, that leaves you with Melody." He went and stood over Toddy, who was still sprawled out on his bed. "Now, listen, Toddy, because this is important. You have to actually *speak* to Melody, instead of doing what you normally do and just staring at your feet."

"Whatever, Max," said Toddy dryly. "Just because I'm not blessed with your incredible conversational skills." He was trying to make a joke of it, but I could tell he was nervous about having to hang out with Lauren and her friends. I was nervous too. Something about those girls just encouraged nervousness.

"Yeah, Max, can you chill out with the game-plan stuff?" I said, shooting Toddy what I hoped was a supportive grin. "Let's just go there and see what happens."

Max frowned. "No, Jack, we *need* a game plan. Because if Toddy doesn't talk to Melody, then Lauren and Scarlett will feel bad about leaving her out, so they'll talk to her instead. And if they're chatting to her, that means they can't be alone with me or you."

"Can't we all just talk to each other?" I suggested.

"We're not supposed to be talking at all!" Max yelled. "We're supposed to kissing them! We're supposed to be trying to win the bet!"

"Well, why don't me and Toddy talk to each other and you can kiss all three of them. How does that sound?"

Max sighed and said, as if speaking to a little kid, "In an ideal world, Jack, that is what would happen. But this is not an ideal world, so I need you and Toddy to concentrate on Lauren and Melody so I can do my moves on Scarlett. OK?"

"'Do your moves'?" I laughed. "Are you trying to kiss her or take her square dancing?"

Me and Toddy lay groaning in pain on our beds while Max spent a whole hour pacing the room, deciding what he was going to wear. He tried on about six different outfits, but in the end it was all totally pointless, because it was so cold outside that we had to keep our puffy ski jackets firmly zipped up. So, really, Max could've been wearing a bright-pink leotard for all it mattered.

The ice rink was about a minute's walk from our hotel, in Mercier's main square. The whole thing was lit up with millions of little fairy lights, and there were stalls scattered round the edges selling steaming mugs of hot chocolate and cinnamon waffles.

We lined up to get our skates and I spotted Lauren, already on the ice. She had switched her all-white look for a tight red puffer jacket and jeans. As we wobbled over to the rink on our skates, she glided across with Scarlett and Melody. Before I even had time to say hi, she grabbed my hand and pulled me onto the ice.

"Whoa!" I teetered crazily, and she held my hand tighter to keep me upright. The rink was really busy—it seemed like every kid in the hotel was here.

"It's easy," Lauren laughed as I skidded painfully into the sideboard. "You'll get the hang of it. We'll stick to the edge."

"It's more that my legs are so sore after snowboarding," I said.

"Yeah, skiing was pretty tiring too. Don't do so many pushes with your feet. Just do long, slow glides. Like this."

I watched her skate elegantly next to me, and tried to copy her.

"You're really good," I said.

She nodded, like she was already well aware of the fact. "I used to do ballet. It's kind of similar to skating."

I wasn't in danger of falling over anymore, but she was still holding my hand. What did that mean? Was she just trying to help me, or did she actually want to hold my hand?

We skated slowly round and round the huge rink, hand

in hand, my heart thudding softly in my chest. All my concentration was going into trying not to fall over. Every so often, I'd look up from my skittering feet and catch a glimpse of Jamie and Ed sneering at me, or Max giving me a not-very-subtle thumbs-up.

And then I saw Mouse. And she saw me. She was with Keira and Connie on the other side of the rink. Our eyes only caught for a split second, but I saw a little flicker of shock—or *something*—in her face. Without thinking, I let go of Lauren's hand.

"Wanna go get a hot chocolate?" I said.

We sat on the bench by the rink, blowing the steam off our drinks. I kept wishing I was with Mouse, but that seemed like a stupid wish, really, when there was another hot girl right next to me. I tried to focus. On Lauren, on Max's bet, on everything that wasn't Mouse. Lauren was looking over at the rink, where Max was talking animatedly to Scarlett. Toddy wasn't even making an effort with Melody. He was just talking to Sarvan by the edge.

"Do you think your friend Max likes Scarlett?" Lauren asked suddenly.

"Uh . . . dunno," I lied. I had no idea how Max would want me to play it. "Do you think she likes him?"

She squinted at them, as if that would tell her the answer. "Maybe . . ." She left it at that.

We kept staring at the rink in silence. Having been

ignored by Toddy, Melody had drifted into conversation with Ed, and Jamie was now muscling in on Max's chat with Scarlett.

Lauren grabbed my hand again. "Come on, let's get back out there."

We skated over to where Jamie and Max were jostling for Scarlett's attention. She seemed to be quite enjoying it. As we got closer I heard the tail end of what Jamie was saying to her. "I don't know what he's told you, but they're not a *real* band. They haven't even got a *name*!"

Scarlett laughed, and Jamie threw a smug smirk at Max. I winced. I knew exactly what was coming next.

Before I could stop him, Max launched himself at Jamie, shoving him hard in the chest and sending him crashing down onto the cold, hard ice.

"Oh my God!" Lauren squealed.

"Shut up about our band, Jamie!" Max yelled down at him. Jamie was too shocked to even respond. He just lay there, flat out on the ice, staring up at him. Instantly, Flynn was there, in full control, pushing away the kids who had crowded round to see what was happening. He put his hand on Max's shoulder, firmly.

"All right, Mr. Kendal. Back to the hotel immediately!"

Max was bright red. "But, sir! It was all Jamie's fault! He started it!"

Jamie was now back up on his feet. "You're a freakin'

maniac, Max!" he shouted. "You should have to wear a muzzle or something!"

Flynn shushed Jamie angrily. "I saw everything, Mr. Kendal. You shoved Mr. Smith, hence you are the one who goes back to the hotel. Now!" He looked at me and Toddy. "All of you!"

"What, sir?" I said. "Why us too?"

"You two are his coconspirators, Jack. You're the ones who are constantly egging him on."

"We don't egg him on, sir," Toddy moaned. "We think he's just as much of an idiot as you do."

Lauren, Scarlett and Melody all laughed, and I noticed Toddy blush proudly.

"Be that as it may, Mr. Todd," said Flynn, "I'm afraid all three of you need to learn that there's only so far you can push me before I break. Head straight to your room, OK?"

Max gave one last cry of frustration and wobbled off. I offered Lauren an apologetic shrug. "Sorry. See you tomorrow, I guess."

"Yeah, cool."

She didn't even seem that annoyed. She looked sort of impressed, actually. Maybe she would like me more if she thought I was some sort of bad-boy troublemaker.

We returned our skates and wandered back to the hotel. I tried to sneak a glance at Mouse as we passed the rink, but she was surrounded by a bunch of girls I'd never seen before, probably eager to find out every detail of what the great Roland was like in real life.

"Jamie's such an idiot," Max huffed. "He just can't stand it that I was gonna get with Scarlett and he wasn't."

"Yeah, well, none of us are getting with anyone now, thanks to you," I said, pushing the hotel door open.

"Where are you going?" asked Max.

"To our room, obviously."

Max shook his head. "No way. If you think we're just sitting in our room all night, you're crazy. Let's go and have a look around town. We might even find a fireworks store."

Me and Toddy hesitated.

"Come on," groaned Max. "Everyone's gonna be at the ice rink for another hour at least. No one will know. We'll just go for a quick wander."

I shrugged at Toddy, and he sighed and nodded. We wound our way up the hill, round the back of the hotel, and past lots of little snow-topped houses until we came to a bench with an amazing view of the town. We could see all the little chimneys puffing away and the lights twinkling. We could even see the ice rink, the tiny figures on it just a blur of different-colored dots. We sat in silence, rubbing our hands and watching our breath billow out in front of us.

"Maybe Jamie's right about our band," I said after a while. "It's a little ridiculous to keep going on about how great we are when we literally just play in your bedroom, Max."

"Don't be stupid," snapped Max. "We're awesome. We

just need a gig. And a name. Then we'll be on our way." A little drop of acid fizzed in my stomach at the thought of having to play live, in front of a real audience.

"We probably need a few more songs, as well," reasoned Toddy. "We should write our own stuff instead of just doing covers all the time."

So far we only had three songs—two covers ("Wonderwall" by Oasis and "London Calling" by the Clash) and one that Max had "written," which sounded pretty much identical to "Smells Like Teen Spirit" by Nirvana.

"Yeah." Max nodded. "True."

Suddenly, from nowhere, a sharp, tinkling sound shattered the silence.

"What was that?" said Max, looking around. We waited a few seconds, and the sound rang out again. This time, I saw exactly where it had come from. In the cluster of roofs directly below us, someone had thrown a snowball at a silver weathervane. It was spinning wildly round and round, its tinkling noise getting fainter with every turn.

"Let's go and check it out!" Max hissed. We crept further along the path as it started to wind back toward the town. A few feet down, Max shot his hand out for us to stop. In front of us, half hidden in the darkness, there was a figure. It had its back to us and its hood up, so it was impossible to tell who or what it was. The figure molded another snowball and carefully took aim at the weathervane. It missed, and muttered something under its breath.

We all widened our eyes at each other. "What should we do?" mouthed Max.

"Let's go back the other way," I whispered. "It could be a serial killer, for all we know."

Max frowned. "I don't think serial killers spend their nights throwing snowballs. Aren't they they're too busy serial-killing?"

"Whatever. Let's just go."

We turned to head back, but suddenly, I felt Toddy starting to tremble violently next to me. Before I could ask what was wrong, the loudest sneeze I've ever heard exploded out of him. "AAAAH-CHOOOO!"

The figure spun round and stood staring straight at us, its face still hidden in the hood. We were frozen to the spot. It started walking slowly toward us.

"Toddy," Max whimpered, through gritted teeth, "if we get serial-killed because you can't sneeze quietly, I'll never forgive you."

The figure arrived right in front of us. He—it was definitely a he—looked weirdly familiar. He pulled his hood down and ran a hand through his floppy brown hair.

"Oh my God!" Max stuttered. "It's . . . You're . . . It's *you*!"

"*Oui,*" said Roland wearily. "I am Roland."

12

MOUSE

"You are definitely drawing more attention to yourself like that," Keira said.

The three of us were skating round the rink in a train, with me in the middle, obscured from view.

"The coolest thing that has ever happened to anyone in our school has just happened to you, and you're acting like . . ." Connie was either lost for words or unstable on her skates.

"Like I danced like drunk Frankenstein in front of a million people *and* a celebrity," I called back at her. I hate people looking at me. I get shy sometimes when I have to order in restaurants. Swaying from side to side awkwardly in front of a huge crowd of people had felt like slowly dying while everyone smiled on. Even now that it was over, the thought of it kept crashing over me and made me want to fold myself up and disappear.

"How did he say it again?" Connie asked for the millionth time. "You keep doing it differently. 'You're *cute,* Mouse,'" she whispered in my ear.

"You sound like Pepé Le Pew." I shook my head.

"You're *cute.*" Keira squeezed my tummy. "It's not how he said it, but how he *looked* when he said it. Was it '*Oh ooochy-cootchy,* cute baby' or was it 'I am consumed by passion. You are *cute*'?" She whistled at the end of the "cute."

"I can't remember," I groaned. I really couldn't. It was like my brain had started to malfunction and remember it a million different ways, so now I had no idea what the real version was. I wish there had been an independent witness or something. The first time a boy had ever said anything to me that could even be vaguely construed as flirty, and the situation had been so weird I couldn't evaluate it properly. That's if Roland had been being flirty at all, which seemed sort of unlikely now.

"You're being very cup-half-empty about this whole thing," Connie said bossily. "I bet most people here would willingly chop their face off to get near Roland."

"It's so true." Keira laughed smugly. "The best thing about it was seeing Lauren's face. It was like someone was ripping her *soul* in half. Are you *friends* with her now, or what?" she asked me.

"I really don't know," I said honestly. I looked over at

Lauren on the other side of the rink. She was ice-skating backwards while Scarlett filmed her.

"Well, you know what *I* think about Lauren Bradley," sniffed Keira.

"Yeah," said Connie breezily. "You absolutely hate her."

"The way she was skating around with Jack was so cringeworthy," Keira carried on. "Anyway, we should just forget about those boys, they're idiots. You're a mini celebrity now, Mouse."

"The best part of today was after the video, when that French girl touched you and started crying." Connie was laughing hysterically. "She touched you like you were a unicorn. Like you were Jesus."

"She *so* wanted you to give her the hat," Keira shouted back to us. "She was blatantly faking it so you would."

I took my hand off Connie's waist and felt inside my pocket for the hat. We had smelled it back in our room. It smelled like shampoo and boys. Which was sort of obvious, really.

It did feel like it should have happened to someone else. Lauren would have loved every single second of it. It would have become part of the thing that made her who she was. The mythology of Lauren Angelica Bradley. But I didn't have the personality to make it like that. I'm too shy. I have always been too shy to make anything work. And ballet was the thing that kind of made it OK. When

I got into White Lodge, everyone stopped talking about how shy I was, even though inside it hadn't gone away at all. It's funny how they took me to ballet to try to "cure" my shyness, but in the end, getting pushed out has made me less confident than ever.

We stopped at the edge and hobbled off the rink. "Should we get a hot chocolate?" Connie clapped her hands.

"You've had like seven today," Keira said, frowning. "I think you might go all Willy Wonka."

We all plonked ourselves down on a picnic bench and watched the rink. Lauren and Scarlett and Melody's energy had changed since the boys left. They were just being normal. Out of my right eye I saw Lauren look over at me, so I smiled. She smiled back and waved, so I did too. Keira rolled her eyes.

"Are you OK about her and Jack?" Keira said. "I mean, you basically snagged a boy who looks like him, but much hotter, today, so . . ."

"Yeah, I'm fine about her and Jack," I said. "I mean, it's not like I like him or anything."

"Lie," Keira coughed.

"OK, well, it's not *just* that. I wanted to be friends with him. Like, get to know him. I would be OK with that. But now he's with Lauren, so I can't even be friends with him."

"Yes you can," Connie said. "He can have a girl who is a friend. Just 'cause he has a girlf—a . . . you know . . . whatever they are . . . that doesn't mean you and him can't be friends."

"I'm OK with her being his girlfriend. I didn't ever really think anything was going to happen. I just . . . now I feel like I'm not even allowed to *look* at him."

I took the hat out of my pocket just as two random French girls walked over, giggling nervously.

"Excuse me," said one. "But you are the girl from the shoot? With Roland?"

Keira and Connie laughed, and I nodded.

"Wow!" said the second girl. "He touched your face, right?"

I nodded again.

"Where?"

I pulled the scarf back and pointed at my cheek. The girls looked at it, in amazement. "Wow . . . Do you mind if I . . ."

She reached up and gently stroked my face. Then she looked at her own fingers in amazement. I made myself fake-cough to distract from the weirdness. Connie and Keira exploded into laughter, but the girls didn't even seem to notice.

"What was he like?" said the first one dreamily. "Did he smell nice? Did you see his new tattoo? Tell us everything."

I thought about it. What had he been like? Really cute? Really clean-looking? In the end, I just said, "He was really . . . tan."

They both looked a little disappointed. "Oh. Well, yes, he has a holiday home in Bermuda, so it makes sense."

Then the other one said, "Can we take a picture with you?"

Keira took the girl's phone and snapped off a picture of the three of us. As the girls were walking off, I saw Lauren, Scarlett and Melody coming toward us.

"Hey, guys," they all cooed together.

"Hey," Connie and me said, smiling back; Keira stayed quiet.

"Mouse, we were wondering if we could talk to you?" Lauren said it looking only at me. "A *private* talk, I mean."

Keira and Connie looked at me. I wanted to say no, more than anything. But it's an unwritten rule that you can't.

I walked next to Melody but we didn't speak. I could tell she was nervous and that she knew what was about to happen. I opened my mouth to ask her what was going on but then thought better. We passed the hot chocolate stalls and walked toward a little playground that was across the square from the ice rink. Lauren opened the gate and we went in. She and Scarlett went over to the swings and sat down. Melody and me followed but there were no swings for us so we just stood in front of them.

Lauren and Scarlett exchanged a look like kids do in plays when they are reminding the other one it's their turn to speak. Like they had rehearsed how this was going to go.

I tried to seem normal, to convince myself something horrible wasn't happening. I glanced over at Melody but she just looked at the floor and bashed her heels together.

"Look, Mouse, this is really awkward," Lauren said. "Especially as, you know . . ." She looked at Scarlett. "Me and you used to be friends."

Used to be friends. Laughing on the slopes earlier, it had felt like things might go back to normal.

"And that's the thing, Mouse, I care about you and I am really worried about you. We were going to go and talk to Miss Mardle, but we're thirteen years old now. We should just be able to talk openly to each other."

I looked at the ground. I just wanted her to say whatever it was she was going to say, so I could leave.

"That's part of it, I suppose," Lauren went on. "We're just . . . It's like you . . ." She looked at Scarlett to help her, to pick up the baton.

"Well," Scarlett said. "And honestly, we are saying this to your face, when lots of people are saying it behind your back. You are a little . . . weird now."

"I mean, I'm sure you would rather we said it to your face." Melody said it like she was trying to convince herself.

"We just wanted to be grown up about it," Lauren said. "And obviously, we don't care about how you and Keira and Connie act or whatever. Everyone should just be themselves . . . but it just seems like you are a little . . ." She looked at Scarlett again.

"To be honest," Scarlett said, "it feels like you are a little obsessed with Lauren. Like it's a little . . . sad."

I put my hands in my pockets. I had forgotten about the Roland hat. I gripped it as hard as I could, until it was almost painful, and told myself to look normal. I have danced when my feet were bleeding before and kept smiling. I didn't want Lauren to see me cry.

"Anything else?" I said, in as offhand a way as I could.

Lauren and Scarlett looked flustered, like they hadn't expected me to speak. Like when they'd practiced their speeches I hadn't said anything.

"Ignoring us on the ferry was rude . . . but whatever." Lauren was talking more quickly, like she wasn't quite as certain of herself as she was before. "We invited you to hang out with us because we were being nice, but you didn't even show up. Since then you have just been acting so strangely." She paused, like she was working herself up to the next bit. "I saw you talking to Jack earlier," she said, "before the Roland thing happened and you dressed up as me."

She said "dressed up as me" slowly. I could feel my jaw tensing. I bit the inside of my cheek so hard that it hurt.

Scarlett carried on. "Actually, it's really not cool to try and get with someone that a friend of yours is with. Today when you were flirting with Jack it was just really cringe-worthy and . . ."

"Sad," Melody said. "Really sad. That you're that desperate."

"We know you're going to ballet school in Paris and that you're used to being the center of attention. Or *like* being the center of attention," Lauren cut over her. "But the thing with Roland today was actually worrying. Mouse, you threw yourself into him when you realized Jack wasn't interested. So awkward, so desperate. And that's the thing." Lauren swung herself back a little. "Jack told me he just thought it was sad. And weird."

"But we just wanted to tell you," Scarlett said, "that it's not OK to act like that. It's actually really strange. And other people wouldn't say it to your face but we wanted to. Basically to just sort this out in a grown-up way."

"Do you get that we are doing this to be *nice*?" Lauren said.

She got up off the swing and held her arms out for a hug. She was actually going to try to make me hug her, like we were friends who had just been shopping together. Even if I wanted to I couldn't have moved. Lauren put her arms down and gave Scarlett a she's-so-immature look.

"I'm glad we could talk about it," Scarlett said. "We wanted to do the right thing, for your sake."

I looked at Lauren and our eyes met. She knew what she was doing. I shook my head and turned around. I walked to the edge of the playground and opened the gate. None of them said a word; they must have just been watching me leave. I didn't go back to the ice rink. I walked straight back to the hotel, passing the stupid Roland posters, and into our room. Mr. Jambon was tucked into a little ball in his cage. I crawled into my sleeping bag and wrapped myself up tight too. I could see *The Teen Witches' Book of Spells* lying on Keira's bunk and heard her voice in my head: "The first rule is to not wish harm on others." I plunged my face inside the sleeping bag to muffle the ugly sobs my body had started making without me even realizing.

"I hope something bad happens to you," I said out loud. "I hate you, Lauren."

JACK

We stood there staring at Roland in silence. We didn't really know what to say. He didn't seem to mind being stared at. He probably gets it all the time. He just stood in front of us, shivering and staring right back.

Close up, he looked exactly like he did on the posters—the floppy, sideswept hair, the huge blue eyes. The only difference was that on the posters he was always smiling; he had this big, cheesy grin smeared all over his face. Now, though, he wasn't smiling at all. In fact, he was glaring at everything, including us. He looked cooler without the smile, I reckoned. Moodier. Less like a Disney-fied boy-band loser, and more like a film star or a punk singer or something. He was so polished he almost looked Photoshopped. If I really *was* a dead ringer for him, I definitely wouldn't still be on zero.

"So," he said, finally. "What do you want? Autographs? Selfies?" His voice was really deep, and his thick French accent gave it this kind of laziness, like he was permanently half asleep.

"Um . . . What's that, man?" said Max.

Roland shook his head irritably. "I come up here for some time to myself, and yet still people manage to find me. So, come on, take the phone out and let's get this over with. I'm not really in the mood for this tonight."

"We don't want a freaking *selfie* with you," sniffed Max. "We'd never even *heard* of you till, like, two days ago."

Rather than being insulted, Roland looked quite pleased. "Ah . . . So you are not superfans?"

"We're not even *fans* full stop," said Max.

"Excellent," Roland said, beaming. He stuck his hand out and we all shook it and introduced ourselves.

"So what are you doing up here, anyway?" asked Toddy. "Apart from smashing weathervanes."

"My hotel is up there." Roland nodded further up the hill. "I just snuck out to have some time to myself to think. Time to myself is quite a rare thing at the moment."

"Yeah," I said. "You're *everywhere*. Well, your posters are, anyway."

He nodded. "I am here to film my new video. But I

can't even walk the street in daylight without being surrounded." He pointed at his hood. "That's why I have to do all this, even when I go for a walk at night, halfway up a mountain."

"Your English is pretty good, you know," said Max. "Better than our French, anyway. We only know *'Ma perruche est dans la zone piétonne'* and *'Monsieur, votre grand-mère était un blaireau.'*"

Roland laughed. "Just the essential phrases, then."

"How old are you?" Toddy asked him.

"Fourteen."

"Whoa, man," said Max, impressed. "You're only a year older than us and you can speak a whole other language fluently."

"Max can barely speak *one* language fluently," noted Toddy, and Max slapped the back of his head.

Roland chuckled. "My managers made me learn English intensively last year, because they want me to 'break England' and 'break America.' They feel I have conquered France. Now they want to take me *worldwide*."

"Sounds pretty terrifying," I said. Roland was conquering the world; I couldn't even conquer Band Night in the dining hall.

"What are you talking about?" said Max. "Sounds awesome."

Roland somehow managed to shrug with both his body

and face. "Being famous . . . it's not what you expect it will be. Sometimes . . . it's not so easy."

"Oh yeah," said Max sarcastically. "I'm sure it must be awful to have millions of screaming girls throwing themselves at you every five seconds."

Roland smiled gloomily. "I guess it is difficult to explain. On the one hand, you have the fame, the money, the snowmobiles—"

"You've got a *snowmobile*?!" Max interrupted.

Roland nodded impatiently. "Yes, yes, I have three. So, on the one hand you have these things, but on the other . . ." He broke off and looked at us. "You no longer live life like a normal teenager, you know? Going on dates, spending time with friends . . . you can't do these things anymore." He looked down at the little town below. "The only fun you have is throwing snowballs, alone, in the darkness."

Max wasn't interested in this sort of deep, soul-searching stuff. "But you must have gotten with tons of girls, yeah?"

Roland laughed. "I do not kiss and tell, my friend."

"We don't kiss *or* tell," sighed Toddy, and Roland laughed again.

"So, like . . . have you got any tips?" asked Max. "For getting girls to like you?"

Roland ruffled his hair as he considered this. "Just be yourself, I guess."

Max grunted. "I'm sure 'being yourself' works if you're

a billionaire pop star, but we've been 'being ourselves' for years and it's gotten us literally nowhere." He stroked his top lip. "What about mustaches? Do you think girls like mustaches?"

Roland frowned. "Maybe. Why, are you thinking to grow one?"

Me and Toddy cracked up as Max jabbed a finger at his own mouth angrily. "I've *already* grown one, mate. What do you think *this* is?"

Roland peered closely at Max's top lip with a slightly disgusted look on his face. "Yes . . . I see. Very . . . sophisticated." He straightened up and patted Max on the shoulder. "I'm sure the women will love it." Max bristled proudly.

We all stood in silence for a bit, looking down at the little town below us. It felt weird how un-weird it was having Roland with us. He didn't seem like the most famous dude in France, or like the cheesy, strutting poser off those posters. He just seemed . . . normal.

"You know," he said, "I met an English girl today, actually. At my video shoot."

My heart suddenly spun into double speed. Max jabbed me in the ribs. "We know her!" he blurted. "That was Mouse!"

Roland's massive blue eyes got even wider. "Yes! Mouse. I was thinking of her today. You know her, really? You are friends with her?"

Max shook his head. "Nah. She hates us. No idea why.

She's crazy. So are her friends. Cute but crazy. They dress insanely, they keep rats and hamsters in their cupboards and they shun you for no reason. Steer clear, if you want my advice. Eh, Jack?"

I nodded. I really hoped Roland *would* steer well clear. If *he* liked Mouse, I really wouldn't have a chance.

"I mean, you can basically get any girl you want, can't you?" Max carried on. "So I don't know why you'd settle for a crazy one."

Roland shrugged. "She seemed much less crazy than most of the girls I meet. Sometimes it is nice to find a girl who is *not* obsessed with you and constantly screaming at you and writing insane fan fiction about you. A girl who is just . . . normal."

"You're mad," said Max. "Why would you pick a *normal* girl over one that totally and utterly *worships* you? You obviously could've gotten any of those girls at your video shoot thing."

"You were there today too?" Roland asked.

Max nodded. "We're sort of in the music business as well, actually."

"Yes?"

"Yeah. Well, we're in a band."

"Ah, cool. Would I have heard your music?"

"Unless you live next door to Max, probably not," said Toddy. "We've never actually played a gig."

"Yeah, but we're gonna play one soon," Max snapped. "We'll probably be touring France this time next year."

"Very nice," said Roland. "Do you all sing?"

"No, just Jack," said Max, slapping me on the back, hard. "He's our front man. And not just because he looks like you."

Roland smiled and sized me up. "It is true, actually. Except for the eyes, I guess. And what is your band called?"

"We're sort of between names at the moment," Toddy said.

Roland shook his head. "No good. You must have a name. You will never get anywhere without a name."

"Yeah, well, we're working on it," muttered Max, and then his eyes lit up. "Maybe you could help us, actually! I mean, you could pull some strings, talk to some of your people, maybe get us a record deal or something?"

Roland laughed and bent down to scoop a handful of snow from the ground. "I'm not sure about the record deal, but I guess I could try to help you." He patted the snow into a little round ball. "If I do that for you, though, maybe you can do something for me in return."

"Obviously," said Max. "Anything."

Roland aimed the snowball and hit the weathervane dead on, sending it tinkling round and round. Then he turned to us, his blue eyes half white in the moonlight. "Can you help me see Mouse again?"

13

MOUSE

"Winter picnics are the best," Connie said, ripping her sandwich in half and handing one of the halves to me. That was the thing about Connie. The essence of her was good. She didn't really know how to be anything other than nice. She had welcomed me back into her life like I had never been away. We were beginning to feel like a group. Like we belonged. Whatever the gene is that most people are born with that gives you the ability to be mean, Connie just didn't have it.

I have it, though. Before the trip, I had worried people would judge me for hanging around with Connie, and last night, alone in the room, every single part of me had hated Lauren.

Keira sprawled on the snow. "I'm in so much pain. Skiing this morning was hard core. I wonder if we'll ever get the hang of it." She looked over at Lauren, Scarlett and Melody eating their lunch at another picnic table.

"Have any of them spoken to you?" she asked, staring down at her marshmallow-loaded hot chocolate and back at them. I wanted to tell Keira not to look over. I didn't want Lauren to think we were talking about them.

I shook my head. "They're just acting like I don't exist."

"Good. We should *actually* forget *they* exist," Keira said. "Do I have a whipped cream mustache?"

Connie nodded. "Mouse, I wish we had gone with you. The things they said to you were really awful."

Keira sighed. "She wouldn't have said it if we had been there. I keep telling you both. It's not complicated. She's just nasty. She's jealous of Mouse because she's going to school in Paris and is prettier than her and cooler or whatever. Who knows, whatever, she's just one of *those* girls." In her boyish, offhand way, Keira made it sound like this simple, explainable, tiny thing.

Going to school in Paris. I pushed the lie away again. I just wasn't allowing myself to even think about how big it was getting. Lying to Keira and Connie on the first day had made me shiver, but not feel guilty the way I did now.

"We should hex her," Keira said. "I know we're white witches, but I'm pretty sure in this kind of situation they must make exceptions."

"Who's 'they'?" Connie asked.

Keira shrugged. "I don't know. The parliament of . . . I haven't read the whole book yet."

"No way," Connie said. "We're not into the dark arts. We're white witches. We're into the light arts."

"That makes us sound like we make lamps," Keira said, and handed Connie and me a Reese's.

"No, I would feel bad," I said. "And anyway . . ." I lowered my voice a little even though there was no way they could hear. "I sort of did hex her already."

"What do you mean?" Keira sounded impressed and surprised at the same time.

"Well, I didn't really. Just . . . last night before you guys got back. When I was upset . . . I was staring at your book on the bed . . . and I just thought about how much Lauren had upset me and . . . I wished something bad would happen to her. Which obviously I don't actually wa—"

"That's totally a hex!" Keira said. "You've hexed her. We formed a coven and became witches. Obviously now you have to be careful."

"Don't be ridiculous. So, what, if I *think* I want an avalanche to happen it might—"

"Nooooooooo!" Connie yelled, and launched herself at me, covering my mouth with her hands.

"OK," Keira said. "Maybe not thinking it, but saying it out loud would definitely count."

I kept quiet.

And then Tania saved me. "Come on, guys, gather round."

Keira lay back in the snow and groaned loudly. "Every part of my body hurts."

Everyone was complaining constantly about the way skiing was affecting their muscles, but it made me feel good, like my body was being used again. I liked going to sleep feeling like I had made it work, like I was training and getting better.

"OK," Tania said, taking off her hat to reveal gold glitter in her pixie cut. "I get it, guys, you are all tired. So this afternoon, we are going to go on a little adventure up the mountain."

"Can we build an igloo?" Connie put her hand up as she said it, like she had meant to wait to be called on but couldn't quite contain herself.

Some girls rolled their eyes or made she's-so-weird faces and laughed, but Tania's eyes lit up.

"Yeah, I know the perfect, secret place, at the top behind the snowboarding park, where no one goes. We can watch some cute guys do tricks at the same time."

Building the igloo took all afternoon. Most people drifted off to watch the boys doing tricks or to practice their skiing. We collected snow and made it into bricks with a bucket and then Connie and Tania laid them in a circle. We did it again and again until the sun started to turn pink in the sky. We laid the last brick in the top and stood around and admired it.

Keira, Connie and me crawled in and Tania followed us.

"It feels really magical," I said. "And warm. Like we really could sleep here."

"A good place for a lamp-making workshop," Keira said meaningfully, looking at us.

"Headquarters for our coven," I whispered to Connie when she looked confused.

"So," Tania said, pointing at my hat. "Is that the famous Roland hat?"

I shook my head and reached into my pocket and handed her the real one.

"I'm not into Roland, but this is pretty cool," she said. "And he is a cute guy."

Keira did a double take. "Um . . . when you say 'cute,' do you mean cute like a little kid, or cute like hot?"

"Hot," said Tania, and Keira shot me a triumphant smile. I couldn't help smiling back.

"He said Mouse was cute," Connie said proudly. "So, do you have a boyfriend, Tania?"

Keira tutted at Connie. "You are so inappropriate." Then she looked at Tania. "But do you?"

Tania shook her head. "No. I am over guys. Completely. I hate them."

None of us knew what to say. It was a little early for any

of us to think about being done with boys; we needed to get started first.

"This place does feel a little magic," Tania said, changing the subject. "Do you wanna write something on the wall before we go?"

"Our names, maybe?" suggested Connie.

"I was thinking more like the names of your crushes," Tania said, smiling.

"I thought you hated men?" I said.

"Yeah, I hate them. That doesn't mean I can't like some of them as well."

"Complicated," Connie sighed.

Keira started battering Alfie's name into the wall with the side of her phone, while Tania began scribbling a long list of weird-looking German names. Connie was scratching RON WEASLEY with the key to our room.

I wanted to write "Jack" but I knew I couldn't. Because he was going out with someone who hated me, who had told me he thought I was a weird stalker.

"I know who you're going to write," Tania said, patting the Roland hat.

"Mouse, you're so cute," Connie said in her Pepé Le Pew voice. I took a pen out of my backpack and slowly and painstakingly wrote ROLAND across five bricks. He was good-looking, so I suppose objectively speaking I did like him.

"Let's go, guys," Tania said, admiring our workmanship.

We started to walk slowly back to the snowboarding park. The sky was getting darker and it felt colder than it had since we arrived. Suddenly I didn't want to leave the igloo like that. It felt unlucky, like I was tempting fate.

"I left my scarf. I'll catch up to you," I shouted, and turned back. I crawled into the igloo, carved JACK as quickly as I could and crawled out again.

I knew straight away something had happened, even from a distance. Everyone looked serious. People were very still and not talking to each other. And then I heard the screams. Tears and pain and fear all rolled into one. I pushed myself along with my poles to go quicker.

Everyone was staring at something on the ground a few feet away. Staring at the screaming. Something about the sound was familiar. I realized who it was the second before I saw her. She was lying on the ground with Tania next to her. Our eyes met, tears rolling down her face, contorted with pain. Lauren.

JACK

"Okay, so, seriously . . . we need a plan. How are we going to do this?" Max asked.

The three of us sat on the edge of the beginners' slope, watching the rest of our class wobble and slam and smash into each other. The second day of snowboarding was turning out even worse than the first. More pain, more frustration, more constant falling over. And absolutely zero progress. We were nearing the end of the afternoon session, and it was still only Jamie Smith that could stand up on his board for more than thirty seconds at a time.

Not that we cared, particularly. All we were thinking about was Roland.

Ever since we crept back to the hotel last night, he was basically all we'd talked about. Max kept going on about the crazy randomness of how we'd met him, and how he would *definitely* get us a record deal and make us famous. But I wasn't thinking about all that stuff. I was only thinking about the fact that he liked Mouse. Because *him* liking her meant that *I* didn't stand a chance. And now I'd agreed to help get them together. Honestly, what the *heck* was wrong with me?

Max repeated his question. "Seriously, come on . . . what's the plan? How can we help Roland see Mouse again? How *exactly* are we supposed to ask out a girl who hates our guts, on behalf of France's number one mega pop star? I mean, any ideas are welcome."

"Mouse doesn't hate our guts," I muttered. "*Keira* hates *your* guts. I don't think Mouse has any strong feelings either way about our guts. Anyway, we could just *not* do it."

Max gaped at me. "*Not* do it? Are you insane? Didn't you hear what Roland said? If we can help him out with Mouse, then he can help us out with the band!"

"*How* is he gonna help us out, though? I mean, seriously. You really think he's gonna bag us a record deal? We've never played a gig!"

Max wafted my words away like they were a bad bus-fart. "Jack, all I'm saying is, it's not gonna *harm* us, is it, having a massive star dropping our band's name in some influential circles?"

"We don't even *have* a name!" I yelled.

"Yeah, well, we will once I kiss Scarlett." Max winked. "Psycho Death Squad." He held his arms out in front of him, as if imagining those ridiculous words on a huge Holly-wood billboard. "All we've gotta do is figure out how to ask Mouse out for him."

"We don't even really have to ask her out," Toddy noted. "He just wants us to tell her that he likes her and see what she says. Then maybe try and get her to that press conference thing he's doing tomorrow."

Roland was coming back to the ski slope tomorrow lunchtime to speak to a bunch of journalists. He'd asked us to try to get Mouse there so he could talk to her afterward.

"Yeah, OK," said Max, chewing his bottom lip, as we all watched Sarvan crash face first into one of the padded barriers. "To be honest, I think the best way is just to come straight out with it. We'll find Mouse this evening and just say, 'Look, Mouse, do you want to get with that Roland dude? Because we met him last night, and he's well up for it, if you are.'"

"Very eloquent," said Toddy. "Could've come straight out of *Romeo and Juliet,* that."

"Yeah, maybe I should tell her," I said. The idea of getting to chat to Mouse alone was weirdly appealing, even if the only reason was to try to set her up with someone else.

"What will your *girlfriend* think about that, though, eh?" Max said, smirking.

"What? Who do you mean?"

Max thumped Toddy on the arm and nodded at me. "Look at this guy—so many girls drooling after him he doesn't even know which one I'm talking about. Lauren, *obviously.* The one you were holding hands with all last night?"

"Oh, right. Dunno." I'd barely thought about Lauren since we left the ice rink. She wasn't constantly muscling in on my thoughts like Mouse was. "Do you think she actually *is*?" I said, rubbing the latest bruise on my thigh. "My girlfriend, I mean?"

Toddy laughed. "Surely you must know?"

"Well, that's the thing . . . I don't. I mean, she was holding my hand and stuff. And the way we she was acting toward me, it was like we were . . . going out. But . . ."

Max finished my sentence for me. "But . . . you can't be going out with a girl if you haven't even kissed her, right?"

"Well, yeah, exactly."

Max hauled himself up and clicked his left boot back onto

his snowboard. "Maybe we should ask Roland. He'll know. We'll ask him tomorrow at the press conference thing." He broke off and squinted across the mountain. "What the hell is that?"

In the distance, we could see a huge red snowplow creeping up one of the other slopes below us.

"That's the snow ambulance," Basti announced to the whole group, with a worried frown. "Means someone's had an accident." He glanced at Sarvan, who was still lying on the ground, rubbing his forehead. "Please, please, please . . . no one get injured. I'll have to fill in, like, all these forms. Honestly, it'll be *such* a hassle."

We got back to the hotel at around five to find the lobby crowded with people. I noticed Melody and Scarlett near the reception desk, and it surprised me just how relieved I was to see Lauren wasn't with them. Then, on the other side of the room, huddled on a bench, I spotted Mouse, Connie and Keira.

"Ah, nice," whispered Max. "They're right there. Let's go and talk to them, and then, Jack, you can ask Mouse about Roland."

As we walked over I caught Mouse's eyes, and she flashed me a quick, brilliant grin. It hit me suddenly, hard and fast, like a punch in the stomach, just how much I liked her. What was I doing trying to ask her out for another guy?

Keira was staring down her nose at Max, like he was a

fly that had just landed on her lunch. "And what *exactly* do you three want? I thought we'd agreed not to speak to each other for the rest of this trip?"

"Well, *you've* just spoken to us, haven't you?" Max said. "So, *you're* the one breaking the agreement."

Keira rolled her eyes. "Ugh. You're ridiculous. You're honestly the most ridiculous boy I've ever met. OK, let's agree to not speak to each other from *now* on."

"Fine," said Max. "Fine by me."

"You're still speaking," said Keira.

"So are you," said Max.

Keira sighed and turned to Connie and Mouse. "I can't be bothered with this. Let's go."

"I gave Mr. Jambon some nuts," Connie said to Toddy as they were leaving. "He liked them. Good tip."

Toddy went bright red, and just said, "Oh, cool, good."

Keira shot Connie a disapproving frown and then said, "Come on, let's go back to the room."

Before they could leave, I blurted, "Um . . . sorry, Mouse? Do you have one second? So I can quickly ask you something?"

Mouse stopped dead, and glanced at Keira, who looked more disapproving than ever. But then Mouse said, "Sure. I'll see you guys back in the room in a sec."

Keira shrugged, and she and Connie walked out to the hall, followed closely by Toddy and Max, who gave me a not-so-subtle slap on the shoulder as he passed. Suddenly there was only Mouse in front of me, looking at me intently with her big gray eyes.

"Sorry . . . ," I said. "That was a little weird."

"It's all right," she said. "It's actually hilarious watching Keira and Max fight."

"Yeah. They're both ridiculously stubborn. They're basically made for each other."

We both laughed. I noticed Scarlett and Melody watching us closely from the other side of the room. Mouse shuffled uncomfortably on the spot.

"Uh, so listen, Mouse. There was something I kind of wanted to say to you."

"Yeah?"

"Yeah . . ." *Roland likes you.* The sentence was right there on the tip of my tongue, but it wouldn't unstick. I couldn't say it. I didn't *care* that Roland liked her. Because I liked her more.

"What are you up to tomorrow?" I spluttered, not even thinking what I was saying. "I mean, I just wondered if you wanted to get a hot chocolate with me or something?"

It was out there, between us, before I could take it back. I'd just asked her out. Not for Roland. For me.

Mouse's big gray eyes got even bigger. Her cheeks flushed and her mouth opened, but no words came out. I felt like I was on some cheesy reality show, waiting to see whether or not I'd been voted off.

She shuffled on the spot again, shifting her feet inward

and then out. Then she said, "Um . . . I'm sorry, Jack. I'm not sure . . ."

My face flooded with heat. I didn't even let her finish the sentence. "No, no, obviously. Sorry. It was stupid to ask."

All I could think was, *Please, God, let something happen now to end this moment—a fire alarm, an avalanche, a rip in the space-time continuum . . . Anything.*

And then something *did* happen. Lauren walked into the lobby. On crutches.

I turned back to Mouse. "I'd, um . . . better see if she's OK." She nodded. I felt the humiliation of the last few seconds all coiled up inside me like a spring, ready to explode painfully as soon as I thought about it properly. So I didn't think about it. I just walked toward Lauren.

I joined the back of a whole line of girls who were clamoring to get to her. She waved them all away and hobbled over to me.

"Lauren," I stuttered. "What . . . what happened? Are you OK?"

"She's been very brave," her teacher said.

"I just fell badly and twisted my ankle. It's not broken, but it was really horrible."

"That's so bad. So you can't ski anymore, right?"

Lauren laughed sarcastically. "Yeah, Jack, *obviously* I can still ski. I'll just use my crutches as ski poles."

A group of girls burst into fits of giggles nearby and I became very aware of the fact that I was having a conversation in front of a live audience. I wanted to turn around to see if Mouse was still there, behind me.

"Oh, OK . . . Yeah, sorry," I mumbled. "That was stupid. Well, I'm glad you're OK, anyway."

She laughed and said, "You're so sweet, Jack." Then she leaned in toward me, and for a seriously terrifying split second I thought she was going to kiss me. That I was going to win Max's bet right there in the hotel lobby.

But just as I was certain that it was really happening, and I was about to move past zero, she turned her head sideways and just brushed her lips softly against my cheek. The girls around us all made this weird, whispery noise at the same time—like a cross between a giggle and gasp.

I didn't really know what to do. I just stood there, feeling my face get hotter and hotter. The Maria Bennett memory started flickering dimly in my head. I wondered if I'd somehow managed to miss my chance. Again.

"Uh, thanks," I said.

Our little audience all laughed, but Lauren wasn't even looking at me; she was looking directly behind me. I turned around just in time to see the back of Mouse's head as she slunk out into the hall.

14

MOUSE

Lauren hobbled into breakfast to a kind of medieval fanfare. Scarlett and Melody walked ahead of her like footmen, clearing everything in her path and throwing exaggerated you-can-do-this smiles behind them every so often. A group of girls left their table so she could sit down, and Miss Mardle brought her a huge tray of food.

Keira rolled her eyes. "She hasn't even broken it. And even if she had, you don't become a nice person when a bone fractures. You're just the same person, but a little crappier."

"Don't look," Connie said. So I looked over. Jack, Max and Toddy were sitting with Lauren and the girls at the Royal Table.

"He may as well start peeling her grapes." Keira shook her head.

"I still don't think he's that bad," I said. The thought of

how nervous he had been before he asked me out for hot chocolate, and the look on his face when I said no were still imprinted on my brain. Along with the way Lauren had looked at me when she saw us together.

"He's a total player," Keira said, jabbing her fork into a melon chunk. "He is the worst kind 'cause he acts all shy and clueless. So he flirts with you at the movie night—"

"He barely even looked at me!"

"Flirts with you, then literally breaks into your bedroom."

"He knocked."

"He *did* knock," Connie said, nodding. "A burglar with manners."

Keira prodded her with a fork and turned back to me. "So he flirts with you, breaks into your room, tries to *kill* Mr. Jambon, then literally leaves and gets together with Lauren. And *then,* yesterday, he tries to ask you out when he already has a girlfriend! Who incidentally was in the hospital at the time." She held the fork up and pointed it at us. "Really. Nice. Guy."

"Do you really think he wanted to kill Mr. Jambon?" Connie whispered. "Should we report him to the National Hamster Council? I *am* a member."

I put my head on the table. It was damp and smelled like cleaning products. I didn't know how to explain it. When Keira laid it out like that, it did sound pretty conclusive.

"I don't know," I said. "I feel kind of . . . like it's fair. I wished something bad to happen to Lauren. . . ."

"Yeah, don't say that too loudly, or ever again," Keira hissed.

"But you know what I mean? It's like karma. I *did* hex her. And if she gets to be with Jack to teach me a lesson, then . . ."

Keira ate a piece of cheese and looked over again. "Look at her, she's loving it. It's like she's at the Oscars. You've done her a huge favor. She's the center of attention now and will be for the rest of the trip."

After breakfast, we headed for a different ski lift. This one took us further up the mountain, to a slightly steeper slope, and it wasn't the normal, easy, conveyor-belt style. It was like a garden swing seat, but dangling sixty feet in the air.

"I'm not sure we're ready for this," Keira said to Tania, in the line. "I mean, we can barely ski along on the flat. How are we supposed to jump off a moving chair?"

Tania laughed. "It will be fine. I'll be on the one in front of you. Just watch me and do what I do."

We stood on the red line and let the chairlift sweep us up off our feet. Then we were whooshed upward, and it felt amazing to be sitting in midair, shunting slowly up the mountain.

"I feel like we're at Six Flags," Connie said.

We talked about Roland and whether our igloo was still

intact and whether other people would be carving the name of their true love in it for centuries to come.

Sitting in between Keira and Connie, tightly packed inside layers of padded jacket, I felt kind of amazing. Lauren wasn't dead, and even if Jack's behavior was impossible to understand, it was there in my mind to obsess about.

"We're actually doing it now," Keira said. "No more boring green-slope snowplowing for us, we're going down a real blue slope today."

"This is where *The Sound of Music* is set," Connie shouted to the mountains. She started doing an impression of a goat and yodeling while Keira swayed the lift violently from side to side. We sang as loudly as we could all the way to the top.

Then we saw the sign that the unloading zone was approaching.

"I'm scared," Connie said. "I've forgotten what to do."

On the lift ahead of us, we saw Tania effortlessly lift the bar and glide down the little slope. She made it look easy.

"Keep your ski tips up," Keira said.

"Stand up and glide," I said.

"Yes, but *when?*" Connie was starting to sound frantic. The unloading zone was getting closer and closer.

"Hold my hand," Keira ordered as the bar released.

"Tania said not to hold hands!" Connie shrieked.

"Connie, come on!" Keira lifted the bar over our heads and started to stand up. "Now!"

I launched myself down the slope and somehow stayed

upright. I came to a wobbly stop just a few feet down. Keira was next to me, but when we looked back, Connie was still on the lift, swinging her way back down the mountain. She looked over her shoulder and yelled, "I'll get it right next time around!"

Scarlett sighed loudly. "So, what, now we all have to wait for her?" she said, to no one in particular.

Keira and I sat down on the snow. "Ugh, I hate them," she said. "You know, Connie never got it about Lauren. Why you were friends with her."

"I dunno, it's hard to believe now, but she used to be really nice." I shrugged. "She was my best friend."

"Well, you've got us now," Keira said. It felt so good to hear. "I think you're thinking too much about the wrong things."

"You're right," I said firmly. "I'm putting a lid on it. Let's never ever talk about Jack or Lauren again."

"Agreed," Keira said with a nod. Jack popped into my head a second later. I *had* said "talk," not "think."

"There she is!" Keira shouted. In the distance, the bright orange outline of Connie appeared. She was still alone on the lift.

"If she couldn't do it when we were next to her, she *definitely* won't be able to do it now," I said. We stood up and edged toward the little lump of snow you were supposed to jump onto from the lift.

Everyone else in our group had now made it to the top and people were milling around, waiting for things to begin. Connie definitely had an audience this time.

As the orange blob became more and more Connie, I could see how scared she was.

I held my arms out like a mum waiting to catch a toddler. "Close your eyes and jump!" I shouted.

"Don't listen to Mouse!" Tania yelled. "Keep your eyes open! It's very important you keep your eyes open!"

Connie started screaming, "I can't do it! I can't!"

"When I shout 'jump,' JUMP!" Tania yelled.

Connie started to lift the bar. She was just a few feet away from us. Tania shouted, "JUMP!"

Connie reacted by shrieking and lowering the bar back down onto her lap. We all stood and watched as she circled right around and headed back down the mountain.

She turned and yelled over her shoulder again. "I can't do it when you're all watching!"

Tania put her head in her hands. "Oh my God. This girl is ridiculous."

Me and Keira laughed, but I could see Melody and Scarlett rolling their eyes.

By the time Connie was in sight again, the crowd had doubled in size. There were whole families and other random ski groups all waiting eagerly to see whether she would make it off the lift.

"There she is!" shouted Tania, pointing at a little orange speck swinging toward us again. All at once, everyone was yelling instructions at Connie.

The dad of a random Scottish family was screaming, "Take a deep breath and jump, sweetheart!" while another ski instructor was shouting, "Eyes on the horizon! Don't look down!"

When Connie was close enough, we heard her shouting, "I told you, I can't do it when you're all looking at me!"

Tania turned to the crowd. "Everybody turn around. Now!" she yelled. Everyone laughed and then did as she said. Connie now had about twenty-five backs facing her as she trundled toward us. I heard Tania shout, "OK, Connie—nobody's watching you now. Just lift the bar and jump off!"

"Maybe we should try a spell to get her off?" I whispered to Keira. "They do seem to be working quite well for us on this trip."

Keira laughed. "Sorry, I left my copy of *Spells for Teen Witches Who Can't Get off Ski Lifts* at home."

We all stood there with our backs to the lift, waiting and listening. I heard the metal creak of the bar being lifted, and then Connie's screaming war cry. Then nothing. "What happened?" said Tania.

We all turned around to see the lift swinging back down the mountain, empty this time. Connie was lying, face first, on the ground in front of us.

She looked up, her face a white mask of snow. "Third time's the charm," she said, grinning.

The whole crowd cheered, and me and Keira helped her to her feet.

Tania led our group across to the point we'd be skiing down from. Even though the slope wasn't that steep, or even that long, it still looked really scary. I took my goggles off and the sun dazzled me. I rubbed sunblock into my cheeks and looked out across the endless mountains. I had moved away from Connie and Keira to psych myself up for what we were about to do.

"You OK, Hat Girl?" Tania swished to a perfect stop next to me.

"Um, not really. From up here it looks really terrifying. It's *insane*."

"I know. But that's what makes it awesome." She looked so relaxed about it all.

"I hate being scared," I admitted. "I don't even watch scary movies. I don't think I'm, like ... a thrill seeker. 'Mouse' didn't stick as a nickname for nothing."

"Well, there's nothing you can do now. There's only one way down. You can't stay up here forever."

I looked down the mountain and it was like every single part of me recoiled. Like my whole body was screaming *Don't do it!* "You don't understand. It just doesn't feel natural. It's totally against my instincts."

I thought about the barre at White Lodge and the mirror I had stared into every day for years. I looked down at my feet. Even in ski boots they wanted to turn out. My spine wanted to be straight, not crouched. My whole body rejected what it was being told to do. Tania didn't say anything and her silence pushed me on.

"Everyone thought I would be great at skiing because I'm . . ." I stopped myself before I said "good." "Because I dance a lot. But skiing is the opposite of dancing. It's like my instincts are telling me not to do it."

"Yeah, but is it your instincts or is it your *fear*?" Tania said.

I pulled my helmet down over the bump my bun made underneath it. "How do you know which is which? Like, surely your instincts are there to protect you from things that can hurt you? That's why you have them."

Tania lifted her goggles and looked at me. "Maybe, but it sounds kind of boring. Maybe you should go against your instincts just once and see how it feels?" She smiled. "Are you gonna wear the Roland hat for your first proper run?"

I put the black beanie on underneath my helmet. "May the force of Roland be with me. . . ."

We stood in a line looking down at the mountain, and one by one, like jumping off a diving board, people suddenly felt brave enough to do it. Keira pushed off with no warning and Connie followed with a scream. I stared down at the little figures slowly zigzagging back and forth. Then I realized that I was the only one left.

I edged forward until it just sort of happened. And then I was doing it. It was like the speed made me feel everything without really thinking about it. I went faster and the wind hit my face hard and it was like I was pushing myself to make it even scarier than it already was.

I saw the bottom coming and remembered to snowplow just in time. Tania was standing there, smiling up at me, and as I waved at her, I realized I was laughing.

"Hat Girl comes in first!" Tania whooped. "You looked great up there. It may *feel* wrong but it looks really right."

"I did it!"

"Yeah, you did."

"Am I really first?" I looked back up at the slope. Connie was flat on her back and Keira was wobbling along inches at a time.

"Yeah. Gold medal. And do you know what your prize is?"

"What?"

"You get to see your boyfriend again. . . ."

JACK

All I could think as we traipsed across the tough, crunchy snow was What am I going to say to Roland?

We'd told Basti that we wanted to spend our free after-noon time watching Roland's press conference. Despite seeming a little confused that we were more interested in French pop singers than snowboarding, he'd said that was fine. So now we were making the long trek back up the mountain to the music video set.

I hadn't exactly been honest with Max or Toddy about what had happened with Mouse. I couldn't bring myself to tell them the humiliating truth, so I'd just lied and said that she wasn't interested in Roland. Max had just laughed. "Not surprising, really, is it? After all, he *does* look like *you*."

Lying to those two was one thing, but lying to Roland was going to be a whole different matter. What was I sup-posed to say? I could hardly tell him the truth. "Sorry, Roland—I know I was *supposed* to ask Mouse out for you, but in the end, I just asked her out for me instead. And, in case you're wondering, she said no. So we're both screwed, really. Anyway, can you get our band a record deal now, please?"

Max didn't even seem particularly upset about the Roland stuff. He was just going on and on about Scarlett and Lauren.

"I honestly think Lauren busting her ankle is the best thing that's happened on this trip," he said as we joined the line for the lift. "I mean, breakfast this morning was amaz-ing. Did you *see* the look on Jamie's face when we sat down with them?! Lauren was all over you, Jack, and Scarlett was absolutely *loving* my witty repartee. And, Toddy, you even *spoke* to Melody!"

"I asked her to pass me the butter," Toddy said.

"Yeah, and did she pass it?"

"Yeah."

"Well, there you go! There's a connection! You've got this whole butter thing going on between you now." Me and Toddy glanced at each other. "I honestly think we'll all definitely be past zero by the end of this week," Max carried on. "Now it's just about who gets there first."

It did feel like something could happen with Lauren. I had no idea why she liked me, but she definitely did seem to. I kept telling myself to forget Mouse and just focus on trying to get Lauren, but it was impossible. Even though she'd rejected me, I wanted her more than ever. How was that fair?

After a few minutes' wait, we finally got onto the belt and whirred our way up the mountain. The video set looked pretty much the same as it had two days ago, except for a wobbly-looking stage that had been set up in the space where Roland and Mouse had been dancing. The area around the two massive white trailers was still cordoned off, and all around the cordons were huddles of serious-looking French guys, with cameras and voice recorders, jostling for position next to the crazed, glitter-faced Roland fans.

We followed Max as he barged his way to the front of the crowd, where a terrifying-looking bald man in a black suit and sunglasses was standing.

"Uh . . . *bonjour,*" Max said to him. "Do you speak *anglais?*"

The bald man nodded. "Cool," said Max. "Well, basically, we're close friends of Roland's. So if you don't mind letting us through, that'd be great."

The bald man pushed his sunglasses up onto his dome-like head so he could examine Max more closely.

"You are Roland's friends?" he said, in his thick French accent. We nodded. "*Everyone* here is Roland's friends," he laughed.

"No, but we *really* are," Max insisted. "Honestly, he told us to come. Ask him."

A few girls around us piped up, pleadingly, in broken English. "Yes, he told us to come too! We're his friends too!"

The bald man laughed another big, booming laugh. "You see? *Everyone* here is Roland's friend. And *everyone* here is staying behind this barrier." Then he flicked his sunglasses back down, as if to indicate the conversation was over.

Max whipped out his phone and shot a selfie of the three of us. Then he handed it to the bald man. "Please, sir . . . just show Roland this picture and say we're outside. Just see what he says, honestly."

The bald man sighed. "Do you promise to go away and not come back if I do this?"

"Yeah, cross our hearts," Max said, grinning.

The man took the phone and slouched off into the trailer. A couple of seconds later, he came shuffling back. He looked at us for a second, then shrugged, handed Max his phone back, and lifted the plastic barrier so we could duck underneath it, triumphantly.

We opened the door of the trailer to find Roland slumped grumpily on a red sofa, in his artfully weathered leather jacket, a pair of huge sunglasses pushed up into his floppy hair. He was getting yelled at by a tiny, but very loud, American woman with long blond pigtails.

"I don't *care* if you don't want to do it, mister! You're *doing* it!" she shouted. "If you think I'm canceling a press conference at the last minute, you can think again! And as for you and Hayley Kwarseany, as far as the press goes, you're an item! And that's *final*!"

She spun around violently, and saw the three of us, her already angry face getting instantly angrier. "And who the *hell* are these guys?" She squinted at me and then looked at Roland. "Are you related or something?"

"It's fine," muttered Roland. "They are my English friends."

The woman eyed us cautiously. "Right, well, whatever. They need to be outta here ASAP, Roland. Press conference starts in thirty minutes." She stormed past us and flung the door open. Just as she was about to step through, she turned back and glared at Roland. "And don't even *think* about moving from this trailer, buddy. Remember, I can see you through the window." And with that, she slammed the door so hard the whole trailer shook.

"She seems nice," said Toddy.

Roland laughed. "It's good to see you guys again." He stood up and sighed. "Cooper is just angry because I don't want to do the press conference. I am getting sick of being this puppet who has always to do what he's told, you know? They are now even trying to put me in a 'showmance' with some American singer I've never even met." He paused. "'Showmance'—is this the right word?"

"Well, it's not *actually* a word," Toddy said, frowning. "But, yeah, I think it is the right word."

"Anyway, we don't have much time," Roland said. "Did you speak to Mouse for me?"

Max cleared his throat nervously and glanced at me.

"Uh . . . yeah," I started. "I did speak to her, Roland."

"And?"

"Well, she . . . um . . . well, it's sort of difficult." I frowned, to show just how difficult it was.

He stared at me, unblinking, his expression unreadable. "What?" He sounded impatient.

"She . . . uh . . . I just don't think she was interested, that's all."

He looked at me in silence for a few seconds. "Did she misunderstand you? You told her I liked her?"

Not exactly, I thought. But I said, "Yeah."

"And you're telling me she wasn't interested?"

I shook my head.

"In *me?*"

I nodded.

He blinked quickly a few times, like he was trying hard to understand this, but he just couldn't. Then he shook his head. He didn't look sad, or even annoyed. Just totally, totally confused.

"But I'm . . . *Roland,*" he said blankly.

"Yeah, we know," said Max.

"It's just . . . this doesn't normally happen to me with girls," said Roland, examining his hands, as if to check he wasn't disappearing. "Maybe I have lost my touch. Or even worse . . . my looks."

He stepped sideways, in front of a full-length mirror, and stared at his reflection.

"No," he said, after a second. "My looks are still good." He turned to me. "You must have done something wrong, Jack. She must have misheard you." He exhaled loudly, frustrated. "I should have tried to do it myself!"

"Well, why don't you?" said Max, peering out the window.

"What do you mean?"

"I mean, she's outside now."

We all clamored to join him at the window. There, at the

side of the still-growing crowd, were Mouse, Connie and Keira.

Roland suddenly started pacing the whole length of the trailer excitedly. "This is it! I'm going to speak to her!"

"But didn't your crazy lady say that you couldn't leave the trailer?" said Toddy. "And won't you also get, like, swamped by crazed fan girls the minute you go out there?"

Roland sighed and slumped back down onto the sofa, defeated. "It's true."

Toddy nodded at me and grinned. "You could always get your stunt double here to stand in for you."

Max laughed, but Roland was suddenly staring at me with a scary intensity. He stood up and walked over to me. "Jack . . . Yes . . . Would you do this for me?"

I blinked. "What? You're not serious?"

He was pacing the trailer again, more excited than ever. "Yes! You would just have to sit here, just so Cooper thinks I haven't disappeared. Then I can go out and speak to Mouse, and I will be back in ten minutes, maximum."

"But I don't even look *that* much like you!" I laughed. "I mean, what about our eyes? They're completely different."

He pulled the massive sunglasses out of his hair and slipped them onto my face. The whole world went coffee-colored, and Toddy whistled. "It's true—without the eye thing, you really are dead ringers."

"It's perfect!" Roland said. He reached up and started sweeping my hair sideways.

"Hey!" I whacked his hand away, but he kept doing it.

"Just to make it a little more convincing. Please, Jack."

I looked at Max and Toddy as Roland continued to side-sweep my hair. "It would be quite hilarious," Max said, grinning. "And it's only for ten minutes."

I looked at Roland, and the guilty twisting in my stomach reminded me that I really did owe him one.

"Fine," I said. "But you'd better be quick."

"Great!" He peeked out of the window to see Cooper barking orders at some frightened-looking women. "Let's do this, quickly."

I gave him my hoodie, and he gave me his black leather jacket. He pulled the blue hood right up and grabbed another pair of sunglasses off one of the racks. "You two better come with me," he said to Max and Toddy. "Just so Cooper thinks all three of you are leaving."

"This is crazy," said Max, shaking his head. "Brilliant, but crazy."

"Back soon," said Roland.

Toddy gave me a thumbs-up, and then the three of them were gone.

I stood there in the empty trailer, my heart tap-tap-tapping under Roland's black leather jacket, wondering what I'd got myself into. I tried to imagine what Roland might be saying to Mouse. Whether anyone would figure out it was really him. But mainly I just prayed that he'd come back as soon as possible.

Then, after what seemed like twenty years, the door finally opened.

But it wasn't Roland. It wasn't even Max or Toddy.

"Right, change of plan, buddy," said Cooper, beckoning me frantically toward the door. "Press conference starts *now*."

15

MOUSE

"Keira, I'm not that heavy. It's because you aren't *thinking ogre*. Think ogre," Connie said.

"Try and lock your core. Like clench your tummy muscles," I said.

"I don't have any muscles in my tummy. Why don't *you* carry her?" Keira made a kind of Marge Simpson groaning noise and swayed unsteadily. For a second I thought Connie would tumble forward into the snow again, but she didn't. Keira inched herself upright and Connie sat resplendent on her shoulders. She waved like the queen at no one in particular.

"I feel like a pigeon," Connie said. "Or Google Maps. I can see everything from up here."

"Can you see Roland and a trailer full of pastries and cheese toasties?" Keira said. "Because that is where we could

213

be right now. Eating crème brûlée and watching Roland tell you you're *cute*." She turned a bit too quickly toward me and Connie squealed.

Some girls next to us started whispering to each other and looking at me, and then one not-very-subtly took a picture of me on her phone. I pulled my hood up and looked down.

"He probably doesn't even remember me," I said. He probably didn't. He'd probably kissed about fifteen people since then, including a spattering of models and some pop stars.

"Or he could have killed himself," Connie said matter-of-factly. "You know, out of dreadful grief at not seeing you again."

"Which would be a good excuse for not being here. Does it look like anything's about to happen? Because I'm getting bored."

Connie squinted and shook her head. "Still just a mountain and a stage without Roland on it." She sighed.

It wasn't just us who were getting antsy, everyone was sick of waiting. Scarlett and Melody had even wandered to the edge of the crowd and started taking selfies and talking to a random group of boys. There were about the same number of people as there had been the day of the shoot, but there were fewer screaming girls and more adults. Photographers and journalists stood around holding microphones in one hand and cups of coffee in the other.

It finally felt like something might be going to happen.

"Walk to that tree," Connie said. "I think my wand is calling to me."

Keira swayed unsteadily and turned around.

"Onward, steed!" Connie shouted.

I turned but Connie and Keira had vanished. The crowd was jostling with people trying to get closer to the front. Someone squeezed in next to me. I noticed the thumb poking through the ratty sweater and for the first time I didn't panic but felt this rush of excitement. It was Jack. I wanted to speak to him about yesterday. I opened my mouth—

"Mouse." A loud whisper came through the scarf. "Mouse. It is me."

The accent was unmistakable. And then he pulled his glasses down his nose like a teacher finding everything really tiresome.

His blue eyes twinkled like he was a mischievous child who had outwitted the grown-ups. The crowd surged and we were thrown even closer together. My face was inches from his.

"*Roland?* What are *you* doing here?" I hissed. Suddenly there was an enormous cheer and some screams. "And if you're here . . ." I pointed to the stage. "Who is *that?*"

JACK

Through the weird coffee-filtered glaze of the sunglasses, I could see a boiling sea of people. Guys with microphones, screaming girls, confused-looking families who'd clearly just come along to see what the fuss was about. And, right at the far edge of the crowd, Toddy and Max, their mouths hanging open, their eyes practically bugging straight out of their heads.

I tried to think straight. To process exactly what was happening to me. But all I could hear was a strange hissing noise inside my head, like a teapot boiling. Something had gone spectacularly, monumentally, *unbelievably* wrong. I was standing on a stage in front of more people than I could even count. And they all thought I was France's biggest pop star.

Cooper had ushered me up the little set of stairs to the stage, and a weaselly-looking guy I'd never seen before put his arm around me, smiling at the audience. I was terrified he would be able to feel me trembling and suddenly figure out that something was wrong. The real Roland definitely didn't tremble in these kinds of situations. But the weaselly guy just patted my shoulder, and then walked forward and said something to the crowd in French.

Most of the faces in the crowd were suddenly replaced by cameras, and I stood there, grinning like an idiot as the bulbs flashed at me, hoping that this was how Roland grinned. I scanned the crowd frantically for a way out.

Then the weaselly guy handed me a microphone.

One photographer in the front row yelled something in French at me, and suddenly it went deadly silent. Everyone was staring straight at me. I glanced over at Cooper but she just gave me the "OK" sign with her thumb and forefinger.

I had to say something. As Roland. My mouth was so dry it took a couple of seconds to unstick my tongue. I screwed my eyes shut and desperately tried to think of any French words I actually knew. Then I remembered.

Before I could stop myself, it rolled out of my mouth, coated in my best, thickest French accent.

"Avez-vous ma trousse?"

The silence seemed to get louder somehow. The man who'd asked the question furrowed his brow and looked around at his neighbors, who were also furrowing their brows and looking around at their neighbors. I felt myself going red, and was suddenly extra glad of the ridiculous sunglasses covering half my face.

The crowd was muttering in what sounded like total confusion. The only thing I could understand was the occasional repetition of *"Avez-vous ma trousse?"* The weaselly guy, who was looking just as bewildered as everyone else, yelled, *"D'accord—encore une question pour Roland?"* and another photographer shouted something else at me in French.

It was like my brain was on sleep mode. Like I was someone else, watching things happen from above my body, just sort of interested to see how it would all pan out. The only thing I could feel was my stomach, grinding and whirring, and my heartbeat pulsing thickly in my chest. I opened my mouth and this came out: *"Votre grand-mère était un blaireau."*

The furrows on the photographers' brows got even deeper, and their confused whispering even louder. Which was fair enough, really, since I'd just informed them that their grandmothers were badgers.

I saw Max literally fall to his knees and out of sight, and Toddy crumple down on top of him. Then I saw Mouse. While the rest of the crowd were looking at me in forehead-wrinkled confusion, she was staring at me in full-on, open-mouthed horror. Next to her was the *actual* Roland, whose face was hidden by the sunglasses and scarf, but I presumed there was a similar expression going on underneath it all.

Both Cooper and the weaselly guy were exchanging looks that seemed to suggest that their perfect megastar had completely lost his mind. Another photographer shouted something else out, and just as it was dawning on me that the only phrase I had left up my sleeve translated as "My parakeet is in the pedestrian zone," I saw Roland lean in and whisper something to Mouse.

16

MOUSE

Cooper looked like a deranged marshmallow at the side of the stage. Her teeny frame was swamped by a giant pink faux-fur coat and she was trying desperately to get the fake Roland's attention. I looked at the real Roland next to me, trying to figure out what was going on. His sunglasses had fallen slightly to reveal his blue eyes widened in complete shock. No one around us gave him a second glance, they were so transfixed by the fake Roland's onstage car crash.

"Is that . . . Jack up there?" I whispered so quietly it was almost inaudible.

Roland nodded.

"How do *you* know Jack?"

He didn't answer, just slowly started shaking his head in horror, then turned and looked at me.

"He just asked the entire French media, 'Do you have my pencil case?'"

"*What?*"

Roland wasn't listening; he seemed like he was talking to himself more than me. "And then he told them that their grandmother was a badger."

"Whose grandmother? Seriously, Roland, *what* is going on?!" I grabbed his arm.

Cooper shouted something to Jack in French. "What is she saying?" I whispered, without taking my eyes off Jack.

"No more questions. She is telling him to get off the stage."

"Roland!" Cooper shouted. Either Jack hadn't heard her, or he was unable to move. His face was half hidden by the sunglasses, but he looked terrified.

"Mouse. Please do something," Roland hissed. "People around us are saying I am ill. That I have gone insane!"

I started to push through the crowd toward the tiny pink outline of Cooper. Jack had gone silent. I stopped and looked right at him, willing him to move. Cooper was clearly trying to do that too, flailing about like a miniature flamingo at the edge of the stage. Why wasn't he moving? Because he was in shock? Because he didn't know how to explain to Cooper what was happening?

Then I looked at him again. He wasn't moving because he was scared. I clenched my whole body and hurled myself forward through the crowd like a little compact bullet. In front of the stage there was a tape, and behind it were four burly-looking men wandering up and down. I took a deep breath and plunged forward, under the tape and toward the stage. The crowd erupted in laughter, clearly thinking I was a superfan overcome with emotion. I jumped up the stairs and grabbed Jack's hand but kept moving.

"Run!" I shouted, and dragged him down the stairs. One of the burly men was on the stage now. The others were looking at Cooper. We could hear the cameras clicking and people yelling behind us, but we didn't look back.

"Keep going!" I shouted. I hurled myself into the confused crowd, dragging Jack behind me. People seemed to part to make way for us. For a second our hands were pulled apart. When I looked behind me, Jack was there, and was jamming Roland's sunglasses into his trouser pocket. He took my hand again and we emerged at the edge of the crowd. The people toward the back hadn't seen what happened, and were murmuring in confusion, but without the glasses, Jack didn't look like Roland anymore. We almost toppled over the little hill that led down to the ski lift station as Jack shrugged off the leather jacket. I sat down and slid to the bottom and he tumbled after me. At the bottom, we hid behind the ski lift station wall, panting. We'd lost them—for now. We stuffed Roland's sunglasses and jacket in my backpack.

There were people milling around, drinking hot chocolate and taking off their skis, unaware that we were fake-celebrity fugitives on the run. I straightened up and walked as quickly as I could to the lift, trying to look casual. We stood in line together and the lift swung under us and lifted us up into the air. We turned and looked back at the swarm of people on the ground, Cooper's pink outline freaking out below us.

The lift chugged along and the mountain spread out beneath us and we just stared ahead, shell-shocked by it all. Then we turned to each other, and Jack was smiling.

"So, what . . . what actually happened there?" I asked. "What were you *doing*? Do you, like . . . know Roland?"

"I didn't until two days ago . . . but, yeah . . . I do."

I couldn't believe it. What would Keira and Connie say? What would everyone say? I pictured Lauren's face, finding out that I had run off with Roland. And then I pictured her face finding out that I had run off with Jack, her boyfriend.

"What, and you just met him and he asked you to pretend to be him? Why? What for? I don't get it."

"Mouse. Honestly. I had no idea how I was going to get out of there. You're like . . . a superhero."

"You're the one with the alter ego." I smiled. Right then, grinning and laughing in disbelief, he had never looked so unbelievably cute. He was actually cuter than Roland. The few freckles that fell over his nose and his browny-green eyes looking at me would usually have made me feel shy and scared, but I just felt excited.

"Just call me Superman," he said. "Except I don't save anyone, I'm an utterly pointless superhero. Unlike you, who actually *did* save me." He grabbed my hand. "I was losing it, Mouse. You are a legend. You're insanely brave. Super-Mouse."

He didn't take his hand away and I didn't move mine.

"Good thing Super-Mouse was there," I said.

"Super-Mouse is my hero," he said.

"Your knight in shining armor," I said, swinging my legs and making the chair rock. The unloading point came into view. It was higher up than we had ever been with Tania. "Neither of us has skis."

"We'll just have to jump," he said. We held hands and I screamed as we launched ourselves onto the little mound of snow. We walked to the edge of the slope and sat down.

"It's snowing," I said. I held out my hand and a few snowflakes fell on the top of my glove. Jack looked up at the sky. It felt lucky.

"It's weird it hasn't snowed until now," he said. "I was thinking that earlier. How there is all this snow everywhere but we haven't seen it actually come out of the sky."

"Like it only snows once a year and then the same snow just stays here. I really love snow." I looked up at the sky and closed my eyes, letting the giant snowflakes fall on me.

"Me too," he said. "That's part of the reason I wanted to come here. I've never been anywhere cold on vacation. The only snow I've seen is the crappy kind that turns gray and icy and melts within a day."

"Yeah, me too."

I felt in my pocket, took out my hat and put it on.

"Is that the hat Roland gave you?"

"No, I doubt Roland would wear a baby-blue Topshop pompom hat." Then I pictured Roland. "Although . . ."

"Exactly, are you kidding me? Have you seen some of the stuff he wears? I mean, he has whole racks of stuff way more ridiculous than a pompom hat."

"That's true." I unzipped my bag and we looked at the leather jacket. On the inside it had ROLAND printed a million times all over it. "But I think his, you know . . . manager probably makes him wear it."

Jack snorted. "That's what you all want to believe. You and all those trillions of other girls who love him. You want to believe it's not his choice, but I think he'd be wearing stuff even more insane than this if he could."

"Like a big, giant bear costume."

"A bear costume?" Jack started laughing even more. "I meant like weird pants with slashes and diamonds and stuff. A *bear costume?*"

It was so ridiculous that I started laughing in a hysterical way. We both did. I was almost crying and I couldn't breathe.

"But then, if he had a bear costume he could roam around freely," Jack said, quite genuinely. "Maybe we should suggest it to him. All celebrities could do it. Imagine, you would think it's just a normal guy in a full-on chicken outfit, but inside it's Taylor Swift."

"Yeah, but Roland would have to be careful. They might think he was a real bear and shoot him."

"That's true. As a celebrity, you would have to be careful to choose an appropriate but not deadly costume."

"What would you choose if you were a celebrity?"

"Well, you actually *are* a celebrity. I mean, if you weren't already, for being in Roland's video, you definitely are now, for basically kidnapping him."

"OK, well, I would pick a platypus costume. And *you'll* definitely be a celebrity when they find out you impersonated him."

Jack shook his head. "Well, in that case, I choose a panda."

"They are going extinct. And they find it hard to get pregnant." And then I blushed immediately.

"I'm not *currently* trying to get pregnant, so . . . ," Jack said, and we both burst out laughing again.

"Want to get some hot chocolate?" I said. It was getting cold and the sun was beginning to go down. After I said it, I remembered him asking me for hot chocolate and wondered if he was thinking about that too.

We walked over to a little wooden hut full of serious

black-diamond-slope skiers and ordered two extra-large hot chocolates with whipped cream and marshmallows.

"This is awkward," Jack said. "I don't have any money. Toddy's got my jacket."

"That's OK." I smiled. "I'm a modern girl." Then I blushed again, because it was like I had said we were on a date. All the time we had been talking, I hadn't thought about the fact I was looking at him, but I suddenly felt really aware of it. Like every time I looked at him it was as if I was shouting, "I like you!"

We carried our hot chocolates to the deck at the back of the café and sat down.

"Do you like skiing?" Jack asked, wrapping his hands around his cup.

"Actually, I really do. Which is weird because it's the opposite of dancing, really."

He looked a little confused.

"I used to go to Bluecoats, and then I left to go to ballet school at Christmas in fifth grade."

"Wow, you must love ballet. I thought you might be a ballet dancer."

"Really? Why?"

"Because you always stand up really straight and tall. I thought either a ballet dancer or a soldier. But a ballet dancer seemed more likely." I laughed, and then he said, "But I mean it in a good way. Like, it makes you look really . . .

nice." And then, even though it was freezing, I saw him blushing slightly.

I looked down and smiled inside. But I didn't want to be one of those girls who try to steal people's boyfriends. However awful the person had been to me. I edged away a little. "Yeah, to be honest, it's been my whole life for like . . . ever."

"How come you left?" he said, and I knew I should tell him the truth. I wanted to. It felt right, but I'd trapped myself with my own lies.

"I got into ballet school in Paris next year, so—"

"Oh my God, Mouse, that's amazing." He looked so impressed. "I'd literally love to be that good at something. To have a talent. Super-Mouse strikes again."

"I don't know if I'm talented, but I do love dancing." That was true, at least.

"Show me a move, then," Jack said. "One move. That I can do at parties to, you know . . . impress Max and Toddy."

"Ballet isn't really like that. It doesn't really help you in a party situation."

"Just show me one thing."

"OK, but I'm not dancing unless you dance too."

I stood up and offered him my hand to help him up.

We were standing opposite each other. I put my snow boot heels together. "This is first position." I held my hands in first position too.

Jack copied and looked ridiculous. His fists balled in the air and his feet splayed out.

"You look like a penguin," I said, and rearranged his hands. "Stand really tall, like someone is pulling you up to the sky."

He straightened up and smiled.

"OK, second position." I rearranged myself and then him.

"So, do you think I've got talent?" he said.

"Yes," I said as I showed him third.

He studied me closely and tried to copy. "How come I look ridiculous but you look amazing?" he asked, and then smiled and looked down sheepishly at the ground.

"You having a dance party?" the boy working in the café shouted over at us.

We both laughed.

"Yes," Jack shouted back. "We're having a snow-boot, enormous-padded-jacket, freezing-cold ballet dance party."

The guy laughed and ducked back into his hot chocolate counter, and some weird, electronic-sounding music started booming out. The boy leaned out from the hut and started waving his hands around in the air wildly. "Dance party!" he shouted at us.

We waved our hands back at him, and then both of us started dancing. It was snowing more heavily now. I almost couldn't see Jack through the snow, so I just went crazy and let myself get carried away in it all. I started spinning in circles, like kids do, and got faster and faster.

And then I collapsed in the snow and Jack collapsed next to me. Underneath the ski suit, I was boiling hot from dancing, and as I lay back the snow hit my burning face and melted on it.

We were lying next to each other, inches apart. I turned my face and he was looking at me. I almost reached out to hold his hand again but I knew that was weird. So I just smiled. I didn't want to suggest leaving, so I just stayed there, looking at him and then up at the sky.

"That was the first time in a really long time dancing has felt fun," I said.

"Same for me," Jack said. "Dancing is normally a phobia of mine."

"Sometimes it feels like it's mine too," I said. "I don't want to go back yet."

"Me neither," he said, reaching out and catching snow-flakes on his fingers. Then he sat up. "I've got an idea." He crunched across the snow and went to the pile of trays outside the café. He picked one up and waved me over. I went across to him and got one too.

"Are you going to turn into Roland again?" I said.

"It's not a magical change like a werewolf." He started walking away with his tray. "Try to look normal."

"We're only carrying trays," I said. "We just look helpful."

"Now we need a good slope," he said, looking out across the impossibly high mountains.

We trudged through the snow, which was getting fresh new layers every couple of minutes.

"What about here?" I said.

We put our trays down and sat on them side by side, looking down the slope.

"Let's push off on the count of three," Jack said.

"OK."

"One . . . two . . . three!" Jack started to slide, so I wriggled my bum forward a little and then I was sliding too. I could hear Jack's whooping and I started screaming. I was going faster and faster until I got to the bottom and slowed down.

"That was amazing." Jack was dusting the snow off his pants and standing back up. "These trays are way better than snowboards."

We ran up a different bit of the slope this time, picking our boots out of the new snow and plunging them in again. It was snowing heavily now, our tracks covered almost as we made them.

"Right, on three again," Jack said.

"One . . ." But Jack pushed off early and started to slide. He reached his hand out to stop himself and I grabbed it. And then we were hurtling together. We held hands until Jack was going too fast and we crashed into each other at the bottom.

"This is amazing!" I shouted across the snow.

We started to walk up again but the wind had got stronger and it felt almost impossible to take just one step. I couldn't see more than a few paces ahead, and even then all I could see was snow.

"Are you OK?" Jack shouted.

"Yeah, but maybe we should go back and come again tomorrow."

"OK," he yelled. Even though he was next to me, I could barely hear him. We turned to go back down the slope. The snow was really deep, and picking up a foot and moving it forward seemed to take forever.

"Which way is back?" I said.

We both stood looking around us but everything had turned white and it was impossible to see which way the nearest lift was.

"I think it's this way," Jack said, pointing, so we started to walk. The wind was freezing and it was hitting my face so hard it hurt, as if I was being punched every time. I couldn't feel any of my body anymore.

We stopped and looked around us again. And I think we realized at exactly the same time how frightened we both were.

JACK

The amazingness of the last hour was being replaced quickly by a feeling of nasty, cold dread.

I tried to act like that Bear Grylls guy my mum likes

from TV; he never looks scared—he just seems confident and totally in control. But then, that's probably because he always has a camera crew with him. Anyone can look hard when they've got tons of people and equipment around them. I'd like to see Bear when he's on his own in a blizzard armed only with a lunch tray. Then we'd see how tough he really is.

I looked back up the slope we'd just sledded down. I could barely even see the top of it. The only people around were bobbing along on ski lifts way above us. But there was no sign of where the lifts started or finished.

The snow was making everything look fuzzy, thick white blotches blurring my vision at every turn. A chill was spreading fast from my fingers and toes to the rest of my body. Mouse was staring at me, eyes wide, her nose and mouth buried under her jacket collar. I guessed it was up to me to make a suggestion.

"Um . . . We should keep going down, maybe?" I said. "I mean . . . *down* is the definitely the right way when you're on a mountain, isn't it?"

"I guess so . . ." She didn't look convinced. "Is that, like, a survival motto or something?"

"Yeah, I think so," I lied. I hugged my arms round myself. I was starting to feel seriously cold. "Can I get Roland's leather jacket back? I'm not trying to look cool or anything. I'm just absolutely freezing."

She handed it to me, smiling, but there was no humor behind it. "What do you think we should do?" she said.

I had literally no idea. We started traipsing downward, each footstep more difficult than the last as the snow deepened steadily underneath us. I could feel freezing water squelching in my right boot.

"We've definitely seen that tree before," said Mouse, after a few minutes.

"That could be any tree."

"No, it's all bent and buckled, like the Whomping Willow in Harry Potter. I remember seeing it before."

"So your navigation method is based on fictional trees?"

She didn't even crack a smile. Which was fair enough, as the situation was far from funny.

"Jack, I'm serious. I think we're just going around in circles. Are we even going down?"

It was hard to tell when the snow was so thick. I could barely see three feet ahead of me. "I'm not sure," I yelled over the wind. "We might be going sideways." My teeth were chattering from the cold. I didn't want Mouse to know how frightened I was. We'd spent most of the afternoon trying to get lost, and now all I wanted was for us to be found.

It was getting darker, and the huge white floodlights above us started to flicker. A few came on, dragging long spidery shadows off the trees and across the ground. But most of them just sputtered pathetically and went out again.

I looked up and instantly felt another dull thump of fear in my throat. The ski lifts had stopped. There was no one on them now, and they just hung eerily in midair, creaking in the swirling snow. We couldn't even follow them down to safety; the cable stretched across two slopes, leaving the chairs dangling over a ravine that must have been over a hundred feet deep.

"Jack, do you think we're in trouble?" Mouse shouted.

"What, you mean, like, with our teachers?"

"No, I meant more than that." She bit her lip. "Like . . . *real* trouble?"

She tried to step toward me, but stumbled and fell into the deep snow. I rushed to pick her up and felt her trembling even through her thick ski jacket.

"We need to keep going," I said. "We'll be all right."

We kept walking. I had no idea where, or even in what direction. It just felt better to move than to stand still and actually think about how terrifying the situation was.

Out of the corner of my eye, I spotted a dark, round shape on the edge of the slope. "What's that?" I said, pointing.

Mouse squinted at it through the flakes. "Oh my God . . . is it? Wait. I think . . ." She started marching off toward the shape. "I know where we are!"

"Hang on!" I stomped after her. The snow was now spilling in over the top of my boots. I couldn't even feel my feet.

"Yes!" Mouse turned round, beaming at me. "I was here yesterday—this is the igloo we built."

The blurry shape was indeed a rickety, not-very-stable-looking igloo. It was about the size of a two-person tent, and its entrance was half blocked by snow. Mouse dropped down in front of it.

"Let's get in here and wait till the snow stops. It'll be warmer."

"How will it be warmer? It's made of ice!"

"Just trust me!"

She started digging at the snow around the entrance. I got down and helped her. We knelt there, shivering and shoveling. Soon we'd got rid of enough snow that Mouse could crawl in through the entrance. I followed her and scrambled into the weird, echoey cavern inside. The ice blocks tinted us a glassy, light blue color. The wind was muffled. It *was* warmer in here.

"If we get out of this alive, I'm going to Google 'Why is it warm in an igloo?'" I said.

"At least we've got some shelter. What are the other things you're supposed to do in a snowstorm?"

I thought about it. "I think you're supposed to grab hold of someone, for the body heat and stuff."

Mouse smiled awkwardly and stared down at the ground. I immediately felt my cheeks get hotter. There's a good tip for Bear Grylls's next series: If you're ever worried about freezing to death in the Alps, just say something unbelievably embarrassing to a girl you like. Your face will warm up in no time.

"We don't have to do that, obviously," I said.

"Sure." She grinned. "I don't think things are that desperate yet." Then she winced. "Not that it'd have to be desperate for us to . . . I just meant . . ." She shook her head. "Oh, sorry. You know what I mean."

I nodded, but I had absolutely *no* idea. I wish girls were just a tiny, *tiny* bit easier to understand. I looked around and saw there were loads of names scratched into the ice blocks.

"What's with all these names?"

She seemed like she was thinking carefully about how to answer. "Um . . . it was just, some of the girls thought it'd be funny to write the names of people they like on the walls. That's all."

"Oh, right."

There was silence while we listened to the wind whistling outside the entrance. From somewhere, I got the nerve to ask, "Did you write anyone?"

More silence. "No. Not everyone did it."

I spotted ROLAND scratched in massive capital letters near the entrance. Maybe Mouse had written it. I suddenly remembered how we'd got into this mess—because Roland had wanted to speak to her. He liked her too. He liked her enough to basically risk his whole career by running out into a crowd to find her. How could I compete with that?

"Not surprising that someone wrote Roland's name," I

said quietly. "Everyone seems to love him. Unless it's another Roland."

"There's only one Roland," Mouse laughed. Then she nodded at my jacket. "Well, *two*, actually."

She stared back at the same spot on the ceiling. I followed her gaze and saw that, among the jumble of boys' names up there, one was written very neatly and carefully in the center—JACK.

I felt a little rumble in my chest. It could have been written by anyone, about any Jack in the world, but seeing her stare at it the way she was felt weirdly great.

"I guess you'll be able to become a real Roland fan when you're living in Paris," I said. "You can join the fan club and everything."

She looked at me, and her face was suddenly heavy with worry. "The thing is, Jack ... the Paris school ..." She breathed out slowly. "I'm not really going there. I lied."

There was a pause. "Oh," I said. "Well, that's all right." Another pause. "So, where *are* you going?"

She was staring blankly at her ski boots, stretched out in front of her. "I'm not going anywhere. I'm back at Bluecoats now for good. I got assessed at my old ballet school. I wasn't good enough, so they asked me to leave. I guess I just wanted to ... pretend that hadn't happened."

I kept silent. I could feel that she wanted to say more.

"I guess ... My mum thought coming on this trip would

be good for me. Like dancing was interchangeable, and I could just get into skiing instead. Or if not skiing, then, I don't know, tennis or chess or whatever. The thing that gets to me the most is that I know she's really disappointed too."

"How do you mean?"

"She framed my first pointe shoes and put them in the kitchen. And going up the stairs there are these pictures of me dancing. At the bottom it's me in a tutu when I was three, and you get to the top and it's just blank wall. And I know what she wanted to put there. Me dancing at the Royal Opera House. Her daughter, the ballerina. And now she doesn't know whether to take them all down or whether to leave this blank wall to remind us that it's not going to happen."

She was breathing quickly, angrily.

"What do you want her to do?" I asked.

She shrugged. "I don't know." She didn't sound angry anymore, just sad. "I just want it to still happen. So badly."

"Is there any chance it still could?"

She shook her head and opened her mouth to speak but then didn't. Instead, she started to cry.

It was soft at first; it was like she didn't even realize she was doing it. I sat there beside her, blinking, paralyzed by panic. My first thought was: What if someone found us now? It wouldn't exactly look great. Me and a crying girl, alone in an igloo.

I shuffled closer to her and put my hand on her shoulder. I could feel her whole body shaking. I wanted to put my arms around her so badly, but I knew I would never have the nerve. I just wanted her to not feel like this. I wanted to somehow take the sadness out of her.

She didn't even seem to notice my hand. She just gave this long, heavy sigh and said, "The worst thing is, I feel like I don't even belong in my own house. I haven't lived there for two years. It's like I'm a guest."

I squeezed her shoulder a bit tighter. Without looking at me, she put her hand up, on top of mine.

"You must miss your friends," I said.

She nodded. "I shared a room for over two years with the same girls and now I think they feel weird about it. Embarrassed that I had to leave. There is this day just before Christmas when everyone gets a new color leotard to show they're going up to the next level at school. And I just didn't get one. And they all put theirs away so I couldn't see. And I knew they wanted to start dancing in them but they couldn't until I left."

There was another silence while I felt her shoulder shivering.

"That's why I said that stuff about Paris. I wanted to pretend, I guess. To pretend I was still good at dancing."

"What do you mean?" I said. "You *are* good at dancing! I saw you with my own eyes this afternoon, Super-Mouse.

You were amazing. And that was with ski boots and a huge jacket on. So I can only imagine how amazing you'd be in a real leotard thingy and those tiny pointy shoes." Her frown started to melt a bit at the sides, and she looked up at me. "Plus, you started a *dance party* in the middle of a ski slope! I bet no one in the history of ballet schools has ever done that. So who cares about what anyone thinks? No one can stop you from dancing, if that's what makes you happy."

She laughed and pushed her long hair back behind her ears. The tears had stopped. Her eyes were twinkling now as she smiled at me. She looked *so* cute. "Yeah, I guess you're right," she nodded. "Thanks, Jack."

"Trust me, you've got nothing to worry about. You're great at the thing you love. Think about me. . . . I'm supposed to be the front man of our band, but I'm totally useless. We were down to play our school's Band Night a couple of weeks back, and I totally ruined it. How can I play in a band when I can't even get up onstage in front of people?"

She sniffed and wiped her eyes. "Well . . . you kind of just did. I mean, you stood up in front of pretty much every journalist and crazy superfan in France."

I laughed. "Yeah, but I was pretending to be someone else."

"Well, maybe that's it," she shrugged. "When you're onstage with your band, just . . . pretend to be someone else.

That way, all your worries and fears and stuff don't matter. Because you're not *you*."

I thought about it. It wasn't a bad idea. She carried on. "Pretend to be *Roland,* if that helps. Just think I'm not me, I'm Roland . . . What would Roland do?"

I knew *exactly* what Roland would do in this situation. I wanted to do it too.

Mouse was looking up at me, a little smile tugging at the right-hand side of her mouth. Her eyelashes were still damp from the tears, making them seem longer and darker as they fluttered around her big, gray eyes.

Almost without thinking, I buried all my worries and fears deep in the snow, and leaned in to kiss her.

17

MOUSE

Was he doing what I thought he was doing? I closed my eyes. It felt like I had become my heartbeat because it was so loud. My shivering had turned to nervous shaking. It was going to happen.

And then we heard the noise.

Muffled and far away, but definitely there. The wail of a siren.

Jack pulled back slightly and we both looked at the entrance to the igloo. It had snowed even more since we had dug our way in, and we were going to have to dig our way out even further.

"I feel like we're going to have to climb out of it," I said. "What if they pass us before we make it?"

We both scrabbled at the snow urgently. I climbed out first and gave Jack my hand and pulled as hard as I could to help him out. My legs were so cold they hurt. Sharp, stabbing, intense pain from being so freezing for so long. It was really dark, even against the brilliant-white backdrop. And it was still snowing, but a more gentle, Christmas-card snow.

The siren's screech was almost deafening now. A searchlight danced over me for a second and disappeared before coming back and fixing its gaze. It was on top of a huge, red snowplow. It charged through the powder like a tank and stopped. A man and a woman in uniform got out and ran toward us.

"Are you Matilda and Jack?" the woman said. I nodded. "Was there anyone else with you?" she asked, and we shook our heads.

Before we knew it, we were being wrapped in huge foil blankets and bundled into the back of the plow. The inside was exactly like an ambulance.

The woman took my temperature and asked me lots of questions about how I felt. Realizing we were OK was followed by an awful, gut-wrenching horror about the trouble we would be in when we got back. I wondered if I would be expelled. I had run away. We had run away. It was probably very, very bad. I could tell Jack was thinking the same thing. He was nodding to himself and taking deep breaths. The paramedic man was prodding him and then he nodded to the paramedic woman.

"You're both very lucky," he said, almost crossly, like we

had meant it to happen and now he was missing his late night snack or something.

I didn't know if I wanted to go back down the mountain and face Miss Mardle.

I wondered if Lauren knew I had run away with Roland. Or maybe Roland had now told everyone that in fact I had run away with Jack. He pulled the foil blanket really tight; he must have been even colder than me. I wondered whether he was thinking about Lauren. Did he think about her the way I thought about him? I want to think I'm the kind of person who wouldn't have kissed him. Who would have leaned away dramatically and said I couldn't possibly when he was with someone else. But I would have kissed him, I know I would. I was scared but I wanted to. I wondered how many girls Jack had kissed, and then I realized I had been staring at him for ages and I looked down.

"Do you think they'll call our parents?" he said.

"I don't know. How long were we lost for?"

Jack shrugged. "I mean, we're fine, so nothing bad actually happened."

"I know, but that's never the point with teachers. It's always much more about what *might* have happened. They are obsessed with that. What-if scenarios."

I was a little obsessed with what-if scenarios myself, to be honest.

We both got out of the plow slowly, knowing what was coming. But that's the thing about getting into trouble. It never happens when you expect it to, always when you are sailing along thinking everything is fine.

Miss Mardle and Jack's teacher were waiting together, side by side like a mum and dad. But then, like a mum, Miss Mardle hugged me and I could tell she was relieved. Us dying wouldn't have looked very good for her really, I suppose.

They spoke to the paramedics and took some forms and we walked back to the hotel, still wearing the ridiculous blankets.

Just before we got to the entrance, Jack hung back a little. "Are you OK?"

I nodded. "I feel better, actually. For talking to someone." It was true. I didn't feel embarrassed that I'd cried in front of him. For some reason, with him, it had felt OK.

"Well, come and find me if you want to talk some more," he said.

When we walked into the hotel lobby, I got nervous. Lauren could be anywhere. She could walk around the corner and see me with Jack at any moment. I wondered if he was thinking the same thing. Worrying his girlfriend might see him. The woman at the desk tapped her friend on the shoulder and they both looked at me and whispered to each other. I looked down.

"See, Super-Mouse, the superstar kidnapper, is even more of a celebrity now," Jack whispered.

"I don't know if I want to be famous for being mentally

unhinged," I said, and then we hugged goodbye. Like buddies who see each other all the time, real friends.

At the hotel, everyone wanted to know what had happened with Roland. Had he asked me to run away? Was he having a mental breakdown? Had we kissed? Were we a couple? Jack was right: I *had* become a mini celebrity. But becoming one just made me realize how much it didn't suit me. On the surface everyone was excited and buzzing about it, but there was an undercurrent too. Like they thought I had come back to Bluecoats determined to make everything about me. I wanted to reverse it, but I didn't know how.

I tried to play it down. I calmed everyone down with a story about running off with Roland and him being picked up by his crew ten minutes later. But on the way into town, I told Connie and Keira the whole truth. About the igloo and how Jack had been Roland and everything. Everything except the almost-kiss, because in the middle of finding out that they had been watching Hamster Wardrobe Boy onstage, not Roland, it didn't seem like big news really.

The restaurant was absolutely crazy. It was decorated like a giant gingerbread house, covered in candy and icing. Inside, it was full of wooden toys and giant gingerbread hearts, and all the waiters and waitresses were wearing traditional Alpine costumes. A man was playing an accordion and one wall was covered from top to bottom with cuckoo clocks.

"This is amazing," Connie said, bobbing around to the music.

We sat at long wooden tables and they brought us trays of hot dogs. This ginormous multicolored cuckoo clock started singing, and then a man dressed as a giant moose came out and started dancing.

Just as it felt like the attention was moving away from me, the waitress asked to have her picture taken with me wearing my Roland hat. And then the dancing moose spotted me and held his moose hand out to me to get up and dance with him. I could see Lauren, crutches and all, looking sour-faced at me from the end of the table. I had been shaking my head to try to get the moose to go away, but Lauren's face and the thought of the playground and how silent I had been gave me a kick. I got up. The moose cheered, the accordion man wandered over and I bopped along to the music with the moose.

"Mouse and Moose!" Connie screamed, taking a picture.

The more people asked me about Roland, the more sullen and withdrawn Lauren got. At one point even Scarlett and Melody left her end of the table to come and hear about what he was like close up.

After dinner, we walked back to the hotel and got into our pajamas.

"So, who would you choose if you had to choose one of them?" Keira asked.

"If you had to marry Roland or Jack tomorrow or you would be shot, who would you choose?" Connie said, gently feeding Mr. Jambon a carrot on her bed.

"Or if you had to shoot one of them tomorrow, which one would you shoot?" Keira said, cross-legged, braiding her hair.

I climbed onto the bunk and swung my legs in the air.

"Jack. I'd pick Jack."

"To shoot or to marry?" Connie asked, frowning.

"Marry, obviously," I laughed.

"So you would *shoot* Roland?" said Keira.

"I wouldn't shoot either of them. What is this obsession with shooting? Anyway, guys, I have to tell you something. When me and Jack were in the igloo . . . I'm not actually sure. It's not like I'm experienced in these things, but I think . . . Jack was going to kiss me."

"And?" Connie said. "Why didn't he?"

"Because he has an evil, Regina George–worshipping girlfriend called Lauren Bradley?" Keira said.

"No, because we heard the siren."

"The siren of *luuuuurve*!" Connie said.

They clambered onto the teeny bottom bunk. Me and Keira side by side, and Connie holding Mr. Jambon lying the other way.

"Is he with Lauren, then, or what?" Keira said. "As much as I hate ol' Bradders, it is a little messed up to go around hitting on you when he's with her."

"But *is* he with her?" we all said at exactly the same time.

"And more importantly, would you have kissed him back?" Keira said.

I put the covers over my head sheepishly and they both made second-grade "ooooooh" noises.

"You need to look hot tomorrow," Keira said.

"What should I wear?" I groaned.

"Your witch-self clothes?" Connie said sleepily.

Keira kicked her. "She needs to look *hot*."

Slowly they fell asleep in the bunk with me. I reached over and picked Mr. Jambon up and put him to bed in his cage. Then I squeezed myself back in with them and re-played the moment in the igloo. But in my head I let Jack kiss me.

JACK

I woke up on the last full day of the trip feeling groggy from lack of sleep. Me, Max and Toddy had spent pretty much the whole night talking about the press conference and the sledding and the snowstorm and all the rest of yesterday's madness. Every time we were starting to drift off to sleep, I'd remember something else I hadn't told them, and we'd sit back up in our beds again, whispering and laughing.

The only thing I'd kept from them was the part in the igloo, just before we'd been rescued. I'd been so close to kissing her. And I was *sure* she would have kissed me back. But then the stupid paramedics had arrived. I mean, obviously I was quite glad they'd showed up, but y'know . . . I just wish they'd showed up, like, twenty seconds later.

After breakfast, as we made our way to the ski lift for the final boarding session, we lagged behind the group so Max could get his fireworks. Toddy kept watch for Flynn outside, and I went in with Max. He practically bought the whole store. He bought bangers, Roman candles, waterfalls, Catherine wheels, bombettes, sparklers and a thing called a "Crackling Comet," which genuinely looked like it could take down a plane.

The snow started falling again—much more lightly than yesterday—as we jogged to catch up with the rest of our group, who were standing around waiting for lifts up the mountain.

"Why didn't you just wait until the end of the day to buy that stuff?" I panted as Max tried unsuccessfully to stuff the plastic bag full of illicit materials into his bag.

"That's when Flynn's *expecting* us to buy dodgy stuff," he sniffed. "He'll never suspect anyone of buying dodgy stuff at the *beginning* of the day, will he? You'd have to be an absolute *idiot* to do that."

Toddy eyed Max. "Yep. You're right about that."

We reached the back of our group and Max flung his bag on the ground.

"What's this then, Mr. Kendal? Been shopping?"

Max looked up to see Flynn standing over him, beaming down at the plastic bag half zipped into his backpack.

"It's just some, um, sweets I bought, sir. For my mum and dad."

Ed and Jamie went "Ooooooh" in unison, and Max threw a scowl at them.

"Very thoughtful of you, Mr. Kendal. Ever the gentleman." Flynn reached down and brushed the plastic handles aside so he could see into the bag. Max inhaled sharply.

Flynn glanced inside and pulled out a firework. It was a big long tube with sparks and mad colors all over it and the words LE FIZZER written on both sides. He examined it carefully. Max was watching him, openmouthed in horror. He could be sent home for this. Or even suspended.

"'Le Fizzer,' eh?" said Flynn, after eyeing it for what seemed like hours. Then, suddenly, he dropped it back into the bag. "What will these manufacturers think of next? What is it, Mr. Kendal, some sort of carbonated candy?"

Max exhaled loudly. "Yes, sir," he said, faintly. "Carbonated candy, sir. Exactly."

"Well, I never. I don't see what's wrong with gummies and Toblerone myself, but if you think your parents would prefer a 'Fizzer,' then fair enough."

Max zipped his bag shut and almost collapsed into the snow.

The morning boarding session was amazing, despite

Flynn warning me that, after yesterday's antics, if I left his sight for "one millisecond" I'd be in detention until I was eighteen. On the blue slope, I set a new personal best for my going-downhill-without-falling-over record (one minute twenty-four seconds), and to Max's annoyance, Toddy even managed to pull off a—very small, very slow—one-eighty. The snow kept falling gently throughout the day, and the fresh powder felt amazing underneath our boards.

"We've gotta go all out at the dance tonight," said Max, skidding to a wobbly stop at the bottom of the slope. "Last chance to get past zero. No more messing about now." He whacked Toddy on the shoulder. "Toddy, no offense, but you're probably out of contention. I don't think your one butter-chat with Melody will realistically have persuaded her to pucker up, Romeo."

Toddy just smiled, shrugged and started trudging back up the slope to the lift.

"It's just me and you now, Jack," Max said, grinning, as we followed him. "In terms of the bet, anyway. By the end of tonight, our band will *definitely* have a name. If things go well with Lauren and Scarlett, maybe we'll start going out with them for real. Imagine that: having hot girlfriends in London." He shook his head in wonder. "We'd be living the dream, man."

"Yeah . . . ," I said hesitantly. "I mean, Lauren's great—"

"More than great," Max cut in, almost angrily. "She's ridiculously hot."

"Yeah, yeah. But, like, yesterday . . . with Mouse . . . it felt like something could have happened, almost. I really . . . like her, Max."

Max snorted loudly. "Mate, Mouse is nuts. I'm telling you, you'd be crazy not to go for Lauren. She's super hot, and—for some reason none of us fully understand—she actually seems to like you." He stopped and looked at me squarely. "Don't make this another Maria Bennett thing, Jack, please. In six months' time, I don't want to be hearing about how you *could have* gotten with Lauren, but you just wasted your chance at the last minute. *This* is your chance. *Tonight* is your chance! Don't mess it up, man."

"I guess you're right," I said. But all I could think of was Mouse's amazing smile.

At the end of the day's session, we said goodbye to Basti and all got the main lift back down into town to return our gear. As we stepped out of the board rental store, I heard a loud shout from across the road.

"Jack! Hey, Jack, over here!"

I looked over and saw Lauren sitting on the terrace of a café, her busted ankle resting on a chair.

Max and Toddy raised their eyebrows at me. "Best go and see your lady, huh?" whispered Max. I told them I'd meet them back in the room later, and walked over to Lauren. Her teacher was sitting with her, but she just said, "Miss Mardle, do you mind if me and Jack go for a quick walk around town?"

Miss Mardle looked like she definitely *did* mind, but all she said was, "OK, Lauren, but I need you back in your room in an hour. Be very careful on your crutches, it's icy out there."

"Jack will look after me."

I helped Lauren up and onto her crutches, and we walked away. I prayed that Mouse wasn't currently on one of the lifts back into town.

"I feel like I haven't seen you for absolutely ages," Lauren said.

"Yeah, sorry, it's all been busy lately."

"At least we'll get to hang out at the dance tonight."

"Yeah, definitely."

We stopped to get hot chocolates and waffles at a little shop, and then sat on a bench nearby. It was getting colder as the sun started to dip gradually behind the mountains. She shuffled right up close to me, tucking her arm through mine, and I felt a shiver of nervous excitement. Max was right; if I wanted it to happen with Lauren, it could happen. Tonight. All I had to do was *not* mess it up.

"Must have been a bit boring for you, not being able to ski these last couple of days?" I said.

"It's been all right. My ankle still hurts a lot, not that anyone seems to care."

"What do you mean?"

She unclipped her hair and shook it down around her

shoulders. "Oh, nothing. They're all just obsessed with . . . you know that girl Mouse, from my school, right?"

I nodded.

"Well, I don't know if you saw, but she had this ridiculous thing yesterday with that singer, Roland."

"Yep," I said. "I did see that."

"Ever since then, it's all anyone wants to talk about. It's so annoying. Mouse just *has* to be the center of attention, all the time."

I knew how untrue that was. It felt horrible hearing Lauren talk about Mouse like that.

"Ah, lay off her," I said, trying to sound casual. "She's had a rough time and all that."

Lauren looked at me sharply. "What do you mean?"

"Well, y'know . . . the stuff with her school. That ballet school she used to go to."

"What stuff?"

"You know. How she got . . . what do you call it? Assessed out? Or they made her leave, or whatever. It must be awful when all you want is to dance, and then you get kicked out of dance school. And now she's back at your school, and she won't get to be a professional dancer." I shrugged. "That sucks."

Lauren was watching me carefully with an odd look in her eyes. "She told you that?" she said slowly.

I said, "Yeah," and then suddenly panicked. I didn't

want her to think that me and Mouse had been having a lot of secret talks. "I mean . . . I've hardly talked to her, really," I spluttered. "But she said something about it. At the ice rink, I think it was."

She stared at me for ages, then broke out into a huge grin. "Yeah," she said. "You're right. I guess I shouldn't be so hard on her. After what she's been through."

A weird, uncomfortable silence settled between us. I sipped my hot chocolate and thought about what might or might not happen tonight, while Lauren smiled vaguely into the distance.

18

MOUSE

"I'm gonna change into my pajamas to get ready," Keira said, and walked into the bathroom. I looked out the window. The sun had already gone down.

"We've got three hours before the dance," I said.

"Yeah, so we need to start *now*. You said it takes you like ten hours to wash your hair, so you better get going." Keira peeled off her top. "I've got so many bruises I look like a map."

I sat on the edge of the bath and Connie sprawled out on the floor between the bunks, letting Mr. Jambon crawl across her tummy.

"Whatever I wear, I will look like I've been beaten up," Keira said, examining her array of purple-and-green blotches.

"Or like you've got a disease," Connie said chirpily. "I

love mine. I don't want them to go away." She rolled up her trousers. "This one's my favorite." She pointed at a large purple, yellow and green bruise that almost covered the whole of one of her thighs. "I think it looks like an old man's face. I'll call him Malcolm, the man who lives on my leg."

"Is that gonna be your pickup line tonight?" I said. "'Hi, do you want to meet the old man who lives on my leg?'"

"I don't need pickup lines," Connie said loftily, putting Mr. Jambon on her head. "I just let my allure do the talking."

"Are you nervous?" Keira said, looking at me in the mirror.

I nodded. "Yeah, but I don't know why. I think it's just the thought that he'll be there. And it might be the last time I ever see him."

"Parting is such sweet sorrow," Connie sighed. "But just make sure you find out his last name and then you can internet-stalk him for the rest of eternity."

"He's probably nervous about seeing you too. My mum always says you should think of boys as spiders," Keira said, taking the braids out of her hair and starting to brush it. "They're more scared of us than we are of them."

"And spiders love witches, so the same probably goes for boys," Connie said.

All day on the slopes, I had been thinking about Jack. I went from being deliriously happy and not being able to stop smiling because he had been going to kiss me, to worried about *why* he had been going to kiss me, to thinking about him and Lauren. Nothing could ever happen between me and Jack really, because she had a kind of claim on him that would last forever, even if she dumped him and met the love of her life tomorrow. But by tomorrow we might never see them again anyway.

Skiing for the last time, hurtling down as fast as I could, I had pictured an alternate universe where me and Jack met by accident in Devon on vacation at Easter. My parents would be in a tea shop for the entire time and Lauren would never be mentioned.

"I definitely want to come on the ski trip next year," Connie said.

"Yeah, me too," Keira said, nodding. She put her arms around me. "I wish you weren't going to Paris. Then we could all come together next year. The three witches."

Connie slipped Mr. Jambon into his cage and came and put her arms around me too. "I love you, Mouse," she said. Just plainly and matter-of-factly.

"I love you too," I said, and hugged them both. "Three witches forever."

I didn't actually know what I was going to do about the lie. I didn't even know if I wanted to go to ballet school in Paris anymore. I just wanted to go back in time and erase the moment where I had said it. I closed my eyes and kind of willed it to happen.

"OK, enough of the mushy stuff," Keira said. "We need to get this show on the road."

"Please can I put the *Mamma Mia!* soundtrack on?" Connie said.

"Is that still your favorite album?" I laughed.

"Yes, it is, *actually,*" Connie said. "It's a timeless classic. Sixteen million people can't be wrong."

"Well, they clearly can and are," said Keira, but as soon as Connie put the album on, she was singing along to every track with us.

It took me a whole hour to blow-dry my hair, and then Keira painted my nails lilac and covered them in little daisy stencils. I went into the bathroom to do my makeup. I put eyeliner on for the first time, tracing a thin, dark line right around each eye. When I came out, Keira was lying on the floor with a mirror, drawing flowers on her stomach with a silver pen.

"What are you going to wear?" I asked.

Connie pointed at her bunk, where she had laid out jeans and a pink tank top that still had the tags.

"My mum bought me this," Keira said, and walked over to her bag and took out a short black dress. "She, like, *knew* there was a dance and got excited about it. She's an objectively lame person. If she'd had her way, she'd have given birth to Armenian Malibu Barbie."

"I wish my mum had bought me a dress. And yours must

know you fairly well, because it is black. She could have bought you a pink one."

Keira sighed. "I suppose. What are you gonna wear?"

I took out the flowery top and jeans I had brought for the dance. "What do you think?"

Keira smiled and held up the dress. "I think you should wear the Malibu Barbie. It's not really my vibe anyway."

I pulled it on in the bathroom and looked at myself. My hair reached my waist, with a tiny braid down one side. Keira had drawn a little silver flower on my shoulder. I looked so different from normal, and I felt different too. Like whatever happened, it was going to be fun. And we would be together, and come back and wedge ourselves into one bunk like sardines, and talk about it all night.

I stepped back into the room and Keira wolf-whistled.

"You look like a film star," Connie said.

"You actually *do,*" Keira said. She was wearing flowy black pants and a cut-off T-shirt to show off all the artwork on her belly.

"Is the old man who lives on your leg ready?" I said to Connie.

"Malcolm can't wait." Connie waved her leg at me.

"Are you ready to see Jack?" Keira said, smiling.

"No," I said. "Yes. I don't know."

And then we all squealed out of the room and down the hall.

The main hall had been cleared of all the chairs and was now dark except for the colorful disco lights by the DJ's table. There were little bunches of purple-and-green balloons floating around, and the sugary Europop was already going strong.

As soon as I walked in I scanned the room for Jack, and when he wasn't there I felt disappointed and relieved at the same time.

"When Jack walks in, are you going to act like you see him or like you are so busy and fabulous you don't see him?" Keira asked.

"Shhhhh," I said, but squeezed her hand tight.

"I'm going to request 'Mamma Mia,'" Connie said, and ran over to talk to the DJ, who seemed a little annoyed to be interrupted during his set.

Lauren sat with her crutches on the other side of the room. She smiled at me and waved. I wondered why. She had ignored me last night at the restaurant. Her waves were always to disguise something else she was thinking; I wondered what it was. But it didn't really matter. We could both exist in one room, one school, one universe, and it would be OK. I had Connie and Keira, and they would stick up for me through anything.

"This trip has gone by really quickly," Keira said.

Monday morning sitting next to Mum felt distant but perfectly in focus at the same time.

"I think rejection is the worst thing anyone can experience," I said to Keira.

She nodded. "Me too."

I thought about the day I found out I wasn't good enough. Maybe I'll always think about that before anything good might be going to happen. Maybe it will always be there, waiting. But maybe I'll just learn to live with it. Like a bruise inside that never goes away but just becomes part of you.

Then I saw Jack. I definitely saw him before he saw me, because I hadn't stopped watching the door since we arrived. I gripped Keira's arm and she smiled at me.

A few groups of girls had started dancing in little circles across the hall. Connie ran back over just as "Mamma Mia" started playing. She was clapping her hands in delight. "He's playing it!" she screamed a little too loudly, like all her dreams had come true. We had to dance; it was her favorite.

We slowly shuffled out onto the edge of the dance floor. Connie immediately started dancing wildly. Keira shuffled in a kind of cool sway from side to side. I couldn't look at Jack, but in my head I felt like he was looking at me.

I started dancing, and the more I danced, the more I remembered how much I loved dancing. Jack being there, knowing about the lie, made me feel freer. Like it was OK to have fun dancing. Because he was there, and he knew about the lie, and he still liked me. Whatever kind of like it was, he definitely liked me. I looked over at him and our eyes met. My stomach flipped over and I felt like I might vomit all over Connie there and then. I looked back over at Lauren to remind myself not to get carried away; he belonged to her.

After a few songs we left the dance floor and bought a drink. "Do you think he'll come over and talk to you?" Keira said. The longer me and Jack went without actually speaking to each other, the more nervous I got about it happening.

"Right, Connie, come on," Keira said. "Let's go to the bathroom. If Mouse is alone, he'll have to come and speak to her."

"Please don't leave me," I hissed desperately, but they were already gone.

I was completely alone. I sipped my drink and looked at the floor and then he was there. Keira's boy tactics were obviously well tried and tested.

"Hey," he said.

"Hey." We both looked down at the floor.

Neither of us spoke. It felt awkward and horrible. Not like on the slopes. It felt like we were drowning in silence. The longer it went on, the harder it felt to think of anything to say to break it.

"Did you have a good last day?" he finally said.

I nodded. "Yeah, I didn't know I was going to get so bruised," I said. "Connie has a bruise she has named Malcolm." I smiled as widely as I could to hide it all.

He looked at the floor and shuffled his feet. He didn't even smile. He took a deep breath, like he was about to say something. And then I saw Lauren, hobbling across the room. She looked really pretty, but she always does. She's one of those people, whatever she wears and whatever she's doing, she always looks polished and perfect.

"Hey, guys," she said, and leaned over and hugged me and then hugged Jack.

"Hey," I said, and smiled.

Jack was bright red. He looked younger suddenly, like a little boy.

I looked up for Connie and Keira. I wanted them to come back. I felt outnumbered. I tried to look normal.

"So," Lauren said, smiling. "How's your friend Roland? Have you heard from him since you ... *whatever* that was that you did?"

I shook my head. I wanted Jack to say something to defend me but he didn't say anything. I looked again for Connie and Keira but they were nowhere. Scarlett and Melody crossed the room and hugged Jack.

"Hey, Mouse," they trilled, but neither of them hugged me.

"I was just asking Mouse about her celebrity-stalking," Lauren said.

"You know you can get arrested for that, right?" Scarlett said.

"Maybe you should get a huge tattoo of his face," Melody laughed. "To show what a superfan you are."

Jack was still looking at the floor.

"Are you gonna stay in touch with him?" Melody smiled. "When you live in *Paris*?" Her voice had a mocking edge to it.

"Yeah, when you live in *Paris*, you and him can be utter besties," Scarlett laughed.

"When you're dancing every night at the Paris Opera House. You'll probably be the first thirteen-year-old to ever get the lead in *Swan Lake*," Lauren added. "Being so amazing and everything."

My heart started racing. I had no idea what to say. How did they know? The only person I'd told had been Jack. Jack, who was standing right next to me, staring at the ground like he wanted it to swallow him up. I balled up my fists and dug my nails into my skin. He *couldn't* have told them. . . . He wouldn't. And then Keira and Connie were there.

"Mouse, are you OK?" Connie said.

I looked at the floor. I couldn't speak. I just tried to keep breathing.

"She's fine," Lauren said. "We're just talking to her about ballet school next year."

"*Oui, oui.*" Connie nodded. But I could tell she knew something weird was happening.

"Are you going to go and stay with Mouse in Paris?" Lauren's voice had an unmistakable edge. Connie didn't know what was happening.

"What's your problem?" Keira said.

"What's *your* problem, weirdo?" Lauren said back.

Keira shook her head and muttered something under her breath.

"What was that?" Scarlett said. "At least have the guts to say it out loud."

"I was just saying you're a bunch of rancid, pathetic losers," Keira said, staring Scarlett right in the eyes.

"That's weird. Mouse was saying how much you loved Scarlett's family." Lauren smiled fakely. Keira looked like someone had punched her.

"For the record," Scarlett said, "my brother thinks you're a gross monster and would never go out with you."

Keira stood completely still. It was like time was going slowly. I tried to look at her but she was just staring at the floor.

"You're just jealous that Keira and Mouse are prettier than you and that Mouse is special," Connie said, proudly and defiantly. "You wish you were a good enough dancer to be going to ballet school in Paris."

Keira had started to cry. Connie reached down and held her hand.

"You're such an idiot," Lauren laughed. "I feel sorry for you. She's not going to ballet school in Paris. She's got problems. She's a compulsive liar. She got chucked out of White Lodge. She's an attention-seeking fantasist. She thinks

Roland wants her. She tells everyone she's going to some super-cool Paris ballet school, when really she got kicked out of her old one. She makes up stories, Connie. She's *special,* all right." Lauren laughed, and Connie crumpled.

"Mouse ...? You *are* going to ballet school in Paris, right?" Connie's eyes were huge, staring into mine.

Keira looked at me. "Did you make it up?"

The bruise inside me thumped and thudded. I dug my nails in harder but I knew I couldn't stop the tears for much longer. And then I just ran. As fast as I could. And I let them begin.

JACK

I was frozen to the spot. I felt like I was ten seconds behind everyone else. What the hell had just happened?

I watched Mouse disappear out of the hall, and turned back to see that Keira was scowling at me intensely through her tears.

Lauren leaned in to say something, but it was like my ears were stuffed with cotton balls. All I could hear was a weird buzzing sound and the muffled thud-thud-thud of the awful Euro disco.

"What?" I shouted over the music.

She leaned in closer. "I *said,* sorry about that. She just thinks she's so much better than she really is. You can't go around lying all the time and not expect to get caught out, y'know?"

I blinked in confusion. Surely they all *knew* that Mouse had been kicked out of ballet school? I'd assumed that the Paris lie had been something she'd only told *me*. A horrible, cold feeling started to bleed through me.

Lauren shuffled closer to me on her crutches, until our shoes were touching at the toes. We were at the center of a little crowd that had gathered to watch the shouting match, and suddenly all eyes were on us. She tilted her chin upward, smiling. Then she closed her eyes and leaned in toward me. The weird buzzing in my ears clicked up a notch. My head felt like it had a pillow wrapped around it. This was it. It was happening now. In front of everyone.

Don't ruin it, Jack.

Her lips brushed mine, and I jolted my head back, instinctively. She blinked her eyes open, and a silent bristle of tension seemed to shoot through the crowd. Out of the corner of my eye, I could see Max running his hands over his hair.

"Jack, what are you doing?" Lauren hissed, her smile just wide enough to make it look like nothing was wrong.

I shrugged.

"Look, if this is about Mouse . . . you shouldn't feel bad for her," she whispered. "She had it coming, trust me."

"I don't know if she did, really," I said, starting to feel

hot with anger. "She hasn't done anything except have her dream of being a dancer ripped away from her. I don't think that stuff about Paris was her trying to impress people, or look cool. It was just about trying to convince herself that her life wasn't really over. That she still might have a chance. So, no, Lauren, she didn't have it coming. At all."

Lauren stared at me. I got the sudden impression that no one had ever argued with her before in her whole life. She'd just had thirteen years of people nodding and agreeing. It was like she didn't know how to react.

"Yeah, well, fine," she said slowly. "Whatever. I guess I just don't think it's cool to lie to everyone the whole time. I think, at some point, you've got to stop pretending, and just be who you actually are. . . . You know what I mean?"

I did know what she meant. Completely. I had to stop pretending too. "Yeah. Look, sorry, Lauren. But I don't . . . We're not going out. I mean, I don't know if we ever actually *were* going out, but if you thought we were, then, y'know, we're not." I paused. "Sorry."

She looked like someone had just emptied a bucket of water over her. Like she was too shocked to speak. She just opened and closed her mouth a few times, but no sound came out.

I turned and walked away quickly, pushing through the dense clump of people around us. As I squeezed through, I heard Jamie laugh, "And the lead singer of the Bailers does it again. . . ."

I kept going without even looking back at him. I suddenly didn't care what anyone else thought. It didn't feel like I'd bailed on anything. It felt like, for once in my life, I'd actually been brave.

My whole brain was focused on finding Mouse, and making sure she was OK.

Before I could open the door to the corridor, Max stopped me with a squeeze on the arm. "Jack, man . . ." He was shaking his head, but I didn't even let him start.

"Max, I know what you think, but I don't care. You go and get together with Scarlett. You go and win the bet. I just need to find Mouse."

I wriggled my arm free and hurried out into the hallway. I rushed into the reception area, and was just about to head down the corridor toward Mouse's room, when the main doors swung open and a wall of noise hit me.

The huge bald guy was muttering into his earpiece, and the crazy American pigtails woman was jabbering loudly into her phone. And, at the center of them all, grinning brightly at the starstruck receptionist, was Roland.

"Ah, Jack! Excellent timing."

"Roland? What . . . what are you doing here?"

"We're asking ourselves the same question, honey, trust me," said the American woman, pocketing her phone and shooting a withering glance around the lobby.

Roland tilted his head to the side and looked at her. "Cooper, please. You promised. Just for tonight."

271

"Ugh, fine." She motioned for the bald guy to follow her and sit down on one of the benches.

"So, what *are* you doing here?" I asked him.

"Isn't it obvious?" he smiled. "I came to get my jacket back."

"Oh, right . . . yeah."

"That thing cost more than my three snowmobiles put together. The zipper is made of real diamonds."

"Yeah, sure. Sorry."

There was a pause, and then he exploded into laughter. "No, come on! I am joking with you, Jack!" He put his hand on my shoulder. "I came to say goodbye. The video is now finished, and tomorrow I go on tour. Germany, Austria, Switzerland, and some more countries I can't exactly remember. Maybe Poland? Anyway, after all that happened yesterday, I couldn't just leave without saying goodbye, you know?"

"Right, no, of course. Look, I'm sorry if I made you look a total weirdo yesterday, Roland. I just sort of . . . panicked."

"Don't worry. Like Cooper says, 'All publicity is good publicity.'" He whipped his phone out of his pocket. "I have been trending constantly since your stunt on the stage. People think I have lost my mind, but . . . they're talking about me. And buying my songs. So maybe craziness is the way forward."

"Oh. Well . . . good."

He grinned at me, and I felt a sudden jab of guilt about Mouse. I had to come clean.

"Roland, I've got to tell you something. That stuff I said about Mouse not being interested in you. I was lying. I never even asked her."

His face stayed blank. He didn't even blink. I kept talking. "I was going to tell her, I promise, but, the thing is . . . I like her too. A lot, I think. And I knew she'd pick you over me."

The edges of his mouth flickered upward. "How did you know that?"

"Because . . . well, look at you."

"Yes, and look at you." He shrugged. "We don't look so different, most people seem to think."

"Yeah, but . . . you're a famous singer."

"And you're the front man of a band."

"A band with no name."

He laughed. "I have a feeling you will have a name soon. And once you do, you might get as famous as me."

"Look, whatever. What I'm saying is, I'm sorry I never told her. You should tell her now. Yourself."

I really meant it. At that moment, I just wanted whatever would make Mouse happy.

He just laughed again, and shook his head. "Listen, Jack. Don't worry. Mouse is great. We both know this. But I feel that maybe she is *more* great for you. I'm sure I can find other great girls in Germany, Austria, Switzerland, and all the other countries I can't remember. Maybe Poland." He turned to Cooper. "Cooper, are we going to Poland?"

"You betcha," said Cooper, not looking up from her phone. "Though I have literally no idea where it is."

He turned back to me. "You see? I think I will be OK. . . ."

I grinned, and it felt like a lead weight had been lifted from my shoulders. "OK. Cool. Thanks, man. So, what are you going to do now?"

"Me?" He shrugged. "Maybe I will go to the dance. Cooper has promised me one night of freedom before I am chained to the tour bus for months." He nodded at the double doors through which we could hear the muffled thud of music and laughter. "Who knows? Maybe the girl of my dreams is right behind that door."

"OK, I'll see you."

He leaned in and whispered, "Oh, and, Jack, if you get a chance, I wouldn't mind getting that jacket back. I wasn't joking about the diamond zipper. Twelve-carat."

I laughed. "I'm on it." I hustled into the hall, past Cooper and the bald guy, until I got to Mouse's room. I banged on the door but there was no answer. I tried the knob hopefully and it swung open.

"Mouse? Anyone in here?" The bedroom was empty, but the bathroom door was open just enough for me to see a sliver of what was definitely Mouse, standing over the sink.

"Mouse, it's Jack," I said gently. "Can I come in?"

I pushed the door open and almost screamed in shock. "What the . . . Mouse, are you insane? What are you *doing*?"

19

MOUSE

I was shocked enough to do a full-on horror-movie blood-curdling scream, but only a short little yelp came out. I held the scissors out in front of me and he jumped back.

"What are *you* doing? You don't just walk in on people in the bathroom!" I shouted.

"Sorry!" He took a step back. "People don't usually brandish scissors at you if you do."

"Oh." I stopped pointing the scissors at him. "Sorry. It was my fight instinct coming out. What are you doing here?" I suddenly wanted to turn and look at myself in the mirror. I had this awful feeling that my face was covered in runny mascara and blotchy tearstains. But there was no way of doing it without it not looking obvious.

"I just . . . Mouse . . . I . . ." He looked at me, right at me, for ages without saying anything.

"It's OK," I said. "It's true. I did lie about ballet school. I lied to everyone. You had every right to tell Lauren. It's your choice."

"Mouse. Honestly, you have to understand, I would never, ever do something like that. . . ."

He looked so upset. He seemed annoyed at himself for not being able to find the words. His eyes were shining like he was about to cry.

"It's OK, honestly. It doesn't matter anymore."

"Yes it does. I just . . . I really need you to understand that when I told Lauren that, I thought she knew. I didn't know when you told me about the lie that I was the only person you told . . . the truth to."

I nodded.

"What I should have done is told you how special I feel that you told me," he said really gently. "Because that's how I feel. Honestly."

"It's OK, really. I was going to have to face the lie sometime. When I came out with it first, I think I thought I could make it true. That I could audition for ballet school in Paris and then it wouldn't be a lie."

"Well, why can't you do that?" he asked. "Then it would make it true."

I shook my head. "No it wouldn't." I sat on the edge of the bath and took a deep breath. "I'm not going to be a dancer."

"I don't get it. Mouse, you *are* a dancer. Because you dance."

"You know what I mean. I won't be a *professional* dancer."

"I don't even know if that's true, Mouse. But if you love dancing, you should keep dancing. Even if it's just with me to random techno music on ski trips."

I thought about Lauren saying she hadn't danced since she didn't get in. It was sad, because she had loved it so much. And she had been really, really good.

I nodded. "Sorry I threatened you with scissors."

"It doesn't surprise me." He smiled. "You are pretty fierce. And I wouldn't expect Super-Mouse to do anything else."

He came and sat on the edge of the bathtub next to me, but he sat too far back and fell into it with his feet still hanging over the edge. I laughed and let myself slip back and fall into the tub with him.

I turned to him. "So, Jack, will you help me do something crazy?"

"Is it witchcraft? Because I saw that book by Keira's bed. Are you going to turn Mr. Jambon back into a rat or something?"

I smiled and rested my head against the tiles. He did the same and we turned and looked at each other and for a second the air changed like it had done in the igloo.

"Do I have mascara all over my face?" I asked.

"Yes. I wasn't going to mention it, but you do look a little unhinged. Even without the scissors."

I hauled myself out of the bath and looked at myself in the mirror. "Oh my God." I turned on the tap and started scrubbing at my face. Jack stayed in the bath, smiling. "What are you going to do?"

"Stay at school. Have a reputation for being insane. Try and make up with Connie and Keira."

I turned and faced him. His head was still resting against the tiles. His hair was tilted back off his face. He looked relaxed and effortlessly attractive. How good he looked made me turn back and keep scrubbing at my face. It was overwhelming. I tried to sound offhand, like I was inquiring about the weather.

"So, are you and Lauren . . . going out?"

He tried to sit up, but fell back into the bath again. "No. I don't want to go out with her. Not just because she was so mean to you, but definitely even more now I've seen her be like that."

A new little lump of sunshine grew next to the bruise inside me. I dried my face and caught myself in the mirror, blotchy and damp.

"Are you going to help me or not?" I said, turning and crossing my arms.

He pulled himself out of the bath. "Yes, Super-Mouse, the crazier the better."

I picked up a random chunk of my hair and picked up the scissors and snipped it off. I looked at it lying in my palm.

"What?" Jack shouted. "Are you crazy? Your hair is so cool. It's so . . . distinctive and . . . you."

"Yeah, exactly. I've had long hair since I was five. Since I started ballet. I've always kept it long, to put in buns, to look pretty, to help me look like a dancer. I just want to see how it feels not to have it."

"I just don't think it's good to make life-changing decisions after . . . after being upset," he said.

"Jack, it will grow back. It's hair. I'm not chopping my arm off."

"But what will your mum say?"

"She'll probably cry, but then it's not her hair. Jack, I'm gonna do it, so if you don't wanna watch, then you better leave." I really didn't want him to leave.

"Well, I'm obviously not going to leave *now*."

I handed him the scissors and stood facing the mirror. He stood behind me. I shook my hair out and looked at it, flowing down to my waist.

"Are you *sure*?" he said. He reached out and picked up some of my hair and let it fall back into place.

I nodded. "It's probably best to just try and chop the ponytail off at the top," I said.

I gathered it up into a ponytail. He picked it up and held it up in the air. "Mouse, if I do this, you better not sue me if you change your mind. Or cast a spell on me."

"I won't. Stop drawing it out, just do it!"

I heard the sound of the scissors being opened and him picking up my ponytail. And then the sound again. He laughed. "There is no way these are going to cut through this."

I pulled the elastic out and shook my hair. "Can you do it in sections?" I handed him my hairbrush and he started to brush my hair really gently, like he'd never brushed anyone's hair before, like the hair could actually *feel* how gently he was doing it.

He was concentrating really hard, picking up little sections and running the brush through them. Then he put it down and picked up the scissors.

"Sure?" he asked, and I nodded.

He picked up a tiny length of hair. "How short? Here?" He touched my ear gently. I nodded again.

And then he picked up a little section and cut it. Hair fell softly onto the tiled floor. Then he picked up another and another until I couldn't even see the tiles anymore. But there was still lots and lots to go. Every so often he would brush some hair off the back of my neck or my shoulder. He didn't speak, just worked away. Trying really hard to get it right.

He walked around to the front of me. We were standing really close—he was just a few inches away from me, our toes were almost touching. He picked up the scissors and held up the little braid Keira had done through the front of my hair. I stepped closer to him and he chopped it off at the root and handed it to me.

And then I heard a full-on horror-movie scream.

"What the hell?" I heard Keira say and then, "Whoa."

Connie was still screaming. Keira shook her. "Stop screaming, you lunatic." Then she looked at me, and then at Jack. "Are we interrupting *something*?"

Jack looked at me. "I'll see you back at the hall?" I nodded and he smiled sheepishly at Connie and Keira and left.

"Your hair!" Connie wailed, and picked some of it up and held it by my head, like she thought maybe the situation could be reversed.

"Is this how you want to apologize for lying to us?" Keira said. "Making us a coat out of your hair?"

"I'm really sorry," I said. "I don't know why I said it, or why I didn't tell you. I should have. I just . . . screwed it up."

Connie picked up a mound of hair and threw it in the air and it softly fell over us all. Then she hugged me. "Listen, Mouse. What I wanted to tell you. What I came up here to do—"

"Apart from stopping you from having your first kiss, obviously," Keira interjected.

"I wanted to tell you I'm really happy that you're staying at school." Connie looked almost tearful. "When we were on the ferry. That's what I wished for. What I wrote. That I wanted you to stay at Bluecoats." She looked up at me and threw her arms around me like she had in the bathroom on the first day. Tightly. Really.

"This week has been pretty intense," Keira said, and then came and put her arms round both of us and leaned her head on mine.

"Keira," I said. "I know I lied to you, but there is one thing you need to know is true. Alfie honestly does like you. Scarlett was lying. I don't know why. Well, I do, to be horrible and—"

"Because she doesn't want me as her sister-in-law. Well, I don't want her either." She made a humphing sound. "Alfie probably hates her too."

"Come back to the dance," Connie said. "I'm going to request 'Mamma Mia' again. And *Roland* is at the dance," she squealed. "And he did a move where he looked . . ."

"Like he was dying of chemical radiation," Keira groaned.

"Everyone is going crazy," Connie said.

Keira nodded. "It's true. Mouse, you have gone properly nuts." Keira kicked some of the hair on the floor and shook her head. And then she smiled. "I love it."

We bundled out and down the hall. My hair was about thirty different lengths, and people were giving me weird looks, but I didn't care. What Connie had said was true, everyone had gone crazy. The dance floor was packed. It wasn't little pockets of girls in circles anymore, but literally everybody who was there was dancing. Miss Mardle was even bopping about at the edge with Jack's teacher, and giggling as he pulled off some pretty horrific dad dance moves.

There was a huge crowd gathered in the middle of the room. We couldn't see exactly what they were looking at, but I knew it must be Roland. We pushed into the mass of jumping people and saw him and Max right at the epicenter. They were doing some sort of attempt at breakdancing and everyone was watching and cheering.

Jack appeared next to me and started breaking out some crazy moves that looked like a cross between Riverdance and the tango.

Out of the corner of my eye I saw Lauren, sitting on the edge, alone. Even Scarlett and Melody had left her to join in the Roland-watching.

"Just a second," I shouted to Jack, and muscled out of the throng.

I walked over and sat down next to her. Neither of us spoke. We just watched everyone dancing. People loving it. People who looked ridiculous but didn't care.

Lauren didn't look at me; she stared straight ahead. We could both sit here for a week and she wouldn't crack. "So the only ones not dancing are the two dancers," I said.

She didn't respond, just acted like I wasn't there. Her tried-and-tested power formula. I kept talking even though she clearly didn't want me to.

"Lauren." She had to look at me, I had said her name. I had called her bluff. She turned her head slightly.

"Lauren. I just . . ."

There were millions of things to say. Millions of fragments that had made it all like this. Her not getting in. My going-away party she hadn't come to. Me being angry that she hadn't come. Her being angry and then every teeny break that followed, right up to Jack. Millions of shards all in a heap between us.

We sat side by side, staring at the dance floor. Scarlett and Melody looked over and whispered to each other.

"You don't have to like me," I said.

"I invited you for hot chocolate on the boat," she shot back.

"Lauren, I heard you talking about me in the bathroom."

She flushed ever so slightly. "Don't act like you haven't said stuff about *me*." Her voice had an edge of defensiveness.

I thought about the hex and how much I had meant it.

"You could still be a dancer," Lauren said, still looking straight ahead. "You could try for other schools. You could keep dancing."

"So could you," I said.

She turned and looked at me and a flicker of something ran across her face.

And then Roland was walking toward us. Lauren straightened herself and tried to look kind of demure and like she hadn't really seen him.

"Mouse." He smiled and leaned down and kissed me on both cheeks. "My kidnapper." Then he winked at me. His eyes wandered across to Lauren. "Mouse, who is your beautiful friend?"

"This is Lauren," I said, turning to her and smiling. "She's a really good dancer."

She blushed slightly, and Roland said, "*Fantastique*. I love dancers. But I see you are injured, Lauren? Maybe I can keep you company, since I cannot ask you to dance with me?"

Lauren went even redder, but still just about managed to nod yes to him. Almost as soon as I got up, he had taken my place next to her.

I went and found Keira on the edge of the dance floor.

"Keira, guess what just happ—" I started, but she squeezed my arm tightly to shut me up. She was staring openmouthed at something on the other side of the room.

JACK

"First he steals Mouse, now he steals Lauren." Max laughed. "What's he gonna do next? Burn your house down?"

We were standing on the dance floor, looking over at Roland, who was trying to chat to Lauren in between taking selfies with a gaggle of ridiculously overexcited girls. Lauren looked like her old self again, all her glossy confidence restored, as she sat there beaming proudly round the room, like she couldn't believe her luck. I was glad, really. I hadn't wanted to embarrass her. I just hadn't wanted to go out with her.

"Trust me, he'll be kissing her in about thirty seconds." Max sighed and turned to me. "That could've been *you,* man. I can't *believe* you didn't kiss her."

"Neither can I," I said, completely honestly. "But I'm glad I didn't. It just didn't feel right."

"Well, good luck to you, mate," Max said, whacking me on the back. "You wait patiently until it 'feels right.' You'll probably still be at zero at my wedding." He clapped his hands together loudly. "Anyway, enough talking. Time for me to get with Scarlett and win this bet once and for all. Where is she?"

"She's over there, with Melody." I nodded to the semi-circle of girls surrounding Lauren and Roland. "Where's Toddy, though?"

We both scanned the hall, and I noticed that Mouse was waving to get my attention. She jabbed her finger excitedly at something behind me.

"Oh my God," said Max, following my gaze. "That Connie girl's a man-eater."

Then Connie tore herself away from the boy she was with in the corner.

"Wh-what the . . . How . . . ?" Max wobbled on the spot,

totally stunned, while I leapt into the air and screamed, "Yes! Toddy! You absolute legend!"

He and Connie walked toward us, hand in hand. Connie zipped straight past, and into the mad blur of squeals and outstretched arms that was Mouse and Keira.

Toddy just stood there in front of me and Max, grinning a kind of wonky, half-embarrassed, half-proud grin. His blond hair was all stuck up at the sides. His cheeks were pink and his glasses were resting at a slightly skewed angle on his nose. He almost looked drunk.

Max was clearly too shocked to form actual, coherent words, so I spoke instead. "Uh . . . Toddy. Would you like to kindly explain what just happened?"

Toddy patted his hair down and turned his wonky grin on me. "She just . . . came over and said, 'Hey, so have you got any more hamster tips for me?' And I said, 'No,' and then she said, 'You're cute, aren't you?' And I didn't really know what to say. But then she just started . . . kissing me."

Max looked like he could faint at any moment. "So, you . . . you . . . you . . ." He turned to me. "He . . . Toddy kissed a girl before we did? Toddy won the bet?"

I clapped Max on the shoulder. "Yep, Max, I'm afraid so. Toddy won." I raised my other hand at Toddy and he high-fived me, blinking and smiling.

Roland slipped through the force field of girls that had imprisoned him and threw his arms around us.

"Can we get out of here for a bit, you guys?" he whispered. "That Lauren girl is cool, but there is only so much female attention I can take."

"Tell me about it." Toddy smirked, and Max's face turned an even deeper shade of purple.

"Hey, so, we've finally got a name for our band," I said to Roland, grinning. "The Parallelograms, right, Toddy?"

Toddy shook his head. "Nah, I've had another think. I quite like . . . Never Evers."

I laughed. "Yeah. That's got a nice ring to it."

"That's actually not bad," grunted Max, and Roland nodded solemnly. "Yes, Never Evers. I can see that on a billboard. Or a backpack. Or a *trousse.*"

We all cracked up. He whipped out his phone and shot a selfie of the four of us. Then he tapped at his phone while he muttered, "This—is—me—with—the—hottest—new—English—band . . . Never Evers." There. It's on Instagram now, so it is a real thing." He grinned at me. "You'll *have* to play some gigs now."

"Yeah." I grinned back. "We're going to."

He squinted back down at his phone. "It has already got three thousand likes."

"Oh my God," said Max.

"Oops . . . three thousand one hundred," said Roland.

Mouse, Keira and Connie came over, and I said, "Hey, why don't we all go sledding? Me and Mouse did it yesterday—it was fun. We can go and get trays from the dining hall."

"Yes, sounds great," said Roland, and everyone else nodded too. We headed for the lobby, where the massive bald guy was still waiting and managed to hold back the swarm of girls who tried to follow us.

"Thank God Cooper left," Roland whispered as he looked around the lobby. "She would *not* like me going sledding. I don't think my insurance covers injuries you get while sitting on a lunch tray."

The girls headed back to their room to get some hats and scarves, and Max said he needed to grab something too, so me, Toddy and Roland borrowed some trays from the dining hall and headed out to the little hill behind the hotel.

Outside, the temperature had dropped even further. It was freezing. The girls came running back and dropped down beside us. Mouse handed Roland his leather jacket, which he thanked her for, but I saw him checking the zipper particularly closely.

She knelt down next to me and smiled her amazing smile. I had been worried when we were chopping her hair off that she would look like a crazy woman, but she actually looked even more beautiful than before. You could see her face much more clearly now, and it was like the haircut had given her a new kind of energy, a bright-eyed freshness, like she wasn't hiding from herself—or anyone—anymore.

"Right," she said. "Shall we sled?"

"Hang on. Where's Max?"

As if in answer to my question, there was a screaming "WHEEEEEE!" noise from behind us, and the sky suddenly exploded, shattering into millions of fiery-red sparks. We all turned around to see Max, half hidden by smoke, back up by the hotel. He was holding an armful of fireworks and a lighter.

"There's no way I'll smuggle *all* this back into England tomorrow!" he yelled. "Might as well use some of them now, right?"

He sprinted over and flung himself down onto the tray next to Keira. "So, listen ...," he said. "We haven't exactly seen eye to eye this trip, but I think it's time to bury the hatchet, yeah? I mean ... you can't deny there's clearly something between us."

"Yeah, maybe you're right." She edged over toward him and put her hand on his shoulder. Just as I thought she might actually, genuinely lean in, she shoved him, hard. He let out a high-pitched shriek as he slid, fast, down the slope.

Keira cackled, and yelled, "Come on, let's go!" and everyone pushed off with her.

I went to shove myself forward, but Mouse stopped me. We watched our friends all zip downward, screaming, going faster and faster until the darkness swallowed them up. Suddenly it was just the two of us at the top of the hill.

"Sorry about that," she said.

"It's all right. I'm quite glad you did it."

We sat there in silence for a few seconds, smiling at each other, not really knowing what else to say. I felt my heart head-butting my rib cage. It suddenly seemed like it was really going to happen. This time, there were no paramedics or pop stars or flesh-eating rat-hamsters to get in our way. It was just me and Mouse, sitting on our massively un-comfortable plastic dinner trays, grinning nervously and waiting for something to happen. I knew I shouldn't feel scared anymore, but I did. It *was* scary. Doing *anything* for the first time is scary. But I wanted to kiss her so badly.

I shuffled my tray an inch closer to hers. She laughed and did the same, so that our feet were just about touching over the sliver of snow between us.

Then I closed my eyes, took a deep breath and leaned in toward her.

Acknowledgments

First, a massive, massive thank-you to Rachel Leyshon, who has proved to be equal parts brilliant editor and expert therapist. Sorry for all the phone calls . . .

Big thanks also to our amazing agent, Kirsty McLachlan, and to Barry, Rachel H, Elinor, Kesia, Jazz, Esther, Laura and all at Chicken House.

We also owe at least one drink to everybody who read this book in all its various drafts and gave us invaluable feedback: Anna McCleery, Abi Elphinstone, Emma Shevah, Rob Ellen, Rosie Ivison, Carolina Demopoulos, Laura Allsop, John Bardsley, Polly Cotran, Diana Battle, Halina Malone, Nell Booker, Sheena Wilkinson, Kate Feenstra, Evie De Witt Turle and Katie Heckles. Thank you all!

Cheers, too, to everyone whose brains we picked about real-life ski trip–based hilarity—namely, Robin, Jeremy, Toddy, Harve, Del and Ally. Big fans of you all.

We're very much indebted also to Elena Palano and Eugénie Bakker, because Connie and Keira wouldn't be here without them. . . .

Much love to our families—Rosie, Helen & Will Ivison and Mark, Clare & Rob Ellen.

And huge thank-yous, too, to Kate Sullivan, Alexandra Hightower and Allison Hellegers for all their incredible hard work and support. You guys are the greatest.

Lucy would also like to thank the whole of the FHS staff for being so supportive and AMAZING. Plus, my 10:15 library crew . . . Stephanie Wahl in year 3 for the Draco Malfoy chat alone; Christiane Lesesne in year 4 for inspiring me with her work ethic . . . I can't wait to come to your book launch someday. Rosie Phillips in year 6 for her knowledge of animal-shaped sponges and all the other juniors who come into the library and talk to me about books. Also to all the senior girls who told me their ski trip stories and to Sophie Daya, Manon Abbott, Larissa Guerrini-Maraldi, Chioma Onyegbosi, Yasmin Samrai. And, of course, U6S, my lovely form.

And a big final thank-you to all the brilliant UKYA authors, bloggers and readers. Keep doing what you do!

About the Authors

Tom Ellen and Lucy Ivison met at the end of high school and quickly became sweethearts. Though they broke up in college, they remain best friends. Lucy is a librarian at a girls' school in central London, where she gets most of her inspiration. Tom is a journalist and has written for *Time Out, Vice, ESPN, Glamour,* and many other publications. Their first book, *A Totally Awkward Love Story,* was partially inspired by their own high school relationship, with Tom writing Sam's chapters and Lucy writing Hannah's. *Never Evers* is their third novel together.